Praise

"A very fu[n]
ters . . . Wi[ll]
very intriguing. With Dyce's eccentric bookstore owning parents and refinishing tips added in, *French Polished Murder* is sure to please and leave readers eager for the next Daring Finds Mystery."   —*The Mystery Reader*

"*French Polished Murder* is an interesting, enjoyable cozy mystery that is well written with good characters who work well together . . . [A] fun book with a little romance and enough mystery to keep you interested."
                                                —*Once Upon a Romance*

"[*Dipped, Stripped, and Dead* is] a fun read. I look forward to seeing Dyce's next adventures. An eccentric, entertaining cast of characters rounds out this cozy mystery. Refinishing tips are included as a bonus."
                                                        —*Fresh Fiction*

"*Dipped, Stripped, and Dead* is an enjoyable, absorbing whodunit."   —*Genre Go Round Reviews*

Berkley Prime Crime titles by Elise Hyatt

DIPPED, STRIPPED, AND DEAD
FRENCH POLISHED MURDER
A FATAL STAIN

A Fatal Stain

ELISE HYATT

BERKLEY PRIME CRIME, NEW YORK

THE BERKLEY PUBLISHING GROUP
Published by the Penguin Group
Penguin Group (USA) Inc.
375 Hudson Street, New York, New York 10014, USA

Penguin Group (Canada), 90 Eglinton Avenue East, Suite 700, Toronto, Ontario M4P 2Y3, Canada
(a division of Pearson Penguin Canada Inc.) • Penguin Books Ltd., 80 Strand, London WC2R 0RL,
England • Penguin Group Ireland, 25 St. Stephen's Green, Dublin 2, Ireland (a division of Penguin
Books Ltd.) • Penguin Group (Australia), 250 Camberwell Road, Camberwell, Victoria 3124, Australia
(a division of Pearson Australia Group Pty. Ltd.) • Penguin Books India Pvt. Ltd., 11 Community
Centre, Panchsheel Park, New Delhi—110 017, India • Penguin Group (NZ), 67 Apollo Drive,
Rosedale, Auckland 0632, New Zealand (a division of Pearson New Zealand Ltd.) • Penguin Books
(South Africa) (Pty.) Ltd., 24 Sturdee Avenue, Rosebank, Johannesburg 2196, South Africa

Penguin Books Ltd., Registered Offices: 80 Strand, London WC2R 0RL, England

This is a work of fiction. Names, characters, places, and incidents either are the product of the author's
imagination or are used fictitiously, and any resemblance to actual persons, living or dead, business
establishments, events, or locales is entirely coincidental. The publisher does not have any control over
and does not assume any responsibility for author or third-party websites or their content.

PUBLISHER'S NOTE: Neither the publisher nor the author is engaged in rendering professional
advice or services to the individual reader. The ideas, projects, and suggestions contained in this
book are not intended as a substitute for consulting with a professional. Neither the author nor the
publisher shall be liable or responsible for any loss or damage allegedly arising from any
information or suggestion in this book.

A FATAL STAIN

A Berkley Prime Crime Book / published by arrangement with the author

PUBLISHING HISTORY
Berkley Prime Crime mass-market edition / October 2012

Copyright © 2012 by Sarah Hoyt.
Cover illustration by Brandon Dorman.
Cover design by Rita Frangie.
Interior text design by Kristin del Rosario.

ISBN: 978-0-425-25523-0

BERKLEY® PRIME CRIME
Berkley Prime Crime Books are published by The Berkley Publishing Group,
a division of Penguin Group (USA) Inc.,
375 Hudson Street, New York, New York 10014.
BERKLEY® PRIME CRIME and the PRIME CRIME logo are trademarks of
Penguin Group (USA) Inc.

PRINTED IN THE UNITED STATES OF AMERICA

10 9 8 7 6 5 4 3 2 1

ALWAYS LEARNING   **PEARSON**

To Amanda Green, Kate Paulk, and Sean Kinsell, without whom this series would never have existed.

CHAPTER 1

Another Fine Mess

The first time I tried to run away from home, I was three. I'd packed all my comic books and a box of cookies in a book bag emblazoned with *Remembered Murder*, the name of my parents' bookstore in Goldport, Colorado, and I'd made it all the way down to the bus station, where I realized I didn't have the money for a ticket. I'd sat quietly in a corner bench and eaten my cookies and read my comics until my grandmother noticed I was missing and came to find me.

It never occurred to me that a three-year-old with a mystery bookstore shopping bag would be sort of noticeable. And it was several years before I realized that, even if I had the money to buy a ticket somewhere, I wouldn't have known where to go. My knowledge of geography at the time was limited to my street, the road leading to the kindergarten, and the diner where Grandma took me for *Kids eat free on Mondays* dinner. The only reason I'd found the bus station was that you could see it from the diner.

And I was married before I realized that, even had someone let me buy a ticket and run away by bus somewhere, no one would have given me a job when I got there.

The saddest thing of all was that at thirty-one, this was still about my level of planning. And that I was, once more, contemplating running away from home. Or at least running away from my parents' store, where I sat by the fireplace, in one of the sofas provided for the comfort and convenience of customers wishing to browse mystery books, and listened as my mother and my best friend planned my second wedding.

Ben, aka Benedict Colm, has been my best friend since middle school. He is tall and rugged looking, with a face that's more interesting than handsome and the sort of body that makes one think of Viking ships. He tones down the feeling that he should sport a horned helmet by wearing a selection of impeccably color-coordinated and blandly conservative suits during the week. On the weekend, he dresses down by wearing slacks, no coat, and sometimes shirts with an almost imperceptible pattern, which he convinces himself are garish. Today he was practically slumming, as he wasn't wearing a tie and had unbuttoned the first three buttons in his subtly striped shirt.

I suppose the attire goes well in his job as an investment planner. Unfortunately, I suspect it was one of the things that had kept my mom—a porcelain doll-like woman who could have played a more true-to-life Miss Marple than the rather butch TV series actress—from believing me when I told her Ben was gay. Though if she still didn't believe it as he leaned forward and said, "I'm wondering if perhaps we could find someone to make a tuxedo for Pythagoras, so he can be best cat?" I washed my hands of her.

No, *in any case*, I washed my hands of my mother, whose response was, "So, your pet rats, are we putting them in the specially designed harnesses, so they can be used as boutonnieres?"

It was at this moment I realized my hands had come up of their own accord and clasped the sides of my head, in horror. Cats and rats? Did they hear themselves? And though Pythagoras, who is not so much my cat as a cat I allow to crash at my home, might be nominally my pet, the rats weren't even mine at all. Okay, so I'd rescued them from inside a piano I'd bought to refinish for my fiancé, Cas Wolfe. I'd only nursed them and looked after them because otherwise they'd be snake food. Besides, they were Ben's problem now. Ben had adopted them. I didn't want them in my wedding.

"I don't want anyone in my wedding," I heard myself say. I sounded surly and unaccountably like a teenager. My hand moved, all on its own, making a horizontal slash from side to side to indicate how much I didn't want anyone at my wedding. "At least no one besides me and Cas. No cats. No rats. No tea roses. No boutonnieres and *no* book distributors. Also, no, Mom, my wedding is not the ideal venue to display the covers of upcoming mysteries that can be bought at the store for a discount of twenty percent. And paperback books do not make tasteful wedding party favors."

The two of them stopped talking for a moment and looked at me, for all the world as though they'd completely forgotten I existed. Which, to be frank, they probably had. Then Mom reached over and patted my hand, absently, more like she was fluffing a cushion or something. "There, there," she said. "Brides always get nervous."

"I'm not nervous," I said. I realized my voice was louder than it should be. "This is not my first time getting married. I don't want a dress. It's not a church wedding. I don't want a guest list. I don't want a reception. I don't want—"

Mom and Ben traded a look that implied they were the adults in the room and that I must be humored and cajoled into playing my part. Ben tapped the pen he was holding against his teeth. It was one of the most annoying habits in the world, and I'd told him so several times since sixth grade. "To be honest," he said, "perhaps the mystery books as favors are a bit over the top. They're damn hard to wrap in a tasteful way. Besides, we can't know for sure what the guests will like to read or even if all of them read mysteries."

Mom narrowed her eyes at the unlikelihood of someone *not* reading mysteries, then wavered. "Well," she said, "my husband has said that perhaps tasteful bottles of fingerprint powder . . ."

And like some slumbering warrior awakened from long sleep, my father perked up behind the register, ten feet away, and beamed at us. "It would be handy, you know. Funerals and weddings often result in murder, and when someone kills Sherlockia on her wedding day, we'll be all ready to take fingerprints."

My name is not Sherlockia. Had my name been Sherlockia, I would have run away from home well before the age of three. In fact, probably before I'd learned to walk.

Mom and Dad had almost divorced over what to name me, with my dad wanting Sherlockia and my mom holding out for Agatha. They'd met to discuss reconciliation in the local candy shop, and Mom had gone into labor over the parfaits. Which might explain—but did not excuse—saddling me with the names of Candyce Chocolat. Dad had dealt with the defeat as he always dealt with such things: by pretending it had never happened.

Which meant the only way *I* could deal with this was by running away. I'd take my on-the-verge-of-dying third-hand Volvo station wagon; cosh my fiancé, police officer Cas Wolfe, over the head and stuff him in the passenger seat; and then wait until my ex-husband—All-ex, who couldn't be more ex if I'd killed him, something I often contemplated doing—returned my son, E, whose real name is Enoch (I'm trying to save on therapy bills by calling him E). I'd strap E in his car seat in the back, and we'd drive like bats out of hell to . . . maybe as far as Denver, before my car died.

I revised my plan. I'd cosh Cas *first* and steal the keys to his white Honda SUV. Then drag him to the passenger seat, move the car seat over, and . . .

I paused. I could see E sitting in the backseat, screaming all the way to Las Vegas because we'd left Pythagoras—whom he calls Peesgrass—at home in Goldport.

Right. I'd throw Pythagoras—a mangy and extremely neurotic black cat—in his cat carrier and strap him in next to E's child seat. And then . . .

In my mind's eye, I saw Ben—as opposed to the real Ben, who was sketching something on a paper pad and showing it to my mother—crossing his arms and giving me his *more in sorrow than in anger* look at being left out of my elopement. After all, he'd been left out of my first wedding, mostly because All-ex was jealous of him, which ranked up there as extreme stupidity, even for All-ex. It probably wasn't fair to leave him out of my second wedding as well. Besides, I'm superstitious. The first wedding had been Ben-less, and the marriage had ended up on the rocks. What if the lack of Ben also blighted the second marriage?

My mental self also coshed the image of Ben over the head, dragged him to the car—a monumental feat of strength since he probably weighs double what I do—and strapped him in next to E and Pythagoras. Only in time for me to realize that Ben's significant other, Nick, would probably be very upset if I took his boyfriend away for a few days. And probably even more upset to miss Cas's wedding. Nick and Cas were not only best friends and colleagues in the Goldport Police Department, but also cousins who had been raised almost as brothers. It would be unforgivable not to take Nick along to Las Vegas to see us married by an Elvis impersonator at the Little Chapel of Quick and Regrettable Unions.

Sighing, I coshed my mental image of Nick, too, and stuffed him in the car under Pythagoras's carrier, which probably would keep Pythagoras calmer for the trip, too.

Then, just as I was about to get behind the wheel of my imaginary getaway car, I realized that though my parents had never exactly approved of me since I'd disappointed them by not becoming a private eye, I was still their only daughter, and they—alas—my only parents. They might be—and often were—the world's most annoying people, but they probably deserved to be there when we told Elvis that we did . . .

I'd just finished strapping my mental image of Mom to the roof rack and Dad to the front bumper, like a very befuddled-looking deer, when I realized this wouldn't do. I mentally untied Dad's hands and put a mystery book in them. He wouldn't even notice he was strapped to the front of the car, provided that the book was interesting enough.

And then I realized that Fluffy, Mom and Dad's cat, would be left alone for the whole time. But I had to draw the line somewhere. And Fluffy hated me and had— twice—tried to eat Pythagoras.

"No," I said. "I'm *not* taking Fluffy." And, as Mom and Ben turned to look at me, I realized that eloping while taking all your nearest and dearest was probably not practical and got up. "I have had enough of this," I said. "I'm going to work."

As I rushed out of the store, I heard Mom ask Ben, "What was that all about?" and Ben answer, "She just realized that she couldn't take us all along if she eloped with Cas."

I hated the way the man read my mind. Which did not excuse what I did next.

You see, two years ago, I'd been left divorced, with a year-old child and a very bad case of never having decided what to be when I grew up. In despair, I'd turned to the only semi-marketable skill I'd learned in the course of my very brief marital life: refinishing and rehabilitating used and antique furniture.

Now, my own business, Daring Finds, allowed me to buy food for myself and E—sometimes it even wasn't pancakes—and to keep a roof—in an unfashionable part of downtown—over both our heads. What was going to happen to the roof and how much each of us would contribute to the pancakes were subjects still undecided between Cas and I. It was, however, mutually agreed—at least by me, leaving Cas to hum along with it or lump it—that I would not shut down Daring Finds or stop refinishing and selling furniture. This time, should it all go bad—no matter how much we hoped it wouldn't—I was not going to be left with no experience in anything marketable. So it was likely I would have to rent someplace for a workshop—Cas's garage being taken up with the cars he and Nick fixed and repainted on the weekends.

For now, my workshop was located in a little shed at the back of the place I rented—the bottom floor of a Victorian building near downtown Goldport.

I had it arranged with tall shelves—full of the various chemicals I used to strip old varnish, stain, and the inevitable three layers of metallic paint that covered any garage-sale-bought piece—all around the walls and in the center a worktable formed by using several kitchen cabinets as a base and topping them with a large, heavy plywood board. On that board I set up the smaller pieces I worked on.

But that day, I felt I needed to work on something big. Like . . . the heavy, rough-hewn pine kitchen table that I'd bought at a garage sale last weekend. I pulled it from where it had been standing against the wall of the shed. It was hard to pull, but that was good, because it allowed me to work off some of my frustration, but it wasn't so heavy that it would be pressboard.

I always find it funny when furniture sellers or ads online go on about how this used furniture must be good because it's "heavy." In fact, most of the heavy furniture is made of pressboard. But this one didn't feel quite that heavy. More the weight of oak or maple. Which was weird, since I was fairly sure it was pine.

Not good pine. It looked like it was cheap pine that someone had half-assedly covered up with a darker pine stain—something like Ipswich pine—which had been mixed with a quantity of varnish. People do the stupidest things.

I stared at the lumpy dark-and-yellow mess on the table and sighed. I could spend several days stripping the vast flat surface by dint of turpentine and heat gun. Or . . .

I looked at my worktable. Sitting atop of it, still in its box, all shiny and new, was the belt sander that Cas had given me as a pre-wedding gift and, I think, to show me he still loved me, even if I insisted on continuing to play with old furniture and varnish.

I had yet to use it, since most of my projects were antique, frail, and definitely not the sort of thing on which to unleash a belt sander. I hadn't had the nerve to tell Cas such a tool was more appropriate for, say, floor refinishing. He had been trying so hard.

But this table was just what the doctor ordered for using the sander. I mean, pine is pretty resilient. As thick as this table was, I could easily slough off one-half inch and no one would notice. Heck, judging by the jam-like look of the top of the varnish, it had probably been applied on top of paint and shellac and silver metallic paint and God alone knew what. It was highly unlikely I'd hit wood in half an inch.

So I got the sander, put the finest paper belt on it—no use getting cavalier—attached the little bag to collect shavings to the back of it, not that I'd ever actually seen one work—usually sawdust escapes all around the edges anyway, but this one might be the miracle—and put on my ear protection, goggles, and dust mask.

Then I plugged the sander in and let her rip.

Which it did, biting a gauge one-eighth of an inch thick across the table, and dragging me along by sheer force of its overactive motor to the other side.

I let go as I ran out of table, and it stopped, as its dead-man-switch safety activated.

I barely noticed as it hit the floor with a thud, and I reeled back, to put both hands on either side of the table and stare at the gash.

The first thing I thought was that using that sander on this piece was probably not the brightest thing I'd ever done. Contrary to my expectations, there was no thick layer of finish on finish atop this table. Just a thin, gummed-up layer of two colors of stain mixed with varnish.

The second thing that occurred to me was that this was a very strange table. Look, it's not as if people don't apply different sorts of stains than the wood beneath. Heck, it is almost the rule that people will disguise cheap woods as more expensive ones.

If I had a dime for every time I thought I was buying cherry or walnut and bought pine instead, I'd have . . . a lot of dimes. It happened less frequently now, because I was better at discerning fake grain from true grain and also judging the weight of the piece.

But never, in the whole time I'd been doing this— never, even, in the time I'd heard of someone doing this— had I come across oak disguised as pine.

Yeah, I know that both oak and pine are relatively light in color. They can be worth similar amounts, too, if the pine is much older than the oak. However, it would not occur to even the craftiest of counterfeiters to disguise old oak as young pine. And the person who had jammed up the top of this table was not an expert in wood, refinishing, or anything related to the business.

So . . .

I went to my shelf and selected mineral spirits and denatured alcohol. I mixed equal portions of them with a bit of cornstarch.

No, the denatured alcohol and the mineral spirits do not react to each other, but when you're dealing with an unknown mixture such as I had found atop this table, one or the other was bound to react with it. Applying them together just saved time for now, though probably later I'd just test and use the one that worked. For now, I just wanted to see more of the table without taking off the top layer of it. The cornstarch didn't do anything except delay the liquids drying out long enough to give them time to react.

I applied the mixture to the edge in a long strip next to the furrow I'd carved and waited for it to react before scraping it away with the flat edge of a five-way painter's tool.

The wood thus revealed was not only definitely oak, but it was sanded to perfect smoothness. Any roughness on the top of the table had been the weird refinishing mix some idiot had applied. Before that mix—and my not-so-bright attack with a sander—the table had been sanded to a smooth, fine evenness and probably oil rubbed. I suspected, like my own kitchen table—inherited from my grandmother—this was antique and good quality.

Which meant what I'd done to it with the sander was

criminally insane. But not as criminally insane as what someone had done to it with the mix of stain and varnish. Which had caused it to sell at a garage sale for twenty dollars, which meant I had never expected a piece of this quality.

Yeah, hindsight is twenty-twenty. Yeah, I should have gone slower and been more careful. I probably would have done it, too, if I hadn't allowed my mom and Ben to drive me to near insanity. Now I would have to sand the top level, which, let's face it, would subtract markedly from the value of the piece. It also meant a slow and patient rubbing with oil to return the top to something close to its original finish. And I didn't like slow and patient!

I applied a coat of my finish remover to another strip of the table, picked up the sander, wound the cord, put the whole thing back in its box, and set it on a shelf, feeling that perhaps it should stay there, unless I got, say, a hundred square feet of floorboards to refinish. Or a barn door.

Then I scraped away the layer of finish from the table, and then the next one. It didn't take long to remove the finish, probably because mixing the varnish with the stain meant neither of them had taken properly. Also, because the layer was thin and set atop of oil.

I made much more rapid progress than I'd expected. I'd just discovered some gashes on the table, and what looked suspiciously like bloodstains, when I heard Cas call me.

CHAPTER 2

Making Light

"Dyce, honestly," he said. "Someone could sneak up on you and kill you, and you wouldn't even notice."

I didn't tell him I was quite likely to notice being dead. First off, it wouldn't do me any good. When he was in this mood, he had no sense of humor. Second, I'd found that dating a policeman came with its very own set of issues. One of them was his certainty that everyone, everywhere, was looking to murder someone he cared for. He seemed to think people sat around all day going, *Who does Cas Wolfe like? Oh, yeah, that chick who does the furniture. Why haven't we killed her yet?* It just wasn't sane. I mean, for one, how many people could do this full time? Who would pay them? How would they have money for rent and groceries?

But it was useless telling Cas this. When he spent the night at my place, he would walk all around the house every night, checking the locks in every window and door. He'd die if he knew how many times I'd left the door unlocked through the night. No, he wouldn't die. He'd start foaming at the mouth and raving about murderers and rapists.

Mind you, I didn't leave the door unlocked on purpose—not as such. But it wasn't a big deal, because this wasn't a bad area of Goldport. Oh, okay, so my friend Ben thought that downtown Goldport near the university was a slum and that gangs fought in the street in front of my house every day. But Goldport was never a big town, though it had achieved a somewhat large and definitely rowdy population during the gold rush. That had left its echo in places named Goldpan Alley and Three Shots Street, and the Leather and Lace Hotel up the street, which was a bed-and-breakfast on the site of a famous brothel.

The gold bust had left the town deserted, its fine Victorian buildings falling to pieces, until the University of Colorado (UC Goldport) had moved to town and brought with it a boom in tech and other white-collar jobs.

Goldport was so white bread that it was a wonder no one had ever tried to spread butter an inch thick all over it. Even downtown Goldport was as safe as suburbs in larger cities. If gangs fought on the street in front of my house, it would be the Paperclips versus the Calculators. They'd be hauling some serious numbers and glaring daggers at each other. They could do serious damage with the edges of their sharpened gold MasterCards.

But, of course, Cas thought otherwise, and there was no point arguing. After all, he saw whatever crime there was in town—and for him, even a single crime would be too much. If murders didn't happen, he'd upgrade graffiti to serious-crime status.

"I'm sorry." I gave him something approaching a contrite smile—at least if my acting abilities were up to snuff—while I looked at the table. The table bothered me.

My acting went to waste. Cas was staring at the table. I knew that expression. It was the sort of expression he got when he tasted something I'd just cooked and discovered it wasn't a gourmet meal. This shouldn't be a surprise, mind. Other than pancakes—I had lots of practice on those—I could do a decent mac and cheese and heat up a mean can of soup. But hope springs eternal, and Cas's other major blind spot was his belief I could do whatever I wanted to—including cooking. Which meant each new, bad experience was a shock.

His face now showed agonizing confusion mixed with an unwillingness to hurt me. Kind of like when my vol-au-vents broke the knife he tried to cut them with.

He was looking at the trench in the middle of the table and studiously avoiding looking back at me. Part of me wanted to tell him I'd done that on purpose, just to see how pretzel-like he'd become in his attempt at being supportive. But the other part of me—the part who desperately wished to make this relationship work—took a deep breath. "Uh . . . I shouldn't use the sander on furniture," I said. "Maybe on a large floor."

His eyebrows went up, and he looked amused. "A *really* large floor?" he asked. "Open wide, with an inch of paint all over it?"

I realized that I'd just told him I couldn't use his gift. "I don't mean I won't use it," I said. "I could . . ." Was I really trying not to insult someone who had given me a gift, even though I couldn't use it? When had I become an adult? I didn't like it. I demanded a recount. Surely I still had some childhood left?

He laughed. "It's all right," he said. "You said you wanted it, so I got it for you. I have no idea if it's useful or not. I'll get you something else."

"No, no, you don't need to get me anything else," I said. "I was planning our wedding today," I said, in a desperate attempt to change the subject. If we continued talking about this, we were going to talk about where we were going to live again. We were going to revisit Cas's determination that we should buy a house, preferably in the suburbs, while things were still cheap. My problem is that I was sure the house in the suburbs would not really contain a workshop where I could continue pursuing furniture refinishing. It would be far too messy and stain things and all. And besides, when all was said and done, Cas didn't really want me to continue doing this. And I didn't want to give up refinishing.

No, it wasn't anyone's dream career. Well, at least it wasn't mine. My dream career would be something like getting paid for lying on white, sandy beaches and testing the mixing on fruity drinks with umbrellas on top. Despite careful perusal of the classifieds, I'd yet to find someone looking for applicants to fill such a position.

Refinishing furniture was dirty, messy, occasionally dangerous—perhaps more dangerous than it should be, given that my parents had cursed me with discovering murders. Oh, okay, so I had no proof they'd done this, but then I had no proof they hadn't done it, and it seemed like the sort of thing they would try. It led me to Dumpster diving and driving back alleys looking for furniture discards on certain days. My hands were always scratched, my nails were a mess, and I kept my hair in a style that I could confine without destroying hours of work, because refinisher was really bad hair conditioner. But I had finally, after three years, built my business to where I could make enough to keep E and me in pancakes.

Cas must not have wanted to discuss that again, either, because he said, "Can you make it . . . I mean, is it repairable?"

"Yeah," I said. I scraped a bit of the weird stain away, and I was sure there were more . . . organic stains there, and I was trying to tell myself they were not bloodstains. "It will take time." I didn't even want to think how long it would take. Mind you, the table was worth it, but it would take me the better part of a week to undo the mindless stupidity of a few seconds.

"It's a different wood," he said, as if he were probing. I wanted to tell him that, yeah, it was and that it was weird. Instead, I said, "It happens sometimes." Because the alternative was telling him that it was the first time I'd seen expensive oak disguised as cheap pine. And the problem was that once you told something like that to a policeman, he'd want to know why anyone had done that, and he'd want to know if it was common, and if I started talking about it, I was going to show him the dark stains. And then he was going to accuse me of inventing murder, as if I had come up with the idea that it would be great to find a crime to investigate. Like anyone would do that. Other than my parents.

At which point several things would happen.

If he decided the stains were blood, he might think

he had probable cause to investigate the table and its provenance—only there were certain things the police were not even remotely prepared to do without evidence, and chances were that they would poke around for a while, then drop it when more concrete crimes emerged to occupy their time.

Or—and far more likely—he would either decide the stains weren't blood or that they were blood but really old and not important. In which case, I would have to tell him he had no way of knowing that and demand that we discover more about it and then . . .

And then we'd be right back where we'd been six months ago, when I'd decided the old piano I was refinishing had contained clues to a tragic love affair and double murder. It had, of course, but on the other hand, the murderer hadn't killed again in more than fifty years. Until I started investigating, and she'd tried to kill Ben and myself. And almost succeeded with Ben. So it could have been argued that Cas was right and it was best to let things lie.

This whole being-responsible thing was really, really hard, and I wasn't sure I liked it at all. My instinctive approach to life was rather like taking that sander to the table. Usually with the same results.

"I . . . will have to sand carefully and rebuild a bit," I said. "But it's a good oak table and I—"

The phone rang. My cell phone, which I kept with me in the workshop. I looked for it under a stack of rags, then under a bunch of sandpaper. I swear the thing hides from me. I'd just leaned forward to peer behind the cans of varnish when Cas's hand, holding the phone, appeared in my field of vision. "Near the sander box," he said.

Which figured, since I'd never have put it there. Phones don't like me and conduct a guerrilla warfare against me. It's my cherished belief they're an alien life form, come to drive me—specifically—completely insane. Though it might be argued it's a short road and well paved.

I flipped the phone open and said, "Yeah," before I registered that the number and name displayed belonged to All-ex Mahr. But it was much worse than that. Michelle, the new Mrs. Mahr, was the one who spoke, in her annoying I'll-sound-like-a-little-girl voice. "Hi? Candyce?"

Her habit of calling me by my full name was one of the many, many things that made me want to throw things, not that I held a grudge against her or anything. Certainly not for marrying All-ex, of course. By the time she got him, I was more than done with him. No, it was because she exactly resembled all the perfect little girls whose existence had tormented me since grade school. They were pink and perfect, and their hair was always in the exactly right place. They dotted their i's with little hearts. They never wanted to splash in muddy puddles, climb trees or walls, or go riding their bikes, with no hands, down Suicide Hill.

Their clothes never inexplicably turned up all frayed and torn and they never had to explain to their mothers that, really, through no fault of their own, their book bag had mysteriously been swung around and around by a very small, utterly spontaneous tornado, that really had nothing to do with their swirling it around and around over their head, till the tornado—not *them* at all, of course—had lost control and flung it into the middle of the street where an ill-timed eighteen-wheeler had run over it, but look, you'd managed to salvage two pages from your math book, which had got blown back at you, and wasn't that a good thing? And *their* mothers had probably never given loud thanks over dinner that it had been a full twenty-four hours without their causing either fire or severe property damage.

Girls, and now women, like that always gave me an urge to dip their pigtails in ink—even when both pigtails and ink were metaphorical.

But I gritted my teeth and said, "Yeah?" again.

"Well, it's Enoch, you see," she said, her high little-girl voice changing into the breathy, little-girl, I'm-too-cute-to-be-in-trouble voice.

"What about E?" I asked, refusing to call the kid by the psychosis-inducing name. The last time I'd had this kind of conversation, my son had flushed one of All-ex's precious signed baseballs and flooded most of All-ex's McMansion.

"Well . . . you see, he's not feeling really well, and we've taken him to the doctor, and . . ."

"What?"

"Oh, it's nothing serious. Just this cough thing that's going around, we think, but since he's running a high fever, and we've already been exposed, I was wondering . . . We got the prescription and all, if we could keep him over till next week. You can have him for more time, after that. I mean—"

I wanted to say no. But it didn't make any sense to do so. For some time now, since the new Mrs. All-ex had been included in the joint custody—before that, All-ex hadn't been really good at looking after a sick baby—if E got sick while with one of us, he stayed until he was feeling better. It made more sense than transferring bottles of cough syrup and antibiotics. And besides, they took him to some fancy pediatrician on the other side of town, and since he was already being treated there, I couldn't just go to my pediatrician close to home. Also, this would give me the weekend free with Cas.

It made perfect sense, and yet I felt my hackles rise, and I wanted to demand they give me my son now, as was agreed under our custody arrangements. I figured it must be the pressure of trying to be an adult elsewhere that was driving me nuts. I forced myself to say, "Oh. Okay. May I talk to him?"

"Well . . . no. That is, he's taking a nap. You know how that cough medicine can make kids feel all tuckered out and—"

I swear at that moment I heard E's voice in the background saying something about Peesgrass—Pythagoras, the cat—and another sound, like something rubbed against the phone. Or a hand clapped over the receiver.

I fully expected Michelle to come back and tell me that E was awake after all, but instead there was a long silence, and then the little-girl voice again, speaking very fast, "So, you see, I'm glad you agreed. I'll call you when he can come home—bye." And then she hung up.

I stared at the phone.

"Anything wrong?" Cas asked.

"Other than the fact that I can't strangle her even though she desperately needs it?"

"Well, you can, but then I'd have to arrest you, and you know I'd hate to do that. I mean, if you really want to wear handcuffs . . ." He stopped when he realized I wasn't responding. "I presume it was Michelle Mahr?"

"Yeah." I closed the phone and put it in my pocket and

looked up into his concerned gaze. "She says E has a cough and a fever, and they've already been exposed, so they're keeping him until he's done with the antibiotics."

"But?"

"But I think I heard him in the background."

"Well, he has a cough. He's not dead."

"Yeah, but she told me I couldn't talk to him, because he was sleeping."

Cas's lips twitched a little. "Knowing E," he said, "she might not have wanted him to talk to you, anyway."

"Why?"

"Oh, come on." Cas grinned at me, his eyes sparkling with mischief. "Remember the time he told you they were really aliens wearing human skins and were attempting to cook him?"

I remembered it very well. I wasn't absolutely sure he hadn't been telling the truth. I did my best impression of a mule at Cas. "So? They can't have thought I believed it." Though I'd given it some good, long thought, frankly.

"It can't be pleasant for her overhearing that stuff."

"Why? Is she afraid she *is* an alien and I'll find out?"

Cas's lids came down halfway, and he gave me a reproachful look, though his lips were still twisted upward in amusement. "Uh-uh. Besides, if he heard you, he might decide he wants to come home now and make himself an unholy terror. More than usual, I mean," he said, then looked as if he was afraid I'd be upset with him.

I wasn't about to argue that E could be an unholy—or holy—terror. He'd started getting in trouble as soon as he was capable of independent mobility. You'd think a three-month-old baby couldn't hurt himself or others, but he'd staged a great escape from the bassinet, slithering on his belly up a stack of stuffed animals and—but for my being close enough to catch him—attempting to crack his head by dropping onto the floor. Then, as soon as he'd started walking, he'd perfected the fine art of removing all his clothes and running out stark naked.

Goldport is not the world's largest city, but neither is it the smallest. And we lived near the part of town that had all the bars and diners. Frankly, I still hadn't decided if it was worse to have your toddler run off stark naked along a sidewalk crowded with late-night diners and drinkers or to have him run off toward the darker areas of the neighborhood and cross streets in the dead of night, braving oncoming traffic. Both of those had constituted a great part of my exercise the last several years.

After that, E had decided to make his father—and my parents, when they thought about it—think I was stark raving mad by not speaking to anyone but me, or when anyone but myself was present.

Since he'd finally decided to add speaking to the world-at-large to his accomplishments, he'd immediately used it to get in trouble. He'd honed the fine art of lying, complaining, and wheedling to the point where he could sell rubber boots to a colony of snakes. And probably would if he ever came across a colony of snakes. All-ex said that at three and a half, E should enter preschool, but I would protect the school system from him—and myself from phone calls over the fire alarm being pulled in the middle of a math lesson, or the bugs that had inexplicably found their way into someone's lunch box—as long as I could. The school system might be a mess, but I didn't think it was bad enough to deserve having my pride and joy inflicted on it.

I was very proud of my son. Like Tom Sawyer, he promised to go far, if someone didn't kill him first.

And there was no denying that he drove his poor father insane. All-ex vacillated between feeling proprietary about his son and trying to keep him from my evil influence and sending him home to me early, showing every sign of believing the child was demonic spawn. He was probably right on both counts, since E was a lot like me as a child, and we understood each other perfectly. And my parents swore I was demonic spawn.

Well, not quite like me. At least so far, he had failed to set the cat on fire or cause the backyard to explode. A fact I gave thanks for daily. Just not aloud and over dinner.

"Well, you have more explosives than the Mahrs," Cas said. "With the refinishing stuff. So if he exploded a backyard, it would probably be here."

I refused to believe I was thinking aloud, and I was not about to ask Cas how come everyone seemed to read my mind. Instead, I said, "Yeah, all right," and pretended to be looking for some refinishing fluid on the shelves.

But he grabbed me from behind and turned me around and pulled me into his arms. I know I'm about five foot five inches tall in my stocking feet, and I weigh one hundred and ten pounds, soaking wet and with lead in both pockets. Still, I normally don't think of myself as little. I'm big enough to do what I must.

Yet, when Cas put his arms around me, I did feel little. And though it should have upset me, it didn't. Instead, with his arms around me, I felt as if I'd been walking outside in a storm for a long time and had finally come into a safe, cozy home, warm and welcoming. Where I belonged.

He bent down and I looked up, and he kissed me—very thoroughly—until my knees felt weak. "It will be fine," he told me, as I put my forehead against his chest. "All this mess will pass, and we'll be a family soon enough."

I sighed. "I don't suppose we could elope?" I said.

"No." He kissed the top of my head. "I've gone over it and over it in my head, and I think we could fit Ben and Nick and E and Pythagoras in my car, but there is no way we could fit your parents. We could probably trust my parents to follow in another car, but yours would stop at the first mystery bookstore and not be heard from again for days."

I sighed. "Yeah. And if we tied Dad to the front bumper, the wind would probably rip the book out of his hands."

Cas's chest moved. I think he was laughing. Of course, there was no reason to laugh. I was deathly serious. My father would need that book, or he would not be happy.

Cass kissed my head again. "I have to go," he said. "There's some weird stuff with arson at vacant properties here in town, and Nick and I will probably be working late on it." He met my gaze, as I looked up. "Nah, don't worry, Dyce. It shouldn't be anything dangerous. It's just with so many houses vacant . . . this stuff happens, you know? People get rid of a bad bet. Probably insurance fraud. It's just a bunch of work. It's not like we can investigate as thoroughly as the insurance agencies can. I'll get pizza for dinner, okay?"

The man knew how to bribe me. But when he left, I stared at the table for a long time, then thought of E not coming home tonight, and couldn't help feeling uneasy. I'd swear the table had bloodstains. And E . . .

Well, at the best of times, I didn't like having to give him up to All-ex once a week. Michelle was in the habit of feeding my poor boy an all-natural diet, involving bran and vegetables. Without his daily dose of preservatives, he'd probably have wrinkles by five. And the Mahrs had absolutely no sense of humor when it came to little things, like taking off all one's clothes and legging it out of the house during a dinner with All-ex's employers.

But right then, it felt weirder. All-ex had already expressed his dislike of my marrying a policeman. Of course, he wouldn't like my marrying anyone. His having divorced me hadn't convinced him that he didn't have the right to be jealous of any men around me. He continued to violently dislike Ben on the mistaken belief Ben was a rival. Which—like my mother's belief that Ben was the ideal man for me—took more than a bit of insanity. Cas was bound to drive All-ex insane just by existing.

I bit my lip. I couldn't explain it, but I really felt weird, both about E and about that table. And it wasn't the type of worry I could calm down by just shutting my mind to it and working some more.

Instead, I closed and locked the shed and went through the back door into my home, which took up the entire bottom floor of a stately Edwardian home.

It consisted of a living room carpeted in arterial-blood-red carpet and furnished with a stained sofa and a coffee table made of such shoddy material that I hadn't even considered selling it. The living room led into the kitchen, with an ancient stove, nice tiled counters, and ancient tile on the floor. It had a deep pantry, which was usually empty except for a large box of pancake mix, and my grandmother's kitchen table and matching chairs, looking as out of place here as a duchess in a slum. Cas wanted us to move in with him after the wedding while we looked for another house, and although his apartment was not exactly the stuff of dreams, it would still be several notches above this. At least the carpet was white and plush, not worn down by generations of tenants.

From the kitchen, a narrow hallway led to the back door, past a tiny bathroom. The other way from the living room, a door opened into my bedroom, which led, through a tiny hallway and past a slightly larger but stained and aged bathroom, into E's bedroom.

Pythagoras was sitting mournfully by his food dish in the kitchen. As I approached, he made a series of little mews that clearly meant, "Excuse me, kind lady, but I don't know if you noticed the patent lack of food in this here dish. I wonder, if it wouldn't be too much trouble, if you could possibly remedy that problem."

Pythagoras is to cats what a professional wrestler is to your average office worker. On shape and muscles alone, you'd mistake him for a Bombay, a breed of cat created and maintained to look like miniature panthers. But his eyes look like no wildcat ever—they are green with a circle of intense blue in the center and bear the most self-effacing, apologetic expression ever seen in any living being.

If he were a human, he'd wear glasses taped together in the middle and stammer as he spoke. Since he is a cat, he meows, in tiny little sounds that seem to strangle themselves in his throat out of extreme politeness.

I got a can of tuna, opened it, and gave it to him. He looked at me for a moment, to make sure my feeding him wasn't a mistake, then set to, eating in delicate little bites. After a moment, he looked up at me, and meowed with a questioning tone.

"No," I said. "It's not your fault."

He asked again, just to make sure, and I said, "I don't think there's anything you can do to help. I do think I'm going to have to go look around, see if I can figure out where that table came from and if there's a chance those stains are old. And I need to go see if E really is sick."

He looked at me, with crossed eyes and a worried expression.

"Don't worry," I told him. "I'm sure everything is fine, and I'm just being weird."

Pythagoras looked doubtful.

As it turned out, he had reason to, and I was wrong.

CHAPTER 3

One Fence Too Far

I'd bought the table at the semi-permanent garage sale two blocks from my house, while All-ex lived across town, in one of the new suburbs growing at the northern edge of town.

I didn't realize I meant to take care of last things first until I was on the highway, breezing past the new condo developments and half-finished construction on office complexes. Not that I had any intention of turning around. I mean, I wanted to make sure E was all right, first. That's what a good mother would do. Even if I often thought that the only way I'd know what a good mother would do was to capture one and turn a really bright light on her eyes as I interrogated her.

Turning into All-ex's neighborhood, I felt like just the appearance of my car on the block should send half of the owners of the well-manicured lawns to the phones to call

911. After all, my car was a very late model Volvo—so late, it might in fact be dead—that announced its arrival with the high whine of a transmission belt about to part company with the world. All the cars I could see—that is, the ones that weren't carefully sequestered behind the wide garage doors next to the gleaming white or cream houses—had come out of the assembly line no more than a week ago and had been buffed to a shine no more than an hour ago.

But as I made it three streets into the neighborhood and no one called the police, I started to feel more self-confident. Besides, I called the police station so often to talk to Cas that if anyone called to report me, the worst that would happen is that Cas—or Nick, if Cas happened to be out—would get really worried about what I might be up to.

Cresting the road, I could see All-ex's home two blocks down, and I thought it might be safer to go around to the back. Fortunately, there was an alley that ran behind All-ex's house, all the sprawling four thousand square feet of it.

Back there, a fence ran around All-ex's backyard. And from inside the fence, like music to my ears, came E's voice saying something that sounded like "kaboom," then the zooming sound of his electric bike.

I hoped the "kaboom" wasn't part of his plan, as I took hold of the handle on the gate and pulled. It wouldn't budge. What kind of suspicious people locked their back gates in one of the safest suburbs in Goldport? What were they trying to hide? Who would try to break in? Other than myself, of course.

Well, whatever it was, clearly my son was not asleep. In fact, if he were any less asleep, the neighbors would have sent for the fire department.

You'd think that would make me feel better—at least, you'd think that if you didn't know me at all. But the fact is that I hate to be lied to, and knowing that All-ex had lied to me—Okay, Michelle did the actual lying but I knew who put her up to it. This was nothing new—made me wonder why, what he was trying to hide, and what I could do to frustrate whatever his plans might be. Because, frankly, he thought that was my ambition, and I saw no reason not to oblige him.

So I walked around the side of the house, looking for something to climb. And I found the trash enclosure. Most houses in Colorado have little paddocks for their trash cans. They can look like anything at all, really, ranging from a custom-made wooden box to a little fence all around the garbage. Anything, that is, that would keep bears out.

You see, bears are not all that rare, even in extreme urban environments like, say, downtown Denver. In fact, growing up in Colorado, I'd long ago decided that bears were like college boys. They woke up, they wanted beer and a snack, and they lumbered downtown to look for both . . . At least judging by all the news stories of bears hanging out in downtown areas and doing the bar circuit. I noted there were never pictures of these ursine miscreants posted. This was probably because, by the time they were caught, they were wearing baseball caps with the bill to the back, T-shirts that read *I'd rather be boozing*, and they were carrying countless napkins with numbers pushed at them by hopeful would-be dates. Also never mentioned—but I didn't doubt it for a moment—was the fact that the bears were probably pulling an A in Composition 101.

I'd once told Ben this, and he'd laughed so hard he almost needed oxygen. To this day, I had no idea why,

but the man was at best odd. So it must be one of those
Ben things.

All-ex's trash enclosure—this being such an expensive
suburb that they had probably brought in a designer to
design the size of squares on the sidewalk—was made
of white brick and guarded from hopeful bears by an
elaborate wrought-iron gate that would have been at
home on a Mediterranean estate. At least a Mediterranean estate blessed with Coloradan bears.

The advantages of a wrought-iron gate, for me, at
least, if not for the bears, were the footholds it gave me.
It made climbing so much easier.

Most of the trash structures I climbed, normally, were
the more conventional Dumpsters around town. Those,
smooth metal on the sides, gave me far fewer holds.
Which meant I'd taken a few spills and, once, discovered
a corpse while Dumpster diving for discarded furniture.
And although Cas had made me swear never to do that
again, I wouldn't really promise to remember that when
students moved out at the end of the school year and the
Dumpsters hid good used furniture going to waste. I
mean, after all, rescuing it was the environmentally
responsible thing to do, right? And besides, I was cheap.

So, listening to E yell, "It's a massive chicken attack!"
on the other side of the fence, I climbed up the gate.

As it shook and rattled under me, proving that
although these things might be very pretty, they weren't
exactly sturdy, I hoped that All-ex hadn't taken to keeping chickens, though the idea of the exceedingly decorative Mrs. All-ex Mahr mucking out the chicken house
was amusing enough.

Lamenting the shoddiness of modern construction, I

finally got to the level where I could peek over the fence. Just barely. Just enough to see the backyard.

You know what I said about my successor, Mrs. Mahr? How her stereotypical prettiness and just-so behavior brought out the worst in me and made me want to put a tarantula down her back as I, uh, definitely hadn't done to the female head of the Leaders of Tomorrow club back in high school?

Their lawn, too, brought out all the worst in me. It was dark green, a color that shouldn't have been possible outside a crayon box and certainly not near Christmas in Colorado. Deep green and perfectly even, spreading under the pale Colorado winter sun from the fence to the house. It was a lawn that was crying out for a bottle of gasoline and a fired-up grill, but I was no longer twelve and I could no longer engage in wanton destruction of property just because I happened to find it fun.

As I looked more closely, I saw that the lawn was crisscrossed by lines about as wide as the wheels on E's electrical toy motorcycle. Which meant I was destroying it—slowly and painfully—by proxy.

E—traced by his babbling about dangerous chickens and an army of dinosaurs—raced along the fence, too close to it to be visible, then swerved away and suddenly into view, zooming along at top speed and yelling, "It's all *T. rex* toenails!"

I'd long ago given up on figuring out my son's imaginary life. Other mothers—in the few times I could be coerced into talking to any of them—told me their children had cartoon characters or even nonexistent children as their playmates. Not E. Oh, no.

Three months ago, E had acquired an imaginary llama

whom he called Ccelly—pronounced Cecily—to whom I had to feed imaginary oats before E ate his breakfast. And who had to be invisibly tied with his invisible rope before we could go anywhere.

I had often wondered if he did this to All-ex and his wife also, but perhaps they just stared at him with that total incomprehension that even E's determination couldn't pierce.

One thing was sure, though. This was no sick little boy. As he turned to come within feet of the wall where I was perched, I said, "Pssssssssst," sounding much like a gasbag that had suddenly developed a leak.

He shouldn't have heard me above his yells and the sounds of the electric motorcycle, but he did. He had ridden back to where he was hidden by the wall once more, but I heard the motorcycle come to an abrupt stop and then a sound that seemed to indicate my son had jumped with both feet atop the seat. He said, "Mom?" in a tentative voice.

I dragged myself the rest of the way up the gate, and then, balancing on top of the side brick wall of the enclosure, I looked up, praying that Michelle Mahr wasn't watching me from inside the house. But since there was no sign of intelligent life from in there—not that this was exactly a surprise—I thought I was safe for now. Of course, it was very irresponsible of her to leave E out here, playing, and not to keep an eye on him. I'd have had words with her about it if I could have explained how I knew. I wondered if he'd never escaped from someplace where she'd put him and what magic she used to do this. If I turned my back for a moment, back home, E would be gone and terrorizing the neighborhood. I wondered if they bored E so much that he couldn't think of anything naughty to do, but this didn't seem likely. Then cold terror hit me: *perhaps E just got away with things while he was at his father's*. Perhaps they had no idea how much trouble he got into, much less how they could attempt to curb it. The idea was enough to make my blood run cold. His mischievous creativity left unchecked, the only thing that would prevent E from taking over the world was his preference for taking over an alternate Earth, where *T. rexes* were at war with giant chickens.

I crept along the side brick wall, toward the fence, which formed the back of the trash enclosure. I crawled on my hands and knees, which was probably stupid, because I'd be as noticeable like that as if I'd been standing and balancing on top of the wall. Brick walls don't routinely sprout fully grown women in white pullovers and jeans. It's not like Mrs. All-ex had to call cleaners to remove the women from atop her brick walls so often that she didn't even notice it anymore. And walls are not any less likely to grow standing women than kneeling ones. I don't have an explanation, okay? It's just that kneeling and creeping felt safer.

I poked my head over the edge of the fence, looked down at my three-year-old son, and said, "E!"

He looked up at me with equal rapture, and said, "Mom!"

People who didn't know him very well might be deceived into thinking E was an angel. He had curly blond hair, blue eyes, and the sort of face that wouldn't have been out of place surrounded by a pair of fluffy wings, like those cherubs the Victorians loved.

In fact, maybe those cherubs had been based on boys

like E. In which case it was only sane to give them wings but no hands, no feet, and no body. I'm sure E could still have thought of some trouble to get into without any of those, but it would have circumscribed his capacity for mischief somewhat. I mean, what could you do with wings but no hands? Careen into things? Seemed relatively harmless when compared to the things that E could do with hands and feet.

Right then, he was wearing little blue coveralls covered in chubby yellow cartoon elephants, a puffy yellow jacket—unzipped—and standing on the seat of his bike, smiling up at me. If I were young and innocent, I'd probably think he was, too.

"Do you have Peesgrass?" he asked.

I was fairly sure in the months since we'd acquired Pythagoras E's speech had improved enough that he could pronounce the cat's name. But either because he thought the name Peesgrass made him sound adorable and might lull adults into the necessary complacence for E's schemes to succeed, or because his pronunciation drove his stepmother insane, he always referred to the cat as Peesgrass. And why did he expect me to have Peesgrass, anyway? Where did he expect me to put him? In my pocket? Although Pythagoras was neurotic enough to—maybe—stay put in the pocket of my jeans, how could I possibly fit a sixteen-pound cat in my pocket? And if I managed to bring him with me, what would E do with him? All-ex claimed to be allergic to cats—which was probably All-ex-speak for not wishing to put up with Pythagoras's shedding and occasional nervous piddling. All the same, he wouldn't allow cats in his house, and E knew that. He wasn't stupid, only a great actor.

But the minute I said no, E's face fell with what looked like genuine disappointment. He looked up at me, his angelic brow furrowed. "Oh," he said. Then pouted. "I told 'chelle to tell you to bring him. I told her I wouldn't stay here without him." He shoved both little hands deep into the pockets of his adorable coveralls and managed to look like Tom Sawyer, aged three and working hard on the charm that whitewashed a thousand fences.

It was no use at all to point out that I had, after all, been his mother for three years, and Pythagoras had only been his cat for six months, and that he should be happy to see me, even if I hadn't brought the stupid cat. It's never any use to tell this sort of thing to kids. For one, they tend not to believe you. I figure it's because, day in and day out, hour by hour, they are subjected to so much guilt and "You should like this" nonsense that most of them develop an unerring eye for BS by the time they are two. The other part was that although Pythagoras was small and furry and neurotic and—as far as we could tell—afraid of his own tail, unable to support E and certainly unable to clean up after him, at least he'd never made E eat pancakes or pick up his bedroom.

"You have to get him," he said. "I'm not staying here without Peesgrass."

"Uh," I said. And then, "Are you sick?"

Now his eyes rounded. "What?" he said, as if I'd accused him of something despicable. "No."

I realized I'd phrased the thing entirely wrong. Whether E considered himself to be sick or not was, unfortunately, no true measure of his state of health. "Okay," I said. "I mean does the doctor think you're sick? The doctor All . . . Daddy and Michelle took you to?"

He didn't ask me if I'd taken leave of my senses. He didn't need to. It was written all over his expression as he said, speaking slowly and calmly, in the way of someone addressing a child or a mentally disturbed person, "They didn't take me to any doctor!" Pause. "Well, not since Christmas, when 'chelle thought I'd eaten her cold cream and took me to the doctor. And then Dad found out I'd put the cold cream on his leather chair. 'Cause it was looking dry," he added, cautiously. "An' you always put cream on old leather, to restore it."

I wasn't going to touch that one with a ten-foot pole. It might be a matter of great interest how much of E's astonishing adventures were the earnest errors of a very young child trying to do good and how much were his attempts to drive the adults in his life completely and totally insane— which is where I had the advantage over him, because I didn't need to be driven. According to all the important people in my life, Cas included, I was so near insanity that I could take a short stroll there, down a scenic road.

The fact was I was a wuss. I didn't want to know if my son was a good kid, just inexperienced, or an agent of evil trying to subvert the world. I had looked all over him without finding any suspicious birthmarks, but maybe this was a stealthy kind of evil. I would bet Mrs. Torquemada had been equally content not to think much about the true nature of her son.

"I want you to come home with me," I told E. Which, again, proved everyone's surmise about the state of my mind.

He said, "Yeah?" and smiled his best angelic smile, and started to climb down from the bike seat. "I'll go pack," he said.

"No," I said in my best conspirator voice. "No. Don't go in the house." Since the divorce, holding on to joint custody, I'd tried to keep my disagreements with All-ex from hurting his relationship with E. "Daddy and Michelle were the ones who wanted to keep you," I said. "They won't let me take you. Probably."

E was quicker than I expected, though I'm not sure how much he understood. He blinked at me, and I saw a sly look come to his eyes, the same look I'd seen before, when he was trying to figure out how to do something he thought was forbidden. Then he looked around the fence.

"The gate is padlocked. There's nothing to climb," he said. "On this side."

"No," I said. And I wasn't even slightly startled, since that was exactly the way I would have thought. No. That was the way I still thought. I looked at the trash enclosure for something that might be used to climb and found nothing. Then I looked at those gates.

Fortunately, I always carry my tool kit.

I retraced to the back of the car and got my tool kit, then walked back to the enclosure. The gate was composed of two halves that closed in the center. If I could just remove one of them. . . .

With the screwdriver, I reached through the gate to where it was bolted on the side. Yeah, you wouldn't think that being able to unscrew things really fast was a needed skill. Until times like this. Of course, I'd started unscrewing things long before refinishing furniture. By the time I was E's age, I'd taken apart more furniture and pulled off more doors than you could shake a really big stick at. Sometimes my parents even noticed. Well, at least if what I took apart was a bookcase.

I leaned the half gate against the fence, then lifted it until I could tip it over the top of the fence. I'm convinced it was made of aluminum or something not cast iron, because I hadn't grown super strength, and I was able to lift it, using the fence as a fulcrum, and tilt-drop it, slowly, to the other side, after shouting to E, "Stay clear."

The gate had barely touched the ground when E was scrambling up it, like the monkey that Ben often accused him of being. At the top, he scrambled toward me, while saying, "Quickly, quickly," as if he were in charge of this escape.

It wasn't until we were in the car and driving away from the scene of the crime, leaving All-ex's trash enclosure sadly open to any and all bar-hopping (or not) bears, that my son looked at me, with a slight frown. "I 'spose," he said. "I could have opened the padlock."

I stomped on the brake out of sheer surprise, causing the people behind me to honk madly. "What? You had a key?" Now, Michelle was criminally insane. What kind of woman would leave Torquemada Jr. alone in a back-yard with the key to unlock the gate? How come he hadn't escaped before, just to check out the neighborhood? Was it that there was nothing fun to do in these suburbs, or did E only torment me?

"No," he said, indignantly, before I brought up my worse suspicions. "But I've been practicing opening locks with pins an' . . . an' stuff."

He looked at me with the most angelic of smiles. Of course, devils were nothing but fallen angels. "Uh . . . opening locks?"

"Sure," he said, now importantly. "Cas says that people can open locks without keys, so I've been trying . . ."

I was afraid to ask, truly I was. There was nothing in my house that was locked or needed to be unlocked, except the shed, with all its poisons, and the front door. And the idea of E in my shed was terrifying. Also, I had trouble believing he'd ever got in there and not created the sort of headlines that screamed *The fire near the college has now burned for five days.* "You've never . . ." At the last minute I remembered that if I asked him if he'd ever got into my shed, it would just guarantee he did so. Which just meant I still had some functioning brain cells. The same brain cells that told me I was going to buy the most high-tech padlock on the market tonight, no matter what it cost. "Uh . . . what have you unlocked?"

"You won't tell?"

"Of course not," I said, not worrying about the logic of it. In the minds of children, I suppose all adults are in collusion.

In his eyes was a look of pure mischief.

"Where did you open locks?" I asked. "I won't tell," I added. "And I won't be upset. I just want to know."

He sighed. "It's Daddy," he said in a tone that said this explained everything.

I hung on, wondering what stodgy and conventional All-ex could have to do with this. Had he, unbeknownst to me, started a career as a safecracker? The mind boggled.

"You see," E said, and licked his lips and looked again at me, sidewise, as though sure I'd find something objectionable in this, "Daddy keeps a lot of things locked."

"Yeah?" I said.

"Yeah." E nodded. "And Cas once talked about someone picking a lock and I asked him what it was. And he said they used wire hooks and they . . . they did what a key does.

Made locks open." He frowned slightly. "So I tried . . . and you know? It doesn't work in every lock, but . . ."

"But it works in some?" I asked, making a mental note to tell my fiancé to be very, very careful about what he said around my troublemaker.

"Yeah. An' I got into Dad's office and his locked drawer and stuff?"

"What was inside the locked drawer?" I asked, out of irrepressible curiosity. E and I weren't that different. If my father had kept a lot of things locked around the house, I'd probably have learned lock picking, too.

E looked disgusted. "Boring stuff. Maps and papers." He thought for a moment. "Oh, yeah, and pictures of poor ladies."

"Poor ladies?"

"They don't have any clothes."

I had to bite my lip to prevent myself from laughing out loud, mostly because I knew E very well, and I was sure all the ladies with no clothes now sported moustaches and probably antennae. "Ah," I said. And then, "E, you know you're not supposed to just open all locked doors, right? You could get in serious trouble for that. Police trouble."

"Oh, I know that," he said, glibly, in a tone that made me very sure that he didn't believe me at all. "Besides, you can't open every door! Even with the best hooks."

"Where . . . where do you get your hooks?" I asked tentatively.

A snort. "Earrings!"

I refused to ask whether it was my earrings or Michelle's. Instead, I drove my budding housebreaker to the place where I'd bought the suspiciously stained table.

CHAPTER 4

Very Suspicious Circumstances

The semi-permanent garage sale took place two blocks from my house, in front of what must once have been a majestic Victorian house. It remained vast and squarish, with a funny turret on one end. But its paint was peeling, boards were standing out from its facing, and its roof sagged on one side. There was a collection of items on the front lawn by a sign that said *Garage Sale*.

The house being one of the few residential buildings left on Fairfax Avenue, one of the main thoroughfares of Goldport, it got a fair amount of drive-by traffic, and at any given time, there were one or two people browsing a collection of items ranging from headless dolls to CD storage racks. Most of the time, I wondered if the people running the sale "shopped" in the same Dumpsters I did.

I drove by it almost every day, of course, and my twin

wonders over it were how the people running it managed to turn a profit at all from what amounted to little more than trash and how they never ran out of items.

Normally, I wasn't even vaguely tempted to stop, but the lines of the table had made me suspect real wood and caused me to park and saunter over.

Today's offerings were less impressive, I noted as I parked and told E, "Stay here. Do not come out. I'll be right back. I'm serious. Do not leave."

He looked at me with a scrunched-up face. "We have to go back," he said.

I let my hand fall on the way to opening the door. Had E turned into an adult? Was he going to tell me Michelle would worry?

"I forgot Ccelly."

I took a deep breath. The rules of this game were impenetrable at best, and I never knew when E would take my lead or not, but as I let air out slowly, I decided to go for broke. "No, you didn't," I said, improvising wildly. "Ccelly broke out ahead of you. He's the one who told me you weren't sick and I should come and get you."

E let out air, as though relieved. "Oh," he said. "Oh. That's where he went."

I refused to believe my son had been missing an invisible llama. I rushed out of the car before he could give me any details.

There were several empty flowerpots near me. Further on were two CD racks. Yet further on were a lot of baby clothes, strewn on a plastic bag. There were also a lot of suitcases that looked like someone had paused at a zoo, on a tour of the world, and given them to a bunch of wild animals to toss around.

The man who presumably lived in the house and ran the garage sale got up from the steps where he'd been sitting and ambled toward me, a smile displaying his large yellow teeth. "I see you're looking at them CD cases," he said. "Very fine they are and—"

"No," I said, afraid I'd be forced to buy CD cases if I let him go on. "No, really. I just wanted to know—" I looked up at a weathered face in which two blue eyes looked curiously unfocused, as if their owner were looking into a very distant place, not at someone standing in front of him. "I bought a table from you two days ago," I said. "Big, kitchen or dining table." I made the gestures with my hands that indicated how big the table was, or at least that it was as large as my arms could reach.

"Hey," he said. "Once you buy it, it's yours. We're not no department store. No returns." He laughed at his own joke.

"I don't want to return it," I said. "I was just wondering where it came from."

He looked at me awhile. "We get things from many places," he said. "People who don't have time to have a garage sale sell us things cheap, see, and then we sell them."

"And who did you get that table from?"

The blue eyes focused at me for a moment, taking me in. "Why would you want to know?"

"Well," I said. And then I realized if I told him that there were bloodstains on the table, he'd probably clamp tighter than a clam with constipation. Not only because, doubtless, he didn't want any trouble—who did?—but because I'd sound like a total lunatic, talking about stains on a table. And besides, I really couldn't explain to him that the finish on that table had just been wrong and nothing a reputable refinisher would do to a good piece of furniture. Heck, I would barely be able to explain that to Cas, much less to this addled stranger. On a strike of inspiration, I went with the first convoluted thought in my head. "You see, Castor Wolfe, senior investigator of the Serious Crimes Unit for the Goldport police—"

"Hey!" he interrupted me, which was a good thing, since I had no idea where I was going with this. I surmised saying that Cas slept with me half the nights would probably not impress this man . . . even if it still impressed me, frankly.

"Hey," he said. "I don't want no trouble with the police. If the stuff was hot, it wasn't I who took it and—"

"Of course not," I said. "But see, that's why we must know where it came from."

He ran his fingers up and through his salt-and-pepper hair, leaving distinct canals in the midst of it, which meant it was either drowned in product or—judging by the stale smell rolling off him—very dirty. "Yeah." He squinted at me, as if by focusing he could determine how serious I was. "Yeah. The table, you say?"

"Yes, the large table, that—"

"Only big table I seen in months," he said. "At the sale. And at the time I kinda wondered how come they didn't want it. But it looked kinda rough, and I thought what the hell."

Considering how often I thought *what the hell*, this was perfectly believable. Heck, I was thinking *what the hell* right now. As in *What the hell am I doing here asking this man stupid questions*?

"So I took it."

"You stole it?" I said.

He glared at me. "No. I paid five dollars for it."

"To whom?" I asked, mentally noting he'd made a fifteen dollar profit on that.

"He said his name was Jason Ashton," he said. "That's all I know. Never knew him from Adam, mind. I have nothing to do with it."

"Where does he live?" I asked.

He shrugged, backing away from me as though, by putting distance between us, he was somehow separating himself from any trouble I brought. "I don't know. Only reason I know his name is that I wrote him a check for the table and . . . and a bunch of other things, like those baby clothes."

I resisted an impulse to go and check if there were bloodstains on the baby clothes. The idea of a vast network of baby sacrificers flitted through my mind and made me shudder. But surely if that were going on, someone would have noticed. After all, there was a limited supply of babies, and people tended to care for them. It wasn't like you could buy babies in the department store, like how my mom used to tell me she acquired me. Though to be honest, she'd said she'd found me in the bargain bin up front, at ten for a dollar. It had taken me until I was four to know she was lying, though at least it explained why she hadn't taken advantage of the bargain and bought a couple more.

"But I don't know where he lives," the man said. "Honest. Don't know him from Adam."

"Right," I said. "Thank you." It was entirely possible he was telling me the truth. About as possible as that he was lying, of course. But in either case, I wasn't going to get any more out of him. Not when he thought I was out to get him. Not unless I could bring Cas with me and get him to ask questions, and I hadn't seen ads for the sale of any ski-lift tickets in hell. "Thank you."

I beat a hasty retreat toward the car. Chances were Jason Ashton was in the phone directory. Alternately, I could probably get someone at the police station to find the address for me. Perhaps even Cas, if I came up with a convincing enough lie to tell him.

In the car, I locked the doors. E looked out the window, doing such a convincing impression of a cherub I almost checked his back for wings. But surely no divinity would be so cruel as to increase E's ability to move *while* leaving him in possession of both hands.

I could call directory assistance and get Ashton's address before E got so bored he did something creative.

I fished my phone from my pocket and opened it. But before I could dial directory assistance, the phone rang. I pushed the ON button, and Ben's voice thundered out of it, loud enough to be heard a good distance from my ear. "Dyce! What in hell are you up to?"

I remembered that I had left poor Ben alone with my mother, planning the wedding. As cruel as this might be, he probably deserved it. He was almost as much trouble as Mom, and was probably only mad because I hadn't supported his plan for boutonniere rats. But it still seemed like unwarranted evil to leave him alone with the woman who had been planning to marry me to him since Ben and I had—unwisely—gone to high school prom together, even though Ben had worn a powder-blue tux, which should have served Mom notice that nothing would come of this.

"Nothing," I said, defensively, as I put the phone to my ear.

The sound that came from the other side was a combination of a sniff, a snort, and a sigh of exasperation. It sounded something like the noise I imagined a dying pterodactyl might make, but I knew it was actually the call of the exasperated Benedict Colm.

"Dyce," he said in the world-weary tone that implied he had seen civilizations rise and fall and had never, ever, ever met a woman more exasperating than myself. Which was, at any rate, a gross injustice, since if Ben had seen the civilizations rise and fall, he'd have concentrated on the Greek and Roman and others with shapely young men and not even noticed any of the women.

"What?"

"Nick just called," he said. "They have an Amber Alert out for E."

I looked at my son, who was looking out of the window at a couple of people browsing the trashy garage sale. "What?"

"It appears someone took him from the Mahrs' backyard. Neighbors reported it was a woman in a blue Volvo. Someone who vandalized their trash enclosure."

I sighed. "It's my day to have him," I whined. "They said he had a fever, but he doesn't. And besides, I didn't take him. He climbed out by himself."

"*Climbed* out?"

"I might sort of have removed the gate to the trash enclosure so he could climb out," I said. "But you know, they didn't leave him a ladder or anything, so it's their fault."

There was a long silence; then Ben said, "I see," in a

tone that indicated that he did in fact see and what's more he didn't approve of what he saw. "I'll just call Nick, shall I? And tell him that you have E, and he's fine. Are you sure this is your time to have him?"

"According to the custody agreement it is," I said. I ran the whole thing through my mind and couldn't imagine their being able to stick me with anything more than rudeness and possibly mild vandalism. It was my time to have E, and when it all boiled down to facts, anyone would stick by the word of the agreement.

"I see," Ben said. "I'll call Nick. You call the Mahrs and tell them you have E. *And* I will meet you at your house."

"Oh, you don't have to. I'm sure—"

"I *will* meet you at your house," Ben said, firmly. "I'm already on the way." And he hung up.

I'd often said, and it bore repeating, that of all the exasperating people in the world, Ben was probably the worst and that it was a good thing for all concerned that he had no interest in women.

Oh, sure, an ex-lover of his had done his best to set fire to that portion of Ben's condo that he couldn't throw out the balcony. But a woman would have been more targeted and careful, and Ben would be dead by now. She would have thrown *him* from the balcony, even if it took a lever.

I considered my options. I could call Michelle Mahr at home. The problem with calling someone, though, is that there is more than a good chance they will answer. And if she answered, I wasn't absolutely sure what I'd do. There was bound to be some unpleasantness, and she might ask questions. It wouldn't be a good thing. Or

I could call All-ex at work. It was the weekend, so he wouldn't be there. Granted, he owned the realty company, but that was why he didn't need to work on weekends. He had flunkies for that.

But then I thought that Ben would probably insist it didn't fulfill the spirit of the thing for me to call a number the Mahrs wouldn't check for two days.

Sighing, I dialed their house number. And lucked out. There was a busy sound, and ten seconds later the answering machine kicked up. "You have reached the residence of Alexander and Michelle Mahr. If you're not a telemarketer, please leave a message at the tone."

"Hi," I said. "This is Dyce. Dyce Dare," in case they knew more than one Dyce who sounded incredibly guilty. "I came by and E was . . . in the alley, and he didn't seem feverish at all, so I picked him up. I'll give him back to you on Wednesday." I hung up and leaned against the seat, taking deep breaths and thinking that I'd give him back when pigs flew. If I couldn't trust them not to lie to me and try to keep him, I didn't want to give him to them at all.

I found my son was staring at me with wide open eyes. "You didn't tell them how I got out, did you?"

"No," I said. "Just that you were in the alley."

"Oh, good," he said. "They ask so many questions."

"Yeah," I said, feeling guilty for backing the budding infantile delinquent against my fellow, supposedly responsible, adults. But I remembered being a budding infantile delinquent myself, and besides, I had very little patience for the Mahrs right now. What could they have meant by lying to me?

It might be something as stupid as their wanting to

show E off at some work-related function or other. All-ex liked to convey the impression that he was a devoted father without actually having much to do with E, who mostly got shuttled between myself and Mrs. All-ex. But if that was behind it, why didn't they just tell me that? I'd never given them problems over that sort of thing before.

It was still bothering me as I pulled up in front of my house, right next to Cas's SUV and behind Ben's new—cream, exactly like the last one—BMW.

They both stepped away from their cars at the same time, as if I were a dangerous felon who must be contained. Ben had clearly been waiting beside his car and now walked toward me, as I opened the door, while Cas walked the other way, toward the passenger side of my car.

I thought it best to ignore them both and walk around, to open the door to E. Only E had already opened the door and was getting out. By the time I closed the door and gave E my hand, the two men were so close that I could feel both their sighs of exasperation as they loomed over me.

I looked up at them, with my best confused and innocent expression. "What?" I said. "It's my day to get him."

"I bet you didn't even call the Mahrs," Ben said.

"Wrong," I said. "I left a message on their machine."

"At Alex's work," Ben snapped.

Ah! He could, too, be wrong. His telepathy apparatus must be on the blink. "No," I said with as much dignity as I could muster, turning to walk toward the front door. "At their home."

Since the guys were blocking the logical path between

my car and Ben's, I squeezed between their parked cars. Ben tried to follow me, but he didn't fit, so, with a sound of exasperation, he walked the long way around the car. Presumably, Cas did the same in the other direction, because as I got to my front door, the men were closing in on me, one from either side again.

I put my key in the lock and squared my shoulders. Holding my hand, E giggled.

I considered closing the door in both their faces, but decided that would be a bad idea. I could probably have a wedding without Ben, even if it might jinx it. But Cas was sort of essential to my marital plans, after all. At least unless I forged a proxy document in his name, which of course I would do, if absolutely needed. For his own good, of course. But I'd rather not have to.

So I let them come in behind us, and I went to the kitchen. I let go of E's hand in the living room, fully expecting him to go to his room and play with his toys or pet Pythagoras or draw or whatever it was he did in there. But the little wretch followed me to the kitchen, which could only mean he expected something interesting would happen, in the way of fascinating arguments between three adults in his life.

I pretended I didn't know what would happen and started making coffee. In the living room, I heard the guys whisper at each other, and I suspected it wasn't tips about how to tie a perfect tie knot or how to design a rat boutonniere. I suspected it was either a rousing pre-battle speech or strategizing on how to approach me. Right.

CHAPTER 5

Minding the Home Fires

"Dyce," Cas said, coming into the kitchen. Ben came in behind him and went to sit with E at the kitchen table. The kitchen consisted of tiled counters, an ancient tiled floor, a stove that had seen better days, and my grandmother's beautiful antique kitchen table, surrounded by four matching chairs.

Cas sounded perfectly reasonable, which was just like him. Trying to get around me by being reasonable. Ah! He'd just see where that got him. I could defeat anyone trying to sound reasonable with my sheer lack of reason.

"You know you can't do stuff like this," he said. "When we're married, it will sound like you're doing this stuff because you know you can get away with it and . . ."

I glared at him. "It's my day to have E."

"Well, that's fine," he said, sounding like sweet sanity. Why is it he always does that when I'm spoiling for a fight? It would be so much easier to scream, argue, and then be done. But nooooooo, he has to try to be reasonable. And I couldn't even be mad at him, of course, because he was being . . . reasonable.

My front doorbell sounded, and Ben got up to go answer it, which meant for sure it was Nick. Right. For some reason, the fact that Ben would just open the door to his boyfriend without asking me first made me furious. I mean, he'd had keys to my house since . . . ever. And had I come back from an errand to find him and Nick sitting in my living room or even cooking in my kitchen, I'd have thought very little of it and waited for an explanation. And even if the explanation had been "We're just tired of our kitchen and decided to change stoves," that would be fine, too.

But right then, his taking the liberty to open the door to Nick like that just made me feel taken advantage of.

The fact that the two of them were whispering in my living room didn't help. "I can hear you," I said, crossly, just loud enough for my voice to carry to the living room.

"No, you really can't," Ben said. And Nick said something I couldn't understand. Just proving I couldn't hear him, I guessed. More of that annoying male logic. As if he had to rub my nose in it.

I got another cup from the cupboard and splashed coffee into all of them, thinking I'd much rather be pouring it onto male heads. Cas put his hand on my arm. "Dyce, look, I know it's your day to have E and if you'd told Michelle Mahr that they couldn't keep him, you'd have been absolutely in the right, but the thing is you didn't. And then you went to their house and got him out of the backyard . . . You're lucky they didn't charge you with criminal mischief."

Nick and Ben came in and, wordlessly, picked up their cups. Nick looks like a more casual version of Bacchus. He could have walked out of the friezes in a dozen ancient Greek palaces. Because I guess he was on duty—what part of duty was for both Nick and Cas to lounge around my kitchen—he wore khaki pants and a white polo shirt, instead of his normal jeans and T-shirts. Still, next to Ben's freshly pressed elegance, he looked almost terminally relaxed, a pose not helped by his managing to lean against my kitchen counter, coffee cup in hand, giving the impression he was posing for a fashion magazine.

I glared at Cas, who as far as I was concerned had started all this. "I didn't get him out of the backyard," I said. "He got himself out of the backyard."

"Okay," Cas said. "So he climbed the gate himself. That doesn't mean you're innocent. Who removed the gate?"

"If they didn't want their gate removed, they should have left something on the other side for E to climb. A ladder, for instance."

E nodded vigorously at this.

Cas dropped into a chair and put his head in his hands. "Woman," he said in the voice of a man tempted beyond all endurance. "What am I going to do with you?"

I heard Ben clear his throat and was seized with a horrible fear that he was about to make suggestions. I was almost sure they would be purely theoretical, but I didn't want to hear them all the same. "You don't have to do anything with me," I said, stiffly. "I'm an adult. I can—"

He took his hands down from his face, and I could see him working his lips to say the unforgivable, then realizing it was the unforgivable and pulling back. He sighed. "Look, Dyce, it's just that you have to think of my position, too. I mean, we're going to be married, which means what you do reflects on me, okay? I don't like it, and you don't like it, but it's the way things are. I can't afford to have you going around acting as if laws didn't apply to you. Not that I don't find what you do . . . criminally endearing . . ." I could *hear* Ben roll his eyes behind my back. "But you can't keep doing it. Not and allow me to keep my job."

He looked at my face and sighed again. "Okay, so probably we could live on pancakes and your refinishing, but is that a proper diet for a growing young man?"

I heard Ben clear his throat and had no clue what he would say, but fortunately E put in, "And oats for Ccelly."

"Cecily?" Ben said. I realized he hadn't been introduced to the invisible member of the family.

"Yeah, he's a growing llama," E said.

"You have a transsexual pet llama?" Ben asked.

"Imaginary transsexual pet llama," I said.

"Oh, like that makes it better!"

"Not now," Cas said, echoed by Nick. "Right now, I just want to understand why you felt the need to kidnap E, after telling your ex's wife she could keep him over the weekend."

"Ccelly told her I wasn't sick," E said.

Cas wisely chose to ignore this. "Dyce?"

"Well, I had a strong feeling he wasn't sick, after all. So I had to go check, and then . . ."

"And then?" Cas asked.

"And then he said he hadn't been to the doctor. And I thought, well . . ."

"You thought?" Cas said.

I chose to imagine there was no sarcasm there. "Yeah,

I thought that since they hadn't taken him to the doctor, and he was plainly not ill, there was something weird going on, and I don't trust them."

Cas took two slow, deep breaths. "God knows I don't want to defend your ex and his wife. They seem fairly odd to me, and that's putting it mildly. But maybe they wanted to keep him over because they wanted to show him off to someone? Or maybe—okay, I know, but . . ." He looked at E. "They seem to want to do this fairly often. Who knows why?"

"It's not that," I said. "I mean, if it were that, why wouldn't they tell me? Clearly this happens regularly enough, and I allow it regularly enough. So why not ask me properly?"

"I don't know," Cas said. "Temporary insanity?"

E looked up from petting Pythagoras, who had crawled into his lap while we weren't looking. "They wanted to keep me because of the fires."

"What?" I think the question came from all of us at once. Nick peeled off the counter and would have loomed over my child, except that Ben—who knows my child better—interposed his outstretched arm, to stop him.

E looked up at us. "I don't know," he said, and at that point it was impossible to tell whether he was really that innocent or had just got so startled by our response that he found it easier to pretend ignorance. "I just heard Dad say to 'chelle, late at night, that it would be easier to keep me with her, until the fire thing was resolved. And that he thought that his passport was up to date, but that must have been a joke, because they laughed."

Cas blinked. "How did you hear this?"

"They were in their room," he said. And then, casting

about to explain his presence, "I wanted a glass of water, so I went outside their room . . ."

I sighed. "There is no way all you wanted was a glass of water," I said. "In fact, I'd bet that Michelle leaves water bottles in your room. Filtered, organic, free-range water bottles." I crossed my arms on my chest and looked around at the bewildered males. "I'm sure of it," I said. "It's the type of thing a woman who insists on feeding him fiber and food with no preservatives would do."

E stuck out his lower lip, in the way he did when he knew he wasn't going to get around me. It wasn't so much a pout as a gesture of defeat. "I get bored," he said. "And they do funny things when they're alone. Like when—"

"We truly don't need to know," I said. I traded a silent look with Cas that said, *Now do you understand why I don't want to do anything unless I'm absolutely sure he is asleep?* His look back said, *Completely. Which is why we're going to get a bedroom with a door that has a secure lock.*

I abstained from telling him that, given my son's new-found hobby, we might need to make our conjugal bed inside a bank vault.

"Well, they were talking, and Dad said, he said, what with all the fires, and that the police"—he looked up at Cas—"were investigating, and that until the police came out with a solution, they weren't safe. And then Michelle said something and Dad said that no, he didn't like hand-cuffs, even for play—" He looked at me. "Mommy, do they play cops and robbers?"

I covered my eyes. A *soundproof* bank vault. And if Benedict Colm didn't do a better job of disguising his laughter, he was going to die in the next few seconds.

"Well, anyway," E said, "they said they should keep me, just in case."

I looked at Cas. The look back at me was completely nonhumorous and had a tinge of puzzled worry.

Ben managed to turn his guffaws—behind his hand, of course—into a convincing cough. Nick said, "Hey, E, why don't you come outside with me and Ben for a moment? I have my new convertible out there. You know, the red one."

It was much too cold for convertibles, not that anything born male would believe this. E loved the things as much as the adult males did, and he even managed to sit very still and quiet when Cas consented to take him to spend an afternoon watching Cas and Nick work on one of the convertibles they restored as a hobby. He perked up, jumping from the chair. "Peesgrass and I—"

Ben was back in full command of what passed for his faculties. He took Pythagoras away from E and dumped him on my lap. "No. Pythagoras might run away."

E looked like he was going to protest, but he probably realized this was his one shot at being taken for a ride in Nick's cool car, and he said, "Okay, can I drive?"

"As soon as you have your learner's permit," Nick said, giving him his hand.

"Ben?" E asked, reaching his other hand for Ben. "Can I get my learner's permit?"

They were out the front door before I heard Ben's response.

Cas and I were quiet for a long while after they left; then Cas sighed, and I said, "You said you were investigating arson cases in houses that are for sale. I know All-ex has a realty . . ."

Cas shrugged. "It doesn't mean it was him. Oh, I grant

you, your son heard something. But you know what he hears is filtered through what he understands. And that means . . ."

"He could be totally wrong," I said. "Like mistaking sarcasm for the truth."

"Yeah."

The thing is that although I was capable of suspecting All-ex of ten wrong things before breakfast, arson and criminal intent to break custody and run weren't two of them. For one thing, All-ex was much too attached to being big fish in the little pond of Goldport, Colorado. He didn't even—truth be told—make much of an effort to enter Denver society. And that was a personality thing. He was ambitions but local. It was almost charming how much he loved Goldport. When we'd been in college in Denver and dating, he'd insisted on running back to Goldport as soon as he could every weekend, even if there was something cool going on around college. He wouldn't consider running. And if he did—supposing that my ex had been hit on the head and suffered a massive concussion and considered going off to start life in a new place, just him and Mrs. All-ex, and . . . E?

Let's face it—E somewhere between appalled him and scared him. Not that he didn't love his son. I was fairly sure he did. All-ex was expected to love his son, and in a conventional, down-to-earth way it wouldn't occur to him not to love his son. But I didn't think he wanted his son full time and without my intervention. No, not even if he said he did. And if he was so crazy as to tell Mrs. All-ex he wanted to do that, then she would talk sense into him. Oh, not openly, but over the years I'd come to realize that Michelle was a nice, traditional wife who perfectly obeyed her husband. Provided he told her to do what she wanted to do to begin with.

"So what do you think is going on?" I asked.

"Damned if I know . . ." he said.

"I don't want to give them E again on Wednesday. I just don't. I know, I don't see him as doing this, but . . ."

Cas nodded. "Well, sauce for the goose. I'll . . . talk to him and tell him we need E for some wedding-related fittings or something . . . What is he wearing to the wedding, by the way? What are you?"

"I don't know," I said. "I was thinking of going naked."

He gave me a leer, proving that the man was there, right behind the eyes of the policeman. "Mmm, my favorite. But unless we're marrying in a nudist colony, people are bound to think it looks funny. I thought Ben had found some dresses for you to look at?"

I groaned. "Ben—aka Benedict Colm, conservatively elegant financial planner and man about town—becomes a little insane at the prospect of helping me choose a dress for my wedding."

Cas raised an eyebrow.

"Miles and miles of gauzy tulle," I said. "Held up with little lace roses and pink ribbons. And if I tell him I don't want to wear white or a conventional bride's dress because this is my second wedding, he goes to the Disney-princess-like dresses intended for bridesmaids and starts pulling out pastel pink, pale blue, and"—I made a despondent gesture—"gold."

"Uh . . ." Cas said. "I'll talk to Nick about—"

"Don't," I said. "Last Friday both of them took me shopping after work. I know you think Nick is a sensible man, but his taste seems to run to froufrou, like face-covering veils. With roses. You know, it's not too late to elope . . ."

Cas laughed. "Your parents would hate it on the roof rack, it wouldn't be fair to my parents to ask them to babysit yours all the way to Las Vegas, and, besides, Nick's parents want to come. They've offered to cater the reception."

I didn't say anything. I'd met Nick's parents, of course. We'd gone up to the Golden Fleece, their restaurant in Denver, and met Nick's mother and father and his ten-year-younger little brother, who looked like a copy of Nick but with more cute and less sexy. I even liked the food. And Nick's mother was Cas's only aunt. It was just I hadn't been thinking in terms of reception. In my mind, if I'd visualized a second wedding at all, there were maybe some drinks, and maybe just the ceremony, and then my husband and I left . . .

"If you want another type of food—" Cas said.

"No. No. I'm just not sure I want them to go to all that trouble; I mean—"

"They'll love it. Don't worry."

"I suppose eloping *really* is out of the question?"

He grabbed me around the shoulders and kissed me. Somewhere in the middle of the kiss, I felt my brain melt and run out of my ears. Which was very effective in making me forget all my worries.

As we heard the front door open and Ben and Nick come in with much—surely unnecessary?—scraping of feet and banging of doors and hearty talk of "That was fun, wasn't it?" to E, we pulled apart.

While I was struggling to get my breath back, much less remember my name, let alone any plans for the wedding, Cas took advantage to kiss my forehead. "It will be fine. I promise. We'll find a way to run away soon after the ceremony." He must have caught a flicker of worry in my eyes, as he pulled my hair out of my face and said, "Look, I'll talk to Mahr about keeping E another week. I'll smooth things over. They can't say much, not to me."

No, probably not. Not if they were afraid of the police. But I suspected I was going to pay for all this soon enough, if not openly.

Proving he knew it as well, he sighed. "I'll poke around, okay? But I really don't think he's involved in the fires. For one, not all the houses burned down are listed with his realty company, and besides—"

And besides, Nick and Ben were now in the kitchen and clearing their throats, so we stood a little further apart, as E came and inserted himself between us. I knew this was an attempt to be reassured that we still loved him, and I was capable of rational behavior sometimes, so we hugged my son.

"Cas, we need to go," Nick said. "There's that interview with—"

"I know, I know." Cas kissed my lips and the top of E's head. "E, do try not to be too bad a boy for Mommy, okay?"

"Okay," my son said, back to his impersonation of a cherub, which wouldn't take in anyone who had known him for any amount of time. "I'll take care of Ccelly, too."

"Er . . . uh . . . good," Cas said, getting up and starting toward the door.

Ben cleared his throat. "Uh, before you go . . . Which color rat do you want for your boutonniere?"

CHAPTER 6

Of Rats and Men

Once I managed to convince Cas that they were not
joking about the rats, he put his foot down. "Absolutely
no rodents in the wedding," he said.

Nick's lips were twitching. "This was Dyce's mom's
idea, wasn't it?"

"Uh, yeah."

"Ben! They'd eat the tuxes. Also, have you considered
rat poo—"

"Right," Ben said. "Okay. Okay. No rats."

"And no best cat, either. Nick is my best man, and we
don't need a best cat."

"But Peesgrass wants to come!" E said. He'd retrieved
Pythagoras from wherever the cat had been sunning himself and was holding him clutched to his chest. Pythagoras's little cross-eyed face stared at us in acute

embarrassment, whether at his position or at the idea of being in the wedding, I couldn't tell.

"They make harness leashes for cats," Nick said. "I'll look after him. He's already black; all we need is to attach a little white tie to his collar," he said.

I didn't say anything. If the cat died of embarrassment, the SPCA would be all over us.

I thought lovingly about the table in my shed and wished I could go back there and work. Then I thought of Jason Ashton. And ambled toward the phone book on the counter.

There was only one Jason Ashton, and he lived a few blocks away, on Jefferson Street—in a warren of Victorian streets named after presidents. I wondered if the three men would notice if I left right then. But, as Cas came and put his arm around my shoulders and said, "Don't worry, Dyce. It will be all right. I'm not going to allow them to take E," I had to assume they would. Well, at least Cas would notice I'd left if I crept out from under his arm. He could be quite observant that way. It was the investigative training.

But in one of those bizarre coincidences that real life can get away with, Nick said, "Come on. We have something like twenty arson suspects to investigate. How you're going to figure all of that out—plus the Ashton disappearance—with three of us in the department is beyond me."

"Ashton?" I said, startled at hearing the name spoken outside my head.

"Woman who left her husband and disappeared," Cas said. "Her husband reported her as a missing person, so we have to look, but there doesn't seem to be anything we can do. She seems to be one of the voluntarily disappeared. We still have to look."

"Oh," I said, but I was thinking of that table in the back and the almost-for-sure bloodstains on it.

When the two policemen finished their coffee and left me alone with Ben, I told Ben the entire story of the table and the stains.

"But," Ben said, "isn't it kind of normal for one wood to be disguised as another wood?"

"Yeah," I said. "But not for oak to be disguised as pine. And not for a bad, jammed stain to be piled atop a fine oil finish."

He frowned. "But then you also say there's never any reason for metallic finishes and people—"

"There's never any reason now. In the sixties and seventies, I'd guess the reason was widespread cannabis use," I said.

"Maybe this was—"

"Maybe," I said. "But it looks more recent to me."

"Oh."

"At any rate, I thought I'd go out and talk to Jason Ashton and see if anything rings any bells," I said.

"Oh, yeah," Ben said. "Because we don't have nearly enough trouble already."

"Exactly. So are you coming with me?"

"Wouldn't miss it for the world."

CHAPTER 7

Playing Happy Families

Jason Ashton lived in an area of Jefferson that was just starting to gentrify. This caused near-lethal whiplash, as one tried to figure out the character of the neighborhood.

Elaborately painted and restored Victorian houses, in the midst of immaculate lawns, sat right next to crumbling, shacklike piles surrounded by barbed wire.

In between the two, in spirit—though often not physically—were Victorians painted white and converted into apartments, usually surrounded by dead lawns or front yards covered in pebbles in a vain attempt to look water conscious but really just looking cheap. More often than not, too, the landlords had let the yard go bad, anyway, so that there was grass growing in between the pebbles.

There was one of those on the left side of the Ashton residence. On the other side was an elaborate house in painted-lady style. Ben glanced at it and frowned and looked like he was going to say something, then didn't. He pulled up in front of the house, looking dubious. I wasn't sure why he'd look so worried. There were other new cars on the street, interspersed with rust buckets that might have been abandoned there by the receding waters of the Flood.

"So this is the house . . ." I said.

He just looked at me.

"Are you going to go and ring the doorbell?" I asked. "See what they look like?"

He looked at me again. "Dyce . . . we are in our thirties. We don't ring strangers' doorbells."

I opened my mouth to tell him we didn't need to stay there after we rang the doorbell. But his eyes told me this would be a really bad idea.

"Dyce, we are not ringing strangers' doorbells and running away. And if we did, what in thunder would it gain us?"

"Uh . . . we'd know if the missing woman answered the door," I said. Which was, in a nutshell, the problem. I mean, sure, I read cozies, too. There are all these stories about how people investigating other people and possible crimes they have no business looking into can dress as electric company workers or social workers or poll takers. The problem—I looked over at Ben's impeccable attire and his look of just having stepped out of a magazine on fashion for the discerning businessman. The problem was that no one would believe Ben was a survey taker or worked for any utilities. At least not until fashion sense became a metered public utility. *Hello, ma'am, we've noticed you've been expending rather too much fashion sense lately. No? Ah, I see. You've been advising your husband. Well, we know how it is, but it will cost you.*

As for me, I might pass as a woman collecting for charity. At least if the charity were for single mothers with disturbingly imaginative children, I thought as E said, "Ccelly can ring the doorbell."

But who would give to such an unorthodox charity?

Ben was drumming his fingers on the wheel. He made a face and expelled his breath, with every look of a small explosion. "Okay," he said. "I didn't realize it was just next door. There's an off chance that Peter saw something or knows something about them."

"Peter?" I said. Peter Milano, a violinist in the Goldport Philharmonic, was one of Ben's best friends—the person who usually called to organize Ben's birthday party and the like. Except I suspected this year it would be Nick doing that. At least I hoped so. But though I'd seen Peter half a dozen times, usually at Ben-related occasions, I'd no idea where he lived.

Ben gestured vaguely toward the painted lady, then frowned. "I don't know how late the concert ran last night, though." Which made sense, because the philharmonic usually had concerts on Friday night. "And Collin is probably in finals." Collin was Peter's partner, and I understood that he was a lecturer at the college. "So I have no idea if they'll be up." Which made no sense whatsoever, since it was close to three in the afternoon.

Ben nodded as if to himself. At least I hoped it was to himself, because I had failed to say anything. "Right," he said. "You wait here."

I waited. I knew for a fact that he was only leaving me in the car so he didn't have to take E and the invisible llama. He was probably scared of explaining the invisible llama to his friends. Coward.

He left the car and ran full tilt up the ten or so steps to the front door, where he stopped and, presumably— hard to see from where I was—rang the doorbell.

He'd turned back, as though giving up, when the door opened. Peter—whom I'd never before seen in T-shirt and jeans—came out on the porch. There was some con- versation and Ben's shoulders shook with laughter and then Peter was coming down the steps—barefoot.

Peter Milano always reminded me of those ultra-precious shepherd statues from Spain. The Lladró ones, where people were freakishly elongated and often vampire pale, with dark hair. He was like that, only not taken to the point of looking unnatural. Instead, he was one of those men who seemed to have been designed to wear a tux and who always seemed slightly awkward in anything else. Also, there was white in the perfect black hair, the sort of white men get at the tem- ples and that makes them look suave and sophisticated.

He loped along the—must be cold as all heck— sidewalk toward me, and opened the car door. "Come inside," he said. "We'll have tea or something. Ben said you want to ask us some questions."

Ben, who had followed more sedately, was opening the back car door and getting E out of his car seat. But E refused to go. "Ccelly," he said, commandingly. "You have to let Ccelly in, too."

Peter raised an eyebrow, and I shook my head. Maybe I, too, was a coward. At least I didn't feel equal to explaining imaginary llamas. Instead, I went in the back, and made vague motions, until E said, "You're not unbuckling his seat belt right. Here, let me help."

He leaned over and mimed opening a seat belt. I tried not to imagine the seat-belted and sitting-like-a-person llama there. It would have to be a very small llama; otherwise, it would be poking its head through the ceiling of the car.

E looked approving and picked something invisible out of midair. "Now, take him out," he said, handing me what had to be presumed were imaginary reins.

How do you lead an invisible llama? Seemed like the opening to one of those drinking songs in which you end up counting objects—possibly invisible hooves—before you get all confused and throw up on your own shoes.

However, I did the best I could, until we got to the steps, when E said, "No, no, you're going to pull his head off," and ran back to push the invisible llama behind up the stairs.

Peter raised his eyebrows to Ben this time, and Ben said, "Don't ask me. As best I can tell, it's an imaginary transsexual pet llama named Cecily."

"But it's invisible," I said.

"Because that makes everything much better," Ben said.

I half-expected Peter to run madly up the stairs, but instead he grinned and shook his head. "Cecily?"

"No," E explained, as he'd explained to me weeks ago. "Two *C*s, elly."

"I see," Peter said. "Because he's a llama, right, so he has two *L*s . . ."

E beamed up at him. "Yes, so he needs two *C*s." And added in a professorial tone, "Llamas have two *L*s because all talking llamas stutter."

"Oh?" Peter asked. I couldn't tell if the look on his face was amusement or fear.

"Yeah. That's why all their names have two comeuppances in the beginning."

"Comeuppances?" Ben said.

"Consonants," I translated.

They held the door open while I came in, leading the imaginary llama. The problem with E's imagination is that it's contagious. I could almost feel the weight of the imaginary lead and hear the tiny llama hooves on the floor, all the while Ccelly looked at me with his superior llama sneer.

E closed the door behind us and dusted his hands. "There. He's only scared of stairs." He had the grace to look down at the gleaming waxed antique floor. "And you don't need to be afraid he'll hurt the floors. I got him little llama tennis shoes, because 'chelle gets upset if he leaves hoof marks on the carpet."

The sound of hooves changed to the footfalls of a well-behaved, impeccably shod llama, and I wondered what Michelle had really gotten upset at.

Ben was explaining Michelle and All-ex as we were led down a pale-blue hallway to a very comfortable-looking sitting room, done up in sofas covered in what looked not so much like pastels, but faded jewel tones. Bookcases entirely surrounded the walls, all of them loaded down with books, but without any seeming order. There were leather-bound books right next to garish paperbacks.

"I'll go see where Collin got to," Peter said.

Ben started looking around at the bookcases, and E sat on the chair, petting Ccelly, who, presumably, liked the room and wasn't causing any trouble.

"Did you tell him?" I asked.

"Yeah," Ben said.

At that moment, Peter and Collin came back in,

bearing a tray with tea things and a plate of cookies. Before I had time to think, I was sitting on the sofa with a cup of tea and a cookie. E had a glass of milk and a cookie in each hand. When he tried to give Ccelly a cookie, Collin intervened and gave him an invisible-llama cookie.

When I'd first met Collin, I'd thought that Peter had been robbing the cradle, because Collin looked maybe twenty or twenty-one. Turned out he was my and Ben's age and a lecturer of classics at the euphoniously named CUG—a slight play on its real name, University of Colorado at Goldport.

"So," Peter said, sitting down across from me on one of the sofas, which were surprisingly comfortable for things that looked so prim. "Ben said you wanted to know more about Maria, next door."

I explained about the table and the stains and how it had been bothering me even before I heard that someone had disappeared who had the same last name. "She was Jason Ashton's wife, wasn't she?" I asked.

Peter nodded. He looked circumspect, as though he'd tell me some things, but not all, and would very much like to know why I felt a need to ask.

"It's like this," I said. "The table was a good price, and it looks great, but I'm afraid that if I fix it and sell it, I'll be cooperating in destroying evidence of a crime."

Peter looked grave. "They seem like a very nice couple," he said. "Really. I mean, if you're going to ask us if we heard terrible arguments, or someone crying for help . . ."

"No . . . I just . . ." I shrugged and bit into my cookie. "I'm sorry. I probably shouldn't have disturbed you. I was going to ring the doorbell next door, but Ben thought . . ."

Ben sighed. "Peter, we're not going to repeat any gossip anywhere, and Dyce is not going to go running to the police. If it helps, she's experienced enough with refinishing that if she thinks something sounds odd, it probably is."

"It's the fact that no one would disguise expensive wood as cheap," I said.

Peter looked at Ben, who was looming behind my sofa, teacup in hand. "Frankly, it wasn't Dyce running to the police that worried me as much as . . . How are things with Nick, Ben?"

I glanced back. Was that a slight straightening of Ben's spine, as though in offended hauteur? Why, yes, I thought it was. "Fine, thank you so much."

"Well . . ." Peter said. "Here's the thing. Some couples talk about everything, some don't, and you two are new enough that I barely know him, and I don't know what kind of couple you are."

"I tell him things that are mine to tell," Ben said. "I don't think he needs to know anything pertaining to other people's lives . . ." He frowned a little. "Frankly, I don't think he'd have any interest. I mean, unless you've seen the woman murdered or something like that, I presume, as responsible people, you'd already have talked. But . . ." He looked at E, who was looking like a little cherub sans wings again, soulfully eating his cookies. "Considering what some people are capable of repeating," he said, looking intently at my son, "it is neither here nor there whether I can be trusted. Come on, Monkey. Peter has a doggie who shakes hands and fetches. I think you should meet him."

Peter looked confused for a moment, then smiled. "Thank you, Ben. Chopin is out back. His toys are by the back door. He's very fond of the red ball."

I was fairly sure that my son had heard enough to know we were going to talk behind his back and that he'd like, more than anything, to hear what we were going to say. But I also knew that E was at that age when he'd be unable to resist a friendly animal: cat, rat, or dog.

So, after minimal hesitation, he gave Ben his hand, and Ben led him out back, obviously familiar enough with the house not to ask for directions.

Peter turned to Collin, who sat down beside him, and they looked at each other for a moment before Collin nodded. Considering that I'd seen Nick and Ben do that also, I wondered if there was some sort of gay-telepathy club, and why hetero couples didn't have it. I wanted my dose of telepathy.

Then I thought of how worried Cas would be if he knew half the trouble I got into or threatened to get into, and I decided it wasn't a gift. Or at least not one I wanted.

Collin sighed. "If it helps," he said, "I don't think anything bad happened to her. I'm not saying that there aren't bloodstains on the table, but surely you know how that stuff can happen—nosebleeds or just . . . hamburger portioning or something, and then they didn't know how to remove the stains, so they threw some varnish and stuff at it. It could be as simple as that."

"Yeah, it could," I said, half convinced. "But if you don't think it was anything bad, then why . . ."

Collin shook his head. "Well, see, we think she has a boyfriend. We suspect she left with him. But the thing is, as far as we can tell, her husband doesn't know, and he's a nice guy. We haven't been able to decide whether he'd feel better knowing that she's away and okay or if he'd feel hurt because she never let him know there was someone else."

"And to make things weirder," Peter said, "the boy-friend is still visiting, so maybe, if the husband needs to be told, he will tell him. I mean, it's clear they're friends."

"Or maybe she ran away because she couldn't take the situation with both of them, in which case, by telling Jason, we're removing his support system for no good purpose," Collin said. "And we're friendly. I mean, I'm not going to say we're best friends, but we had a barbecue together in the summer, and they come over when they need something, and we leave the keys with them and ask them to feed Chopin when we're away."

"Boxer," Collin said. "In the backyard right now." He grinned. "Thought he might scare Ccelly. You know what . . . invisible llamas are like."

"But how do you know there was a boyfriend?" I asked. It is deductive reasoning and bulldog-like tenacity like this that have, for the longest time, made my parents sure I should be a private investigator.

"Because we saw them. I mean, he might just have been a friend of the family who comes over to babysit. He seems to be that, but . . ." Peter set his teacup down on the polished coffee table and motioned for me to follow him to the window. He raised the shade on it. "See that window?"

There was a window directly facing this one, across a tiny strip of garden filled with leaf-bare rosebushes. "When the light is on, you can see in there. We don't try to, you know, but if you happen to be in here, and come to the window to lower or raise the blind or something, you can't help seeing. That's a bathroom window, and one day I saw their friend, Sebastian, in there, with Maria, helping her get out of the tub, completely naked."

"And he gasped in such a way that I went to look, too.

So I saw it, too," Collin said. "And I know that we some-times . . . I mean, I don't know what to make of it other than the idea that he was her boyfriend. We started notic-ing other little things after that, like how he came to visit almost every day while Jason was at work. It started both-ering us."

"And then she disappeared," Peter said. "And you see why we'd assume it was voluntary."

"Yeah," I said. And maybe it was. Yeah, the friend still coming to visit after she disappeared was a very odd thing, but then maybe she had got tired of both of them. Maybe she could not cope with the emotional entangle-ment of having two men in her life. Maybe that was why she had left. "What is he like? The husband. Was he very upset?"

"When she disappeared? Yeah, he was. He looked like death for a few days and asked us if we'd seen anything, if she'd told us anything before he reported her missing. But we hadn't. I mean, other than the stuff we didn't want to tell him because we didn't want to hurt him. He's a nice guy," Peter said. "Works down at the lumberyard, takes classes at night at CUG. Young kid—you know, late twenties. Maria used to take classes at CUG, too, but she also dropped out of sight there. No transfer, nothing. Collin looked." He hesitated. "In a way, boyfriend or not, it seemed like a very odd thing to happen. I mean, they seemed like such a nice couple, very attached."

Collin cleared his throat. "The only thing that sur-prised me," he said, "is that Maria didn't make any effort to take the kids. They have three: five, three, and one. And she always seemed very attached to them. Nice kids."

"And what is Sebastian like?" I asked. "Is he nice, also?"

"Well . . ." Again the traded look, this time with a chuckle. Collin mumbled something, and Pete smiled. "His nickname around here is Sex-on-Two Legs. Just on looks, mind you. I don't think he's ever even noticed us."

I must have looked confused, because he said, "Well, if you want a factual description, he's . . . not very tall. A little taller than Collin. Dark haired, dark eyed. I believe he's a handyman, and he spends a lot of time outside—so he's tanned and has an . . . outdoor look."

"And his name is Sebastian?"

"Sebastian Dimas," Collin said.

"And he's still coming by?"

"Yeah. In fact he was here just yesterday, staying with the kids while Jason went to work," Peter said. "Of course the kids know him, and I suppose although they are shocked about their mother's disappearance, it's better to have a babysitter who knows them."

"Yeah," I said.

At that moment, Ben and E came back in, with E saying, loudly, "Ccelly likes Chopin. Chopin is a good dog."

Ben was saying something about how llamas were especially fond of dogs. Then he said, "Do you know everything you need to know?"

I nodded, though what I'd learned opened more questions than it answered.

"Oh, good," Ben said. "Then there's a dress I'd like you to look at."

CHAPTER 8

Froth and Roses

It started with the name of the store. It was called The Pink Rose, and the only sign over the door was a drawing of a bright-pink rose—from which I deduced it was a wedding-dress shop for illiterates.

"No, don't start deciding you hate it already," Ben said. "It's wonderful, really. When I came home last night, they were still open, and I went in and explained that you were tired of all the standard options around town, and—"

The second thing about the store was that it was on the bottom floor of Ben's loft building. In the last year, this bottom floor had housed a Realtor's office, a deli, and a florist. The recession had bit downtown business hard, but still, this location, amid offices and lofts, seemed singularly inappropriate for a wedding shop. My anxiety was not made any easier by the fact that nothing at all showed in the two shop windows. Instead, there were tall pink curtains, closed against the light, hiding the shop. I wondered if it meant they were that ashamed of the dresses, but the look Ben gave me meant I might die for saying it.

Inside the shop, holding E by the hand, I found myself in diffused pink light and surrounded by mirrors. If I'd known that Ben intended to drag me to a shop where I'd be exposed to multiple images of myself, I'd have done my hair and makeup and lost twenty pounds.

But mostly the shop smelled and looked expensive, the type of place where you expect to have to pay a door price just for walking in. The lady who walked toward me was clearly the refugee from some Victorian manor. Tall and spare, her gray hair pulled tightly back into a bun. She wore a gray dress that wouldn't have looked out of place on a dowager in a BBC production of *Pride and Prejudice*. And the way she approached us clearly implied that we were lowborn mongrels of poor parentage.

I looked at Ben to see how he was taking this and hoped E didn't find it necessary to give vent to Ccelly's opinion of the moment. But even E must have felt awed because he didn't say anything. And Ben looked cowed enough as he approached the woman, his head slightly lowered, and whispered to her.

She gave me the once-over, very slowly, as though she didn't think I was quite worth all that. For a moment, as her cool gray eyes surveyed me, it all seemed to hang in the balance, and then she nodded, slowly, and clapped her hands.

After a while, two women came from the back room

and motioned for me to follow them. At this point, I had horror movies running through my mind, and at the back of my brain a little voice was yelling, "Don't go into the back room."

But I looked back at Ben, who only smiled and nodded—encouragingly—at me, and then at E, who could have saved me with a single sharp wail about Ccelly but who didn't. You bring a son into the world, and he fails to rescue you when you need it the most.

I followed despondently, knowing in my heart that back there a tentacled monster was waiting to devour my brain. That's why there were no words on that window. Even the dumbest of brides wouldn't go into a shop called The Pink Rose, Dresses by Cthulhu.

But the back room failed to disclose any tentacles. It wasn't nearly that exciting. Instead, the British manor house theme continued—there was a room with the wallpaper all in tiny pink roses and a settee upholstered in pink-rose fabric. One of the women motioned for me to sit down; the other brought me a cup of Earl Grey tea and a ginger biscuit.

The second woman went out through yet another door and came back with a bundle wrapped in white cotton. It was laid out on a narrow, library-type table and unwrapped.

It was gray. Absolutely and unrelievedly gray.

"Mr. Colm said you didn't want a traditional wedding dress," the first woman said.

"This is very elegant, very unique."

I wanted to tell them gray might be unique for a wedding, but it wasn't elegant. But I didn't. I knew Ben very well, and if I went out there and told him that I hadn't even tried the dress on, he would tell me I wasn't giving it a chance. So I let the two women dress me in the gray dress and then lead me to the front, where I looked at myself in the mirrors.

An excess of gray greeted me. The dress was gray and unadorned, except for a row of gray roses around the waist. I heard Ben say, "Oh," in a tone that meant that this didn't look quite as he'd expected. E didn't say anything, which was terrifying in itself.

I looked at the mirrors again, and realized I looked . . . wilted. Somehow the gray dress made even my hair and my skin look gray. In fact, if I wore this it would look like *Wedding of the Living Dead. We just woke up and ate the gravedigger's brain and came here in search of someone to marry us till bullets do us part.*

I realized in time that saying this would probably be unforgivable. So instead I said, "You know . . . I . . . er . . . don't think this is quite what I was looking for."

Before I could make a fast getaway, I was ushered back to the room again, and another cup of tea was pressed on me. It seemed rude to leave after they gave me tea and all, so instead I waited. Minutes later, they brought out a dress. It was black. Glossy, unrelieved black.

As they were dressing me in it, before I could tell them this was not exactly what I had in mind, I found myself attired in black and brought back out in front of the mirrors.

And then I was faced with a terrible dilemma. I liked the dress. I really did. It was glossy and gorgeous, and it made me look taller and svelte. But for a wedding? *Well, it would have been appropriate for my first wedding,* I thought. *And Dad would like it, anyway, since he thinks there's always a murder at a wedding. I'll be all ready for the funeral.*

I bit my lip. The two women who'd been helping me dress had locked in a holding pattern around me, telling me how elegant and beautiful I looked and adjusting my skirt this way and that.

"It's very beautiful," I said. "But . . ."

"She'll have to think about it," Ben said, hurriedly, as though trying to prevent me from saying something appalling.

As though I would. And just as I thought about it, I found my mouth had a mind of its own and had gone into automatic—and there was nothing I could do to control it. "It's a lovely funeral dress," I heard myself saying and bit my lower lip hard, then tried to fix it by saying, "I mean, I know how wonderful this would be for the murder. I mean . . . My parents own the mystery bookstore and . . ."

I think if Ben could have, he would have physically dragged me out of there. As it was, I almost ran into the back room, before my mouth could think of anything else to say. Inside the room, the two women helped me out of the dress, probably because they were afraid I would hurt myself or it trying to wriggle out of the funereal fabric.

In no time at all, I was sitting in the passenger seat of Ben's car, looking straight ahead.

"You have your sweater on inside out," he said.

I didn't say anything. Ben drove for a little while in silence. Lights were coming on all over, and a cold wind was blowing. Ben hummed a couple of inharmonious notes between his teeth. "Well," he said, in a tone of great heartiness. "Didn't that go well?"

Which was when E burst into tears. It was so sudden that Ben headed for the side of the road and slammed on the brakes. And then we both turned around to find the child doing his best impression of a watering can.

The corollary of "My son looks like a cherub" was that when he cried, I felt truly guilty. His lip was trembling; there were tears chasing each other down his face.

"Why are you crying?"

"I don't want Mo-mo-mommy to die."

Although I completely understood this, I knew there was no way I could tell him that I'd never die. On the other hand, he was three, and this was hardly the time for the we-were-born-to-die speech. So instead, I said, "I'm not going to die anytime soon, sweetie," and hoped very much that it was true.

"Why do you think Mommy is going to die?" Ben asked, baffled.

"When she wears those dresses, she looks like the ladies in the books in Grandma's store. And they all have knives and 'tuff in them. And Grandma says it's because they're dead and someone wrote a book about them being dead." He started crying again.

It took us five minutes to convince him that I wasn't going to be killed. It seemed easier to tell him that I'd not buy the dress, since he seemed to think the two were linked. Once E's tears were dry, Ben looked ahead again. "So," he said. "I was thinking we could go to the George . . ."

"I can't," I told him. "Cas is bringing pizza."

And then Ben looked guilty.

"What?" I asked.

"Oh, I forgot to tell you. Nick called while you were getting into the dress. Or perhaps getting out of it. Yeah, okay, it's not important. There was another case of arson, down by the castle. A row of condos. They went over there, both of them, and they don't know when they'll be done."

"Oh, lovely," I said, because it wasn't, and suddenly, thinking of having to get E out of the backyard and the Amber Alert and everything else that had happened today, I felt as if I could burst out crying just like E. This seemed like the perfect conclusion to the perfect day—not.

"Come on," Ben said. "Let's go to the George."

"You only like going to the George because you like to look at the owner," I said, which was unworthy. The George diner had the best Greek food at a decent price anywhere in the Rocky Mountains.

"Nah, that's just a side benefit," he said. "It's the souvlaki salad and the rice pudding calling me. Come on."

"I don't have money."

"It's okay, Dyce, I'll pay the fifteen dollars. Surely I owe you that much for the gray dress. It looked better before it was on you, I swear."

"Yeah, what I like about you is that you say the sweetest things."

He grinned and slow mock-punched my shoulder. "I'll even get a milkshake for the little monkey," he said.

It was hard to resist a man who offered to buy my son a milkshake, particularly when said man had been my best friend ever since he'd saved me from a half-dozen bullies I had surrounded back in sixth grade. And when he really didn't want anything from me, except to listen to the gossip his friends had shared.

But when we were ensconced in the back booth of the George and Ben was attentively watching Tom, the co-owner of the diner, walk away after taking our order, I realized we couldn't talk. Not in front of E, not until E was asleep.

Which was too bad, because today of all days I felt like I needed to access my exobrain, which often seemed to be held in Ben's head.

Instead, both of us very conscious of E listening to everything and feeding Ccelly his imaginary oats, we watched Tom walk back with our order. He was quite worth watching. Not very tall but with the muscular chest of a weight lifter narrowing to a small waist and, proportionately speaking, very long legs. He wore his hair long, though he tied it back with a scarf, to fulfill food-service regulations. And his face was so cute it was almost pretty.

I was shocked by Ben asking, "So when is the wedding?" until I realized it was to Tom, not me.

Tom grinned. "Next summer, we think. We need to line up someone to look after the diner for a day or two. You'll be coming, of course. We've invited all of the Goldport police and their significant others."

Which for some reason caused Ben to blush and mumble.

As soon as Tom walked away, I asked him, "Ben— how are things between you and Nick?"

CHAPTER 9

A Prickly Investigation

"What?" Ben asked, as soon as Tom was out of earshot.

"How are things between you and Nick?"

There was just a moment of hesitation before Ben said, "Fine. Why?"

Right. Okay, until very recently Ben and I had had a pact in which each of us stayed out of the other's love affairs. But I didn't think that was possible now, when we were dating cousins who had been raised as brothers. "It's just that Peter seemed to wonder if you were still together and—"

"Oh, Peter," Ben said, derisively, as if his friend's name were a swearword. "Peter! He's known me since I was in high school, and he has this bug in his brain about how I'm only dating Nick because I'm on the rebound, and Nick isn't my type at all."

I thought of Ben's ex—small and blond and, let's face it, somewhat effete. I thought of the guys I was almost sure Ben had dated before that, at least the ones I knew. They'd all been smaller than Ben, and they'd all trended somewhere between blond and very blond. "Well?" I said.

Ben shrugged. "He's my type. Or rather . . . he's a type I didn't know I had." He looked up at me for a moment, then looked at E, who seemed totally absorbed in his burger and fries and a conversation with Ccelly, who, apparently, was sitting next to him on the booth. "It's just that he's so damn . . . Greek."

I blinked. The last thing I expected from Ben was any type of ethnic bigotry. "Beg your pardon?" I said. "Do you mean he eats too much souvlaki? Or he wears a toga around the house? Holds Olympics in the living room?"

Ben shook his head. "No, look, the thing is that it's not that . . . I mean, just because someone is gay, if he comes from a very traditional culture, it doesn't mean he has severed his every tie to his culture or every one of the culture's claims on him."

"You're saying he's conflicted about being gay?" I asked.

Ben shook his head vehemently. "No. That was all solved long before I came on the scene. I mean, Dyce, we're in our thirties . . . And no," he said, anticipating my next question, "it isn't even that his parents disapprove. Perhaps they do, but not from what Nick says. I think that battle was fought before we met, too. I mean, he'd bought a house with his ex. And his parents seem to like me. They are impressed with my having an MBA and being an investment planner. Even if I'm not exactly an accountant, I think I can help his parents with the taxes, you know . . ."

"But then . . . ?"

"Oh, it's just that Nick expects to be . . . the man of the house. I mean, he was raised to . . ."

I was out of my depth. In fact, I was out of my depth even if I had had a snorkel available. "You're both the man of the house!" I said. I needed a submarine.

"Oh, yeah," he said. "And that's the other thing—the house. Nick has bought back his ex's half, and the lease on his house is coming to an end, and he wants us to . . . He wants me to move into his house."

"Oh?"

Ben loved his loft. He'd bought it with the money left to him by his grandma Elly, and he'd decorated it just so, all white upholstery, dark wood, and vases and things. I'd have gone nuts living in any place where the only colors allowed were white, dark wood, and red. But for Ben, with his color coordinated, subtly different array of beige ties, the condo was like paradise on Earth. Heck, when he and Nick had adopted the baby rats I'd rescued from inside the piano, Ben had picked ones that color-coordinated with his condo. And he'd refused to adopt Pythagoras when he rescued the cat, because Pythagoras was black.

"Uh," I said. "I suppose it's difficult with both of you owning places. I mean . . . It's not even easy for me, and neither Cas nor I own a place. It's just he wants to buy one, and I—"

"And you?" Ben looked concerned.

"I'm afraid of what will happen if it all goes bad," I said. "As difficult as it is to sell a house right now, you know . . ."

"Oh," Ben said. "But you can't live your whole life on the expectation that something will go wrong, can you? Sometimes you have to let go of your fears and try to make something wonderful of it, don't you?"

I was trying to think how to explain to him all my confused, overlapping feelings—how I really couldn't just leap in, how, yeah, I understood what he was saying, but at the same time, with E's happiness on the line, I couldn't just jump into the first relationship that offered itself, because what would I do if it all exploded? I didn't think I could share custody with two men, and what if I had more children, and—

Only I didn't ever manage to mention it, because E looked up from feeding imaginary fries to the imaginary llama and said, "Cas!"

I looked behind me. Cas and Nick were coming toward us, dodging amid the packed tables. We reshuffled the seating, so they were sitting next to Ben and me, who, in turn, had E between us.

In no time at all, the policemen were eating burgers and fries. Tom, who was clearly familiar with both Nick and Cas—not a big surprise, since most of the Goldport police ate here for at least one meal a day—asked how the arson cases were going, and Cas said, "Bad. Really, really bad. You know those condos behind the castle?"

The pride and joy of Goldport was an eighteenth-century French castle, transported here stone by stone and rebuilt on-site by a dispossessed French aristocrat.

The way I had heard it, the aristocrat had been escaping the French Revolution and meant to re-create the home that his dear old mama had left, so as to keep her homesickness to a minimum. But that was surely too early? Unless the castle was there before the area was part of the United States.

But in the last year, some company had built a complex of condos behind it. I hadn't given it more than one look, except for thinking that using that adobe type of construction right behind something that might have graced the banks of the Loire looked incongruous.

The condos, when completed, had been on offer at a pretty high price for this city. They'd had all the energy-saving innovations and radiant heat and all sorts of goodies. I remember seeing them advertised on the nearest street corner.

"Yeah," Tom said. "We considered buying one of those, but all we could afford was the studio, which is hardly the sort of place for when you're married. I mean they were really nice. I heard they were on fire. Anything left?"

Cas shook his head. "No. But it's worse than that. We found a body in one of the condos."

"Oh, no," Tom said. "Someone was caught in there when the place caught fire?"

"I don't think that was that," Cas said. "We . . . think it was deliberate. Probably. Don't quote me on it, of course."

"Who would I quote you to?" Tom asked. "It's not like we'd talk to reporters, even if they wanted to talk to us." He added, "But it sounds like bad business. I wish you guys all the luck in the world."

It was amazing how Nick and Cas could tuck into their grilled burgers after coming back from a place where they'd found a burned human body. Worse, I knew if I gave them an opening, there would be jokes about long pig. That was part of the way policemen coped with the more unpleasant aspects of their profession.

Afterward, as we were walking out, Kyrie, Tom's better half, stopped Nick and asked him something that sounded like "Did they see anything flying over the area?"

Nick shook his head but was frowning when we got up front. I wondered if Kyrie was a believer in black helicopters.

It turned out Nick and Cas had come in one car, and so they just traded passengers—Ben took Nick, and Cas took a completely asleep E and myself. Ben and Nick didn't look like they were at loggerheads as they got into the car.

"I'm sorry," I told Cas. "It must be tough."

"Yeah," he said. He scratched at his nose. Now that we were in the relatively enclosed area of the car, it was obvious his clothes smelled of soot and smoke. "You know, the thing is . . ." I looked at him. "The thing is that those condos were up for sale with, well . . ."

"All-ex's realty?" I asked. I didn't need the nod from Cas. I already knew it.

CHAPTER 10

Sofas and Susceptibility

I woke up listening to Cas in the bathroom. He is the champion of the silent getting up, but no man born of woman has ever learned to brush his teeth silently. Which is a good thing, as otherwise I might well end up missing his exit most mornings.

As it was, I wasn't exactly awake but in that state in which your still-asleep brain pilots your still-asleep body through motions designed to give the impression you're awake but that, in fact, will give the impression of the living dead to anyone who has ever watched a zombie movie.

I found myself out of bed—shuffle, shuffle—feeling on the floor for my shoes—shuffle, shuffle—finding one tennis shoe and one of the house slippers my mom gave me, which for some reason had a half heel and pink pompons. I felt around with my foot, trying to find the mate of either, but couldn't. However, going without shoes in the house risked an encounter with the dreaded micro Lego blocks E left strewn all over the carpet. This was a well-known tactic of toddlers seeking to get rid of parental authority. I imagine it worked in the Neolithic, too, when an adult crippled by the stone Lego embedded in the foot would get eaten by a saber-toothed tiger in no time.

Considering the trouble I got into even without saber-toothed tigers, I couldn't afford to go barefoot. So I slipped on my mismatched footwear and continued to the bedroom door—shuffle, limp, shuffle, limp—pulled it open and—

There was a mummy on my sofa. It was long and vaguely human shaped and white. I let out a scream before I realized the mummy wasn't so much human shaped as, more specifically, Ben shaped.

The minute my scream sounded, the mummy—that is, Ben—sat up, looked at me, and screamed.

Look, I was too sleepy to stop the automatic reaction. It takes coffee and being somewhat awake to realize you're not in a rerun of a mummy-versus-zombie movie. So I screamed again. I mean, zombies, sure, I'm a zombie every morning before coffee. But mummies are much scarier. Mummies are like zombies who have gone to school and learned all sorts of arcane stuff. Ben screamed, "Dyce, damn it."

And I managed to scream, "What in heaven are you doing here?"

By that time our screams had brought the law down on us. Okay, in this case not so much down as out of the bathroom and across the bedroom, in his pajama bottoms and holding aloft the safety razor of doom.

It would probably have been more impressive if half of Cas's face wasn't covered in white foam and if the safety razor he was holding aloft weren't one of the cheap disposable ones in virulent pink—which meant he'd forgotten to bring a razor and had therefore swiped one of my razors from its pack. However, in his defense, he was holding it like someone who meant business and had jumped into the fray to protect his ladylove. If any threat got near me, it would be well and properly shaved for good and all.

He didn't even make an effort to take a swipe at Ben's whiskers, though—which was a little disappointing. Instead, he stood there, staring from one to the other of us. After a while, he frowned at Ben. "What are you doing here?" he asked, which again proves that Cas can spot the essential wrongness about a situation.

Then he turned on me, in a completely unfair way. "And why are you screaming?"

I pushed my lower lip out, which I realized made me look like a petulant child, but I felt like a petulant child, so that was okay. "He was imitating a mummy."

"No, I wasn't," he said. "I was asleep, and she came in and screamed."

"You're asleep in my living room."

"On the sofa. It's normal for people to sleep on the sofa."

"It's not normal for you to sleep on my sofa," I said. "You have a place of your own."

"Ah! But Nick has a key."

"Right," I said. "And I bet you have a key to his place. Why didn't you go and sleep on his sofa?"

Ben glared, knowing he'd been trapped by my

infallible logic, and rolled his eyes. "Women. Can't live with them, and I don't understand why anyone would try."

Since this pretty much accorded with my view of females, I couldn't say anything, and Cas took advantage of the silence to sigh, audibly, and in the tone of one much put-upon. "If you two are done screaming down the house, I'm going to finish shaving. Some of us have jobs to be at."

"Some of us don't work on Sunday," Ben said, like that made him special.

"Aren't you the lucky one?" I said, shooting him a venomous look, as I eased by to go to the kitchen and make Cas his breakfast. Of course, no way could Ben let me go about my morning business without coming out, still trailing his blanket.

There were several things wrong with that blanket. First, he'd brought it from home, because I do my laundry at a public Laundromat, which means I can't afford to keep anything large and white around. Things have to wait for wash long past the time at which a white blanket near a cat and a toddler would end up gray, long before I could afford to take it to the Laundromat. Second, he had wrapped himself in a modified version of his "full mummy" sleeping posture, so that he looked like a human burrito with feet. I glared at his feet, and hoped he'd step on a Lego but, of course, he never did. Lego toys have magnets that attract them to parental foot soles.

Another annoying thing about Ben and his insecurity blanket was the way he managed to hold it around him and perfectly closed while he—mutter, mutter—washed out my coffeepot, which I had washed the night before, thank you so much, and set about perfectly measuring and grinding the beans to make the perfect coffee. Some people need a dose of reality with their perfection. But I was extraordinarily good and didn't say it. Instead, I decided since he was making the coffee—like he had to impress Cas!—I would make breakfast.

There's only one thing I do well in the kitchen, but that I do very, very well. I had a stack of tender yet crispy pancakes in the middle of the table as Cas came in. "Oh, wow," he said. "Coffee and pancakes? It is my lucky day."

Neither Ben nor I dignified that with an answer. Ben, because I guess he really wasn't trying to impress Cas, and myself because I was never sure if Cas was serious when he praised me for pancakes.

I'd just got him the maple syrup when E came in, carrying Pythagoras as he usually did—as though the cat were a doll—grasped in a hug under his front paws.

"E, you have to support his legs; you're hurting him," I said, automatically.

"He's not complaining," E said, perfunctorily tightening the grasp with one arm, and putting the other arm under Pythagoras's back paws. "He likes it."

To be honest, the cat's amiable and confused expression betrayed neither like nor dislike, just this total confusion best transcribed as, "Kind lady, give me three of the green ones. I am a marshmallow poteen." Sometimes I worried the poor animal hadn't been *completely* insane when we'd adopted him.

I put pancakes, syrup, and a small glass of milk in front of E. Ben was standing by the coffeemaker and drinking a cup of coffee with an expression that would only be justifiable if the coffee had killed all his relatives and attacked his livelihood.

Ben in this mood—as I'd learned fairly early on—is a good analogue to a statue in the middle of a traffic circle. The best you can do is maneuver around him and pretend he doesn't exist. Unfortunately, he was standing in front of the drawer with the silverware needed to eat pancakes. But that was okay.

I gave E a small spatula to eat his pancakes with, handed Cas a cheese cutter, and grabbed a wooden spoon for myself. It says how well they knew Ben that, after a flitting look at him in front of the drawer, neither of them made a comment.

Turns out a small melon baller makes a not-unhandy coffee spoon. In similar circumstances before, I had discovered it could be used to eat cereal with, though it was a pain to put one's finger on the little hole in the bottom of the scoop.

I was halfway through my second pancake and third cup of coffee, and feeling a lot less like a zombie, when the human burrito stirred. He stepped away from the counter, glared at us as if we'd said anything, and lurched out of the room. I heard him go into my bedroom and then slam the door to the shower.

Cas looked at me, "Does he often do this?"

I frowned, hesitating between loyalty and truthfulness. "Only to me," I said.

"Do you think he fought with Nick?" Cas asked, doubtfully.

This was such a stupid question that, frankly, it made me question all those lines in books and movies about the police and their inquiries. I mean, even I, with my untrained mind, could spot that there had been some big row and now Ben was avoiding Nick, which, if I knew anything about Nick—whom I admittedly had known a much shorter time than I'd known Ben—probably meant Nick was avoiding Ben. It was a wonder they hadn't both met here while avoiding each other.

"I mean, what in heck do they have to argue about?" Cas asked. "They laugh at the same stupid jokes, they like the same movies, they—"

"Ben said something about not knowing where to live and Nick's house lease coming to an end," I said, quickly, to forestall whatever else my beloved felt like telling me about his cousin's relationship with my best friend. There are places the mind shouldn't go, and mine tends to go there by default, anyway.

"Oh, but Nick . . ."

"Ben seems to think Nick is being a little . . . how do I put this? Greek."

Cas stared at me, his eyes slowly widening. "But I thought the whole thing was—"

"Cas! No. I mean, you know, Nick is behaving presumably as Nick's dad would. No. Stop. Not that. I mean, *House, castle, why isn't my dinner made?* kind of Greek."

Cas closed his mouth slowly. "Oh." He frowned slightly, and looked vaguely toward where the sounds of the shower running echoed. "Yeah, I could see that would be a problem. But . . ." He frowned again. Finally he shook his head slowly. "At any rate," he said, as though dismissing some elaborate argument, "I have to go to work. We should have the forensic report on the body from the arson case." He sighed. "I hate to say this, but

I rather hope it was the arsonist, and he miscalculated. At least that problem would be done and over with."

He kissed me, perhaps not as thoroughly as he would have if E weren't watching us interestedly as if he intended to pick up tips for future dating.

As soon as he'd left, I told E to stop feeding pancakes to Pythagoras, and gave Pythagoras some of the stinkiest tuna known to man, which only caused him to stare at me in confusion, then hop back on E's lap for pancake. "Fine," I said, darkly. "But don't come complaining to me when you get an upset tummy."

The look in his eyes was *No complaints. I'll just throw up on your pillow.* Which was, of course, par for the course. Lacking access to my own shower, which Ben had claimed, I did the dishes by hand until I heard the shower go off. Eventually, Ben showed up in the kitchen, perfectly dressed and groomed, wearing grayish chinos and a gray-greenish shirt. It being Sunday, he didn't have a tie on, but you could tell he felt uncomfortable without it. I noted the clothes were different from the ones the day before, but I presumed that if Ben had gone through the trouble of bringing his blanket with him, he would— almost certainly—also have brought a small suitcase with a change of clothes and possibly his ubiquitous beauty products. Only he'd learned through painful experience not to leave his beauty products lying about where person or persons unknown could get hold of them.

As he came into the kitchen, he looked sheepish, as he tended to look when he knew he'd been exasperating. "Hey, look . . ." he said.

I'd long ago learned to strike while the iron was hot and impose on Ben while Ben was embarrassed or feeling guilty. "Hey," I said, quickly. "You know, I'm not going to have much time to work, with E here until . . . well, for a week at least, if it works out, so I was wondering, if you don't have anything to do today, if you'd consider babysitting him a bit so that I can get some work done out back, because I'm almost out of stock at the consignment shop, and I have to finish stuff to take in."

Ben opened his mouth, then closed it, then ran his hand back over his hair. "Nick and I were going to . . ." He pushed his lips together. "But he's working all day, because of the arson case, you know?"

I started to see there might be outlines to the problems that Ben and Nick were having that had nothing whatsoever to do with ethnic culture. "Uh . . . You know, it's part of being a policeman. They work all sorts of hours. It's something I'm starting to get used to, but it's hard as hell. It's one of those jobs where the job has to come first, because it's bigger than the person or career advancement or all of that."

He looked up startled. "What?" And blushed faintly. "Oh, that, yeah. I do get it, Dyce. It's just . . ." He shrugged. "When did you become the grown-up in this association?"

I waggled my hand at him. "It comes and it goes. So . . . come on . . . if I shower, and go work a couple hours out back, can you spend a couple of hours with E? Because, you know, I am going to have to watch him the rest of the time. And look, if you brought the laptop, as long as you keep an eye out to make sure he's not trying to teach Pythagoras to waltz or something, you can work on your computer, meanwhile."

Ben started to nod, then said, "Teach Pythagoras to

waltz? Do you mean . . . like waltzing Matilda? I have to keep him from killing the cat?"

"No, no. It's just he hugs Pythagoras and dances around and around in circles, till the cat barfs all over the carpet."

"Oh. That's okay then."

He only said that because he'd never had to clean up one of Pythagoras's impressive pools of vomit. For a cat that spent all day, every day, indoors, that cat managed to conjure up—possibly from another universe—the most absurd stuff to throw up. Oh, okay, fine, I knew that he periodically ate one of E's toys. And I knew that for some reason he sometimes ate small objects, coins, and, on a single occasion, a balloon. Now, I didn't know *why* he ate these, beyond the obvious reason that the poor cat was crazier than a refrigerator salesman in Antarctica. No. The problem wasn't finding odd and unlikely objects in his vomit. The problem was finding impossible objects: things that looked like large semi-digested rats or parts of a squirrel tail.

I lived in fear of the day when Pythagoras would throw up in the living room, and I'd find an elk's hind-quarters in the mess or perhaps even a yucky but still functional 1954 Buick convertible.

But I wasn't going to tell Ben any of that because men tend to get confused if not outright skittish once you start talking about space-time portals inside of a small black cat's stomach. And besides, if he was so foolish as to let Pythagoras throw up, I intended to guilt him into cleaning up.

I got in the shower, cleaned up quickly, got jeans and a T-shirt on, came back out, grabbed a protesting E, gave him a quick shower, and dressed him in jeans and a sweater. I left Ben trying to convince E to put shoes on and hurried out back to my work shed.

Once there, I put my coveralls on, then put goggles on—because it wouldn't be the first time I splashed stuff on them and not my eyes—and started spreading mineral spirits with cornstarch on the surface of the table.

I established several patches, then went back to the first patch to scrape, using the sharp edge of the five-point painter tool and an infinite amount of care. I'd have to patch the huge strip in the middle, but I'd like to try to prevent myself from having a bunch of uneven strips.

Most of all, though, I wasn't sure if I'd be able to do anything with this table—not with its legal status undefined, as it were. I couldn't really sell it while I wasn't sure if there was a crime surrounding it.

Without thinking about that too much, I started scraping the finish around where the stains were and found myself discovering that along with the stains, in a splatter pattern, there was also a rather large pool, as though someone had poured out black liquid.

You don't grow up as the daughter of the owners of the single largest mystery bookstore in Colorado—or possibly by now, in the West—without knowing that old blood dries black, instead of red. There were ways of telling if it was blood, of course—at least there should be, if the varnish and stain hadn't changed the composition. I had a black-light flashlight in the house. The reason for it was obvious, walked on four legs, and was probably crazier than . . . well . . . I had yet to find something it wasn't crazier than.

He was a good cat and didn't often commit

indiscretions of the smelly type, but I suppose when a cat got scared, one couldn't expect him to control his bladder, and Pythagoras could get scared by his own shadow. So, periodically, I had to play "find the tinkle," an endeavor in which a good source of black light is invaluable.

I went back into the house, and was looking through the drawers in the kitchen for the flashlight when Ben called out, "Dyce, is that you?"

"No. It's the tooth fairy."

There was a pause, and I wondered if he was considering this hypothesis, so I cut in, "What's wrong?"

"Your son," Ben said, in ponderous tones, "cheats at Candy Land."

I stuck my head into the door to the dining room, where they were sitting in front of E's game of Candy Land. Now, this was something I hadn't expected Ben to fall for. He'd known E long enough to realize that tying an adult down to a good board game was E's favorite hobby and that he'd do anything to manage it, including but not limited to setting bear traps in likely locations. And once you sat down to a board game, you were doomed. You'd not be allowed to get up again, not even if you faked death. Two weeks ago, I'd spent an hour with my tongue hanging out and my eyes closed, pretending to be dead, before E got worried enough to promise he'd let me do something else if only I came back to life.

But there were some things that were impossible even for E. "He can't possibly cheat at Candy Land," I said. "No one can. The cards don't even have words."

Ben crossed his arms on his chest. "Oh, yeah? He will wait till I'm distracted by something, and he'll stack the deck."

E crossed his arms on his chest, in perfect imitation of Ben, and gave me his best angelic smile. It was very good. It almost hid the suspicions of little horns under the blond curls. "Ben has absolutely no proof."

I smiled at my son. "Oh, cheer up, Ben. He's going to be such a success at politics!"

"It can still be averted," Ben said, hopefully. "You could treat him with aversion therapy."

"Oh, come on, surely you can play a board game with a toddler without getting upset? Perhaps he's lucky."

I think Ben murmured, "Yeah, right. Lucky," as I left the room, got the black-light flashlight, and went back to the shed.

By closing the door and draping a cloth over the small window high up on the wall, I reduced the amount of light in there enough that a black light shining on the table revealed a soft fluorescent glow where the stains were.

Um. Right. So . . . it was blood. Or at least organic materials.

On the other hand, it could be blood but not human blood.

The problem was that the only truly infallible way would be to tell Cas all about it and let him send samples to the lab.

I was standing there, shining the lantern on the table, when there was a knock on the door.

CHAPTER 11

Fire and Chills

"Yeah?" I said, turning off the black light and taking down the cloth I'd put over the window. It was probably Ben, of course, trying to get me to come and make E stop cheating at Candy Land.

But no one answered; instead, the door handle jiggled, and because I hadn't taken the trouble to lock it, the door swung open.

For a moment, there was too much light for me to make out the figure in the doorway, and then I blinked, and my first impression of him—definitely a him—was that I was being visited by a faun. There was something earthy and sexy about the short, muscle-bound man. Then I blinked again and realized he didn't have goat feet or legs. Well, at least not that I could see through the jeans and his big work boots. And I wasn't going to stare at his jeans anyway. I was a grown-up, a mother, and decently engaged to a nice man who was going to make an honest woman out of me. Mind you, if that meant I had to stop telling white lies, it might be a long time before I let it happen.

He was tanned and had deep-set dark eyes, which stared at me in an inquiring way. "Mrs. Dare?" he asked.

I'd never been called Mrs. Dare, certainly not by a man old enough to be a friend or a brother or something. I blinked at him. And realized he was smoking, as he threw the cigarette down and stepped on it, right in front of my work shed.

"Be careful," I said, my voice coming out raspy, as though I was making a threat, which I certainly wasn't. "There are a lot of flammables in here. If a spark should fly . . ."

He frowned at me, then smiled, a smile that managed to be sexy and not particularly nice. "Interesting," he said. "I came here to tell you that, too." And looking at what must be my look of total incomprehension, because I had no intention of smoking in the shed, or anywhere for that matter, "To be careful." He looked as if he expected me to understand what the hell he was talking about, then shook his head. I repressed the urge to tell him *Life is full of these little disappointments*, which was probably a very good thing, as the next thing he said was, "My name is Sebastian Dimas."

It took me a moment to remember who the heck that was, and then, because I remembered the way Peter and Collin had referred to him, heat went up my face, then down again.

He looked gratified, and I couldn't really tell him that it was just because I was speaking to someone I'd heard mentioned as Sex-on-Two Legs and not because I was actually doing anything wrong. I wondered what he thought I was doing wrong, for that matter.

He patted his jeans and pulled out a cigarette. "Listen, lady," he said in that tone that people use when they don't think you're a lady at all and that, in fact, seems to imply you're an old, gossiping biddy. "Jason has had enough trouble, okay? He really doesn't need you poking your nose in, right? Just leave the man alone."

I blinked at him again, which probably made me look like an old, gossiping biddy, too, or at least totally stupid. "What?"

"Jason Ashton," he said, as he lit his cigarette, cupping one hand to protect the flame. I felt a creepy sensation go up my spine, like an overactive caterpillar was crawling on my back. "Look, he and Maria are the nicest people in the world, okay? They've got their kids, and they're not exactly rich, but anyone who is down on their luck or in trouble can be sure of being helped by them. Too much so, in my opinion. Some of the people—" He shrugged. "Never mind. It doesn't matter. If Maria left, she had her reasons. She discovered something about . . . about herself, and she had to go away for a while to cope with it. She'll be back, I'm sure, when she has figured it out. Meanwhile . . . I mean, Jason is worrying enough. You really shouldn't be harassing him."

I'd managed to add two plus two and get three hundred and fifty-four. He wanted to warn me away from looking into Jason Ashton. He'd probably run away with Maria and didn't want Jason to find her. He . . .

He was smoking, inches from the door to my shed,

which in turn was filled with bottles and bottles of turpentine, mineral spirits, varnish, wax.

I stepped outside, closing the door behind me, and hoped that Ben would come to the back door and see what was going on. He was probably too busy preventing E from cheating, of course. The man was never there when I needed him. It was amazing he hadn't gone into the police.

Sebastian stepped away from the shed as I stepped out, which was good; otherwise, I'd have walked straight into his cigarette. I was trying to figure out whether to tell him that the table was in there and that this is what had started me looking into it.

"Look," he said. "I heard about you. I was in school just behind you. And I know that your parents are nu . . . that your parents are the owners of the mystery bookstore, and I understand that your boyfriend is in the police, and you probably think you're some sort of a detective. But it's just a bad idea all around. Jason made a missing-person report only because he has an assistantship offer in California, and if there's any chance, he wants to contact Maria before he leaves." He took a deep pull of his cigarette. "I told him it was misguided. Much easier for me to rent the place after they move out, and then, when she comes back, I'll be there to tell her where he went, right? But he wanted to make sure she was all right, because she hasn't been to her doctor."

He blinked, as though realizing he'd said too much. His lips formed the *S* word, before he shoved the cigarette back in them. I realized that the reason he was surrounded by an unnatural haze was that I was still wearing my goggles. I pulled them up on my head, aware that this made me look like some sort of wild Africa explorer, and said, "I wasn't looking . . . I wasn't trying to harass him, really. I just . . ."

But he frowned at me. "Did your boyfriend ask you to ask questions?"

"No. No, no, no, no. Cas is not even that concerned about it. He thinks that her disappearance was voluntary and . . ." I bit my tongue.

But he didn't seem to get upset. Instead, he gave me a long look. "Possibly," he said. "In a manner of speaking. Probably not what you meant, but yeah."

"But . . . uh . . . I heard they were good people and seemed happy. I mean . . ."

"They are good people, and they seem happy. Sometimes there are problems, of course, for anyone. And sometimes I think they take on . . . well . . . deadbeats. But on the other hand, they took me on when I—" He stopped and shrugged. "It doesn't matter. Just if you don't have a reason to prod and poke and drive around and ask questions, don't, okay? They didn't do anything to you. Let them work out their problems in their own way."

I couldn't say anything. I mean, what could I say? In a movie, I would have said, "Or else what?" but look, things people do in movies are rarely a really good idea in life. Because in movies someone yells, "Cut," and you get to change your makeup and you don't have to go to the dentist and rearrange your teeth.

Besides, even if the taboo against beating women who are smaller and unarmed held—and it's possible it would have because this smaller and unarmed woman had a fiancé who was a police detective—if nothing else, there were other ways he could take revenge on me. For one, just his smoking that close to my shed was making my entire body tense, and not in a nice way. Suddenly and for no reason I could explain, and certainly for no reason I wanted to dwell too much on, I saw the image of the burned condos and heard Cas say there had been someone dead in one of them. My stomach clenched. I looked around at the street, where a parked truck showed what seemed to me to be a flamethrower.

"I do handyman work around here," Sebastian Dimas said. I wondered if he did handyman work up at the condos, too. A lot of the real estate companies hired contractors or casually attached workers to maintain places that were for sale. I wondered what type of work required a flamethrower.

And then I realized he'd been talking all along, as now he removed his cigarette from his mouth, threw it on the ground, and stepped on it. "But you're not interested in my sob story, right? Right. No one said you had to be. Just, without Jason and Maria, I'd probably be in the homeless shelter right about now, so you can say I'm protective of them, okay? I mean, they'll be leaving soon, but they leave me on my feet, and there's debts you can never repay, right?"

He looked at me, and I got the impression he wanted to say something else, perhaps threaten me a little more. But he'd no more opened his mouth than the back door opened and I heard E say, "Did not."

"Did too," Ben said. "Here, we'll ask Mommy."

I turned to look at them for a moment, and when I looked back, Sebastian was in his truck and starting it. This must imply powers of teleportation, since I refused to think that a grown man had run away at the sound of that particular argument.

Then again, perhaps he had. I felt like running away. I also felt a headache coming on, low and tight over the eyes, mingled with an odd and inexplicable relief.

"Mommy, I didn't cheat," E said. "I didn't replace the cards."

"He did too," Ben said. "I caught him."

I looked up, already shaking my head in the automatic mommy shake. "Ben, honestly. What does it matter?"

"We're supposed to be teaching him honesty!"

I wanted to tell Ben to stow it, but of course he was right. The man had the horrible habit of being right.

"Ccelly hid the cards," E said.

"There is no Ccelly!" Ben said.

"Yes there is."

I shook my head again. "Ben, Ccelly—"

"You're going to make it hard for him to tell the difference between reality and imagination."

I put my hands out blindly and rested one hand on E's head and clasped the other around Ben's arm. "Come on," I said. "Let's go inside before my headache becomes blinding."

This was the first time my oh-so-observant friend noticed something was wrong. "Did it have anything to do with the guy who—"

I nodded.

"Who is he?" Ben asked.

"He was the guy who . . . He's a friend of Jason Ashton."

Ben's eyes went really big. "Oh. You mean . . . He wanted to . . . talk about the table?"

"No. He wanted to tell me there was nothing to look at there, and please move along."

"Oh." Now he looked concerned, reminding me that though he could get quite goofy on the subject of three-year-olds cheating at Candy Land, he was often the closest thing I had to a protective older brother.

"Yeah," I said.

"Come inside," he said. "I'll make tea or coffee or something." And then to E, "You'll have to put the game away."

"But we're not done," E said, and stomped his foot.

"Well, no, but I need to talk to Mommy now."

"I hate grown-up talk," E said.

The problem is that I did, too. More so when it had just occurred to me that Sebastian Dimas could only have found out about my snooping in one way. Ben's friends had to have told him. Now, I understood the man was extremely good looking, but all the same, surely they hadn't thought it was a good idea to let him know I was looking into Ashton's affairs.

And if they had done that, how much could I trust what they'd told me? And how was I going to tell Ben about it?

CHAPTER 12

Too Close for Comfort

I woke up with Ben knocking at the bedroom door. At least, I woke up with my chin resting on Cas's chest, my arm thrown across his tummy, and an insistent pounding on the bedroom door, which—when we didn't answer immediately—turned into a cautious turning of the door handle and Ben's voice saying, "Excuse me, pardon me."

My eyes took some effort to open—it had been a late night of debauchery for Cas and myself, at least if debauchery consisted of eating too much pizza while playing Candy Land with the three-year-old con man. Who had cheated. And won. And blamed missing, torn, and hidden-under-the-table cards on Ccelly.

When I managed to open them, and look toward Ben, he was crossing my room, in his pajamas, a hand decorously protecting him from the site of Cas and me. Presumably because he wasn't sure how decent we were. Which was a point, as I was not decent, even if I was wearing pajamas. Cas, on the other hand, was only in his underwear. And clearly had woken at the same time I had. He now opened his eyes, somewhat. I felt him stir under me, and the words "What the heck?" rumbled through his chest and into my ear.

"Ben," I said. "Carrying his clothes, and . . ." Right on time, the door to the bathroom closed and the shower went on. "Taking a shower."

I sat up, and Cas sat up after me. "Dyce, I love you more than life, but we can't have him live with us."

"You think I want us to?"

"No, no," Cas said. "I'm sure you don't, even if he cooks better than you." He stopped as though expecting me to get mad at this. I didn't. Ben lives mostly on restaurant takeout, but I was very well aware that he could cook better than I. Not a big deal. Ccelly probably could, too.

Cas sighed. "Okay, well . . . at least we have to get a house with another bathroom. Which reminds me. I made an appointment for us to see a house this afternoon."

"What?" I asked.

He shook his head. "It's a good price, it has a shed in the back that you can use for your work, and it has a big backyard for E. If we're lucky, any explosions he causes will be contained before they reach the fence."

"But—"

Cas took hold of my hand. "The other part of this, before you say something hasty, is that I want to look at this house. If I'm right about the pattern I've been seeing, they'll be going after this house next—the arsonists. And I have a theory as to why they're going after these houses. I need a plausible reason to look, see?"

"So I'm supposed to help the police with their inquiries?" I asked, which was a bad choice of words, because I remembered the inquiries I had made on my own, and the result of that. And the fact that, as much as I'd managed to convey to Ben, he'd refused to believe and insisted, instead, that Peter and Collin would never have betrayed my confidence. Right. Of course, he'd also told me that what he could see of Sebastian Dimas didn't look all that special.

I'll give you that Ben was, presumably—no one would make as much fuss over arguments as he did, otherwise— a man in love and that his boyfriend bore a decided resemblance to Bacchus while Sebastian was more a Hephaestus, or perhaps a Pan, but I still refused to believe that Ben—let alone Peter and Collin—was completely blind to Sebastian's charm.

"Okay," I told Cas, thinking that he might go easier on me when he found out what I'd been up to. "Only if the backyard is big enough to contain explosions, though."

"Oh, assuredly," Cas said. "Of course, I'm not sure about Ccelly. That's one wily imaginary llama."

I nodded. Ben was now singing something thumpy, with an excess of enthusiasm. He doesn't have a bad voice, but it echoed through the pipes and reverberated in such a way that you couldn't make out the words.

"I'm going to make coffee," I said.

Cas rolled his eyes. "I'll make eggs or something," he said.

As soon as we were out of the bedroom, he said, "You know he's going to wake E."

"Of course."

"Look, it's just . . . I'm not sure he can live with us. Not even in the apartment over the garage. Nick . . ."

"What?" I looked over at Cas, who was chewing the corner of his lip. I wondered what he was about to say that worried him so much. Had Nick told him he was giving up on Ben? Because, Greek or not, a pain or not, I was fairly sure that Ben was still madly in love with Nick. At least I'd never seen him make so much of a nuisance of himself over anyone else. Not even his ex, who had been borderline psychotic.

"Nick is not sleeping. He's really worried, and I don't even know what he's worried about. He's . . . I'm going to have to tell him where Ben is spending the night. Nick has no clue what is going on or why Ben is avoiding him."

I stared at him. "Impossible. Surely they're arguing?"

"Not as far as I can tell. As far as I can tell, those two have fewer communication skills than Clever Hans, the calculating horse. You know, stomp your hoof once for yes, twice for no. They don't seem to be talking at all. Each one just assumes the other's answer and goes on that way." He looked anguished. "I'm very much afraid I'll have to tell Nick what's going on."

"Well," I said, going on into the kitchen and starting the coffee machine. "Of course you have to."

He got eggs and bacon from the fridge. "You mean you're not going to tell me I can't? You're not going to say it's dishonorable?"

"What? Of course not. Obviously, they love each other and are inept. Sometimes you need to give a hand to these things." I turned around and saw him looking at me dumbfounded. "Come on, Cas," I said. "No woman would hesitate twice before doing that."

He shook his head. "Femaleness is another country," he said. "They do things differently there."

"Clearly," I said, as I measured coffee into the basket. And then I wondered if Peter and Collin had a different code, too. Well . . . Ben didn't seem to and he knew them.

At that moment, the phone rang. I looked where it was supposed to be, sitting on the counter, but it was nowhere to be found, and I was about to issue a challenge to the world of wandering phones at large when Cas put it in my hand, returning to scramble a big bowl of eggs. "It's your father," he mouthed, as he handed the phone over.

The number in the caller ID was in fact that of the store. It could be my mother, of course, but she usually called from the house, not the bookstore.

I pressed the button with some misgivings. It wasn't every day that my father remembered I existed, much less called me. Of course, it was entirely possible he'd decided that the Dyce Dare mentioned in his phone pad was some book distributor.

But as I turned the phone on, he didn't ask me about book orders or delayed book shipments. Instead, he yelled, loud enough to be heard all over the kitchen. "Dyce! I must talk to you now."

This was twice as bad, because when my father remembered I existed, he did not remember my name. Of course, perhaps he still thought I was someone else. "Uh . . . Dad?"

"Yeah. I have to talk to you about the murder."

Across the kitchen, Cas looked at me and raised an eyebrow. *Oh, sure, Dad, way to go, mention murder around my fiancé, who thinks I'm at risk of being murdered by random roving bands devoted to the extermination of furniture refinishers.* I took the phone with me—with some alacrity—to the living room, as I said, in a whisper, hoping he would follow my lead, "What murder, Dad?"

I'd underestimated my father's reading of social cues. As my voice dropped, so did his, and it came over the phone in a fumbling whisper I could not understand at all. So I cleared my throat and returned to normal levels of speech. "What murder, Dad? Did anyone get injured at the store?" You have to understand that my father's level of attachment to reality is somewhat shaky. He had long ago eschewed reality for mystery books, and, at this point, his confusion between reality and imagination was worse than E's. It was quite likely that the murder he wanted to complain about had happened on the Orient Express in Agatha Christie's mind.

"No, don't be stupid," he said. "This murder that you committed."

"What?"

"Oh, you know. I'm not about to tell anyone. People take these things much too seriously," he said. "They don't take in account different types of morality. It's something that Raymond Chandler—"

"Dad," I spoke as levelly as I could. "I didn't murder anyone."

"Oh, there's no reason to pretend with me."

E padded across the living room, clutching Pythagoras, and giving me no more than a vaguely sleepy look, as I told my dad, "I haven't killed anyone, Dad. Honestly."

"Oh, if you're going to be that way," Dad said in the tone of a man humoring the mentally ill. And then, sounding sullen and put-upon, "I'm only trying to help."

Ben came out of my bedroom, fully dressed and with his tie on, and headed for his briefcase, which he'd left by the door. I put my hand over the receiver to tell him, "Cas has made eggs." If I was going to encourage Cas to betray Ben's location, I might as well compensate in advance.

Ben hesitated minimally, which he wouldn't have done, I will note, if I had cooked the eggs, then whispered, "Got to go. Late for work. You really should have a working alarm clock."

I resisted the urge to roll my eyes because at this point I was afraid they would stick somewhere up in my cranium. "Ben, you have an alarm clock at home you could—"

Unfortunately, in my enthusiasm, I'd uncovered the phone receiver. My dad heard it, and said, "Is that Ben? Does he know that you killed some woman over a table? Is he still willing to marry you?"

Now Ben's eyebrows went up, and he shook his head as he grabbed his briefcase and headed out the door. Oh, boy, when Dad got hold of the wrong end of the stick, it was usually the wrong end of a stick from another world.

"Come on," Cas called. "Eggs are ready."

"Who is that man?" my dad asked.

"My fiancé."

"Odd, he doesn't sound like Ben."

"He's not Ben."

"You threw Ben over for someone else? Why, just two days ago he was in here, planning the wedding with your mother."

I bit my tongue short of saying that my mother should marry Ben, then. Instead, I said, "Uh, Dad, can I call you back?"

"No. Just come here. We shouldn't talk about this on the phone. The police might be tapping the line."

I hung up, to find Cas looming over me. "Why am I

tapping your line?" he asked. The confusion on his face meant only that he had not grown up with my dad—which was a good thing—and therefore simply couldn't fathom Dad's thought processes.

"I think," I said, speaking carefully, because I probably didn't want to scare the nice man who meant to marry me—I mean, he had to know there was insanity in the family, but he didn't need to know how much insanity—"because I threw Ben over for you."

But Cas, for all his lack of experience with my family, was clearly more resilient than it would appear. He put his arm around me and guided me toward the kitchen. "Good thing," he said, approvingly. "I don't think Nick is into threesomes."

He sat me down at the table, fed imaginary oats to Ccelly, and acted for all the world as though my best friend hadn't spent the night on my sofa and taken first dibs on the shower. As though my father hadn't called to accuse me of a murder that had probably happened only in Dad's somewhat—okay, extremely—delusional mind. As though my son didn't insist on taking an imaginary llama with him everywhere. An imaginary llama that wore sneakers.

Look, I'd understand this completely had Cas been one eyed, one legged, five feet tall, and clinically insane. But he was well over six feet tall and built like your best type of classical god. And he had a smile that made me go jelly inside. Of course, it was possible he was clinically insane, but the police normally screened for that sort of thing, didn't they?

I shoved a forkful of fluffy eggs in my mouth and looked up to find him smiling at me. "I'm going to take a shower. I'll pick you up at one to take you to look at the house, okay? I assume you're going to see your dad?"

"I think I have to," I admitted reluctantly.

"Of course. He's quite capable of escaping town with a briefcase of mysteries bolted to his wrist otherwise. And then your mom would be upset at us and make us go find him. You know that never ends well."

So he showered while I finished breakfast and washed up. Then I bathed E and then myself, resisting the demand that I bathe Ccelly by telling E that llamas licked themselves clean. Someday, in some zoo, my son was going to see a real llama, and then he would never trust me again. It was a risk I was willing to take.

I got him into the car and drove to the store. My parents had started the store accidentally. Or, rather, my dad had started the store accidentally. I was fairly sure my mother had meant to start it. At least I hoped so, as otherwise they would be the first accidentally successful merchants in history. My dad had inherited a three-story Victorian from his grandmother. Being then out of high school, he'd moved into the house with all his books. Knowing Dad and how many books he had, I supposed that was enough to fill every room in the house from floor to ceiling several times over.

There he might have stayed the rest of his life, till eventually someone had found him dead in the pile of books, possibly eaten by bookworm. But somehow, at a mystery convention, he'd met Mom.

I have yet to understand how she got him to notice her long enough to engage in conversation and marry—my conception was an enigma that even I had no intention of prodding—but she had managed this, and, upon coming home with him, she'd hung up the sign *Remembered Murder* over the entrance and started selling books. Eventually, she'd cleared the upper floors enough to have furniture and a somewhat normal house. Oh, we still had bookcases everywhere, including the two bathrooms. If only enough companies had the foresight to print their books in washable paper, we'd probably have books in the shower as well. But there was room to walk around, and there was even some more or less normal furniture.

Now, usually when I visited, I went around to the backyard—which I'd once set fire to, in an unfortunate gas-bottle-on-the-grill accident—and up the staircase that Mom had bullied Dad into building to the kitchen door on the second floor.

Today, I had to go into the store first. For one, I needed to figure out whether the reason Dad was convinced I had murdered someone was because he had murdered someone and was now trying to figure out how to hide the body in the stacks. Yes, I knew it was unlikely. On the other hand, Dad had come up with some interesting notions in the past.

I took hold of E and explained, in as stern a voice as I dared, that he was not to tear, bite, or in any other way do anything that might damage books, including but not limited to breaking the spine by opening them too wide. E nodded meekly.

The thing is, I had no idea how much E could read, and since the time when he'd taken a book into the store restroom to wash, Father had treated him like an entire— very small—invading army.

This time was no different. The moment E stepped over the threshold, Dad pointed a trembling finger at him.

"You," he said. "You have no business coming into a bookstore."

E looked at him a moment, then did his best imitation of an angel, and said, "Hi, Grandad. This is Ccelly." He pointed to the invisible llama he held at the other end of an invisible rope. "Ccelly is a well-behaved llama. I won't let her eat anything. May I sit by the fireplace and play with Ccelly?"

My father seemed completely disarmed by all that charm. He looked at my son and nodded in an almost military way. "Very well," he said. "But mind you, I'll be keeping an eye on you."

E went to the sofas, where he sprawled, talking to something we had to assume was Ccelly. My father stood by the register glaring at him.

"Dad," I said. "You told me you wanted to see me."

He turned to me and for a few breaths seemed not to have the slightest notion of who I was. I'd never actually figured out if this lack of memory was true or an act, because when the situation got dire enough, he remembered my name and even Ben's. Once or twice he even seemed to remember Mom's. But I suspect most of the time the three of us and everyone else just fell into that vast and confusing category of objects that had no covers or titles, which made it very difficult for him to remember exactly who we were and what we were all about.

After staring at me, he said, "Oh, Sherlockia. I didn't see you there!"

"Hi, Dad," I said. The name was a battle I not only wasn't going to fight, but from which I would run as far and fast as possible. "You asked me to come and talk to you."

"Oh, yeah," he said, but he didn't seem to know what

he was saying. I waited for the world to stabilize for him. You see, as far as Dad is concerned, it's not so much that he can't remember people. That's part of it, of course. But the main problem—once he identifies the walking-talking nonbook advantage—is figuring out when it is and what might pertain to it. Sometimes I suspects he views life as a book, where you can advance the pages forward or backward and tune in wherever you wish to. That or he's completely insane, but I'd rather prefer the page thing.

"Oh, yeah. Why did you kill someone over a table?"

"Dad?" Of course my mind was going on about the table, and the stains on it, and what Dad might know about all of it. "Why do you think I killed someone? I didn't, but I'd like to know why you think that."

"Well," Dad said, "it was obvious when he came here and said that he wanted to know where you'd got the table and if what interested you were the bloodstains."

If I had dog ears, they'd have stood up and at attention. "Bloodstains? He . . . Who was he, Dad? What did he look like?"

"Oh, you know him. The guy that you asked about the table."

I tried to imagine the man from the semi-permanent garage sale coming into the bookstore, but the picture wouldn't quite gel. Dad would have kicked him out on smell alone. Mind you, Dad was so protective of the books that he would apologize to those he had to sell, and he often tried to go out of his way not to part with them. A man who smelled that badly and who looked like he'd never read a book in his life would get kicked out of the bookstore on suspicion of intending harm to books. Dad had been known to ask people to leave for looking at a book in a funny manner.

Then I thought of another person the "he" might be. "Was he dark haired, Dad? With his hair in a ponytail? Perhaps smelling a little of tobacco?"

Now Dad looked at me like I'd taken leave of my senses. "No, no. The skinny blond with the pop eyes." He made an expression imitating someone who, if the impersonation was accurate, would have looked like a cartoon character just before his eyes popped out and he had to chase them across the floor. The problem was that I had never seen anyone like that.

I didn't doubt Dad had seen him, though, because, again, Dad talking about a table right now—no matter how erratic his mind or memory—was too much of a coincidence. It strained disbelief. It was obvious someone had been here talking about a table and that the table was somehow linked with bloodstains and, in Dad's head at least, with me. Which meant the person must have mentioned the table, blood, and me.

"What did he say, Dad?"

"Uh? Not much. He said you'd bought a table and you'd . . . No. He didn't say you'd put bloodstains on it, only I assumed you had, because otherwise, why was he so worried about the whole thing? But he said that you . . . that there were bloodstains on it somehow, and he said that if you continued asking questions and putting your nose where it didn't belong, you were going to find yourself in trouble."

"Did he give you a name?"

"Yeah. Yours. He said Mrs. Dare."

Mrs. Dare. The same thing that Sebastian had called me. But even my dad couldn't think that Sebastian was blond and had pop eyes. "I see," I said. "And how did you know he didn't mean Mom?" Though if he did, the coincidence in that alone was phenomenal.

"Nah. He said the young Mrs. Dare."

"I see," I said. It was clear as mud, which of course was about how things got when I was around Dad. All the same, I wondered how person or persons unknown had managed to track me to the bookstore. This time—I was fairly sure of it—I hadn't been toting a bookstore bag around. Unless I had an invisible bag, just like E had Ccelly. I was about to check for any unusual weight on my hands when Mom came in, carrying Fluffy.

Mom is a small, delicate, doll-like woman. Fluffy is the perfect mystery cat: the white Persian that the villain usually caresses. Her actual name was Fluffy the Second, like book two of a trilogy. The original Fluffy was the cat I'd grown up with. We'd been great friends until I was about six and decided to play lion tamer and make Fluffy jump through Mom's quilting frame, which I'd set on fire.

After the fire department had come, and Fluffy had been taken to the vet, most of her fur had grown back in. And yet, she'd never forgiven me. She'd lived well into her twenties, in, I think, the hope I'd die before her. Whenever I stayed at Mom and Dad's, she'd pee on my bed.

When she'd finally died, Mom got a little white kitten she'd named Fluffy the Second, and, in proof that reincarnation might be true beyond silly television shows, Fluffy was born with undying hate for me in her heart.

Now fully grown, Daughter of Fluffy: The Grudge Continues still hated me as much as the original had. She drew herself up in Mom's arms and hissed just as Mom looked at me with a smile so vague and misty that she might be as unmoored in time and space as Dad. At least she did not call me Sherlockia. Or even Agatha, which was her preferred name for me. Instead she said, "Ah, Dyce. I'm glad you dropped by. I've been meaning to talk to you about Fluffy."

"Uh . . . what?"

"Fluffy," Mom said, and made a gesture with her arms as though she meant to hand me the cat. Fortunately, I was wearing long sleeves and a jacket over my sweater.

"It's funny," Mom said, as she looked at the parallel cuts left by Fluffy's claws on my jacket's sleeve. "She almost never does that."

I didn't say anything. She always did that to me. "Yes," I said, stepping back and trying to keep out of reach of the devil cat. "What did you want to ask me about Fluffy? I really don't know any good exorcists." I didn't dare add that fire solved most such problems. For some reason, Mom didn't see Fluffy the same way I did. In fact, for a brief and confused time she'd thought Fluffy would make a good friend for Pythagoras and had tried to bring her by for visits. It wasn't until Fluffy had taken a big bite out of Pythagoras's tail that I'd managed to convince Mom to stop the forced cat-socialization program.

Mom looked confused, as if Fluffy and exorcists didn't go together like bowl and spoon. "What? No, no. I was thinking about your wedding. You know, Fluffy is already all white."

"I am not wearing the cat," I said. "That's final." I had no clue if Mom meant for me to wear her alive or dead, but in any case, I wanted no part of the psycho kitty.

"Of course not." Mom looked offended. "It's not like I have the time to train her, though I submit to you that last year she was in the habit of sitting on top of your dad's head while he worked. It was very warming, of course, but also looked rather stylish, like an exotic hat. But with the wedding, and the music and guests," she said and sighed. "Well, the poor dear would probably get scared and jump off, and we wouldn't want her to get lost. No, what I'm thinking of is far more appropriate. I thought, you know, you don't have a sister."

Which was one of those things for which I was forever grateful. Oh, I'd probably have loved a sister. At least, when I was a kid, I was always jealous of Ben's large family and how busy and happy their household always was. He was the oldest of seven, which was probably where he got all his naturally protective and supervising attitude. And I liked staying at their house and talking to everyone.

But if Mom and Dad had another child, they would have had even more problems getting our names straight, and one of us would probably be forever forgotten. Alternately, they'd try to get us to behave in unison so as to better keep track of us. Synchronized upbringing!

"No," I said. "I don't have a brother, either."

Mom hesitated. In the past, she'd variously claimed that Ben was almost a brother to me and tried to get me to marry Ben. I could see her weighing these options in her mind, right now, but instead, she said, "Well . . . you know . . . the thing is . . . the thing is, Ben can't be your maid of honor."

No, but I would double dare Mom to suggest it in front of Ben, whom Cas had already tapped for his attendant. And the idea of Ben in a pinkish dress with a flower behind his ear was . . . untenable. Even his mental image glowered at me with such intensity that it would burn holes through my thoughts if it went on. "Yeah," I said.

"So I was thinking," Mom said. "Who could possibly be your maid of honor?"

"Uh . . . no idea," I said.

Mom waved Fluffy around again, lifting her a little and pushing her at me. I was smart enough, this time, to step back and plaster myself against a bookcase. Mom, clearly, had a loaded cat and wasn't afraid to use her. "Fluffy!" she said, as if I was completely stupid.

"Yes, I see, that's Fluffy, but what does that have to do with a bridesmaid?"

"Fluffy can be your maid of honor," Mom said. "We'll put a little wisp of silk around her neck, instead of the collar. And we'll put a little crown of flowers on her."

I stared. There are moments when one has to ask one-self if one has gone completely insane or the world has.

In this case, it wasn't even a competition. I might have my moments when I jumped to conclusions, forgot myself, or did some pretty odd things. But compared to the mental space Mom was inhabiting right now, I stood in the polar center of sanity. In fact, my mental state was the opposite of unstable. I was that fulcrum against which the lever that moved reality might rest.

"Mom," I said, aware that this little fact might have escaped her. "Fluffy is . . . How do I put this? A cat."

"Oh, I know that," Mom said.

"But you know what you said. She might get scared. The music, the crowds. And Ben and Nick will probably smell like rats, because, you know, they have pet rats, and—"

"Yes, of course," Mom said. Then, promptly negating this hopeful sign, "That's why we must get a cat harness that color coordinates what your wedding theme color will be. Have you decided on one? Ben said gray, but I was thinking something more . . . joyous, like cerise."

Which was when I happened to look toward the little sitting area, by the fireplace, and noticed that E wasn't there.

"E!" I yelled, and, shoving past Mom and Fluffy— who waved an ineffective paw (all claws out) in my direction—I ran out the front door and down the steps to the street.

Dad and Mom's store is set in what had once been a residential street surrounded by stately Victorians. It was now mostly a commercial neighborhood, the bottom half devoted to the sort of shop that people who lived within walking distance liked to frequent. There was the book-store, a vegetarian restaurant, two art galleries, the sort of dress-making establishment that specializes in dresses made primarily—or at least designed while under the influence—of hemp, a furniture store specializing in antique rugs and lamps, and a doll's hospital that restored antique and hard-to-find dolls.

At this time of the morning on a Monday, the streets weren't exactly crowded, so E should have been easy to see, the more so since I'd put on his little red jacket before we left the house. The problem, of course, was E's height. Although there were only a dozen or so people in the street, they were all taller than E. If he stood in front of one of them, I'd never see him.

Add to that that there were a lot of cross streets and that if he walked down one of the cross streets, he could get so lost I'd never find him. Cursing myself for not having had him chipped when I'd had Pythagoras chipped, and wondering why no one put tracking devices on the ears of little boys at birth, I stood on the sidewalk and said, "E? Ccelly?"

From the recessed entrance of the doll hospital, next door, a small figure emerged, pulling away from the wall in the best style of spy movies.

He looked over my shoulder to the door of the store, then threw himself in my arms. "Sorry, Mommy," he said. "Ccelly wanted to walk."

"Er . . ."

He looked into my eyes and did his best to make his eyes seem honest. They didn't seem to stay that way, but instead a bit of laughter kept lurking at the corners. "Oh, Mom," he said. "I'm sorry. It's just . . ."

"Yes?"

"I don't like Fluffy. I was afraid she'd claw me."

"Yeah. I often am, too."

"And then I thought if I left, they'd have to let you go so you could find me."

"You," I said, "are a very bad boy." But I couldn't keep the laughter from my voice.

E sighed. "I know. Can we go to the Chinese restaurant buffet?"

Well, no. Technically we could not, since I hadn't sold a piece in a long time, and I was edging close to broke. On the other hand, I wanted to. And besides, we could always eat pancakes for a week.

"Yeah," I said. "Let's." At any rate, the Chinese restaurant was near the police station, which would leave me very well situated for my date with Cas. We were going to look at a house together. That idea was a fear I'd face when I came to it.

CHAPTER 13

The Insidiousness of Dreams

I was about halfway through looking at the house when I realized I was in trouble. No, I mean, real trouble. At some point this had gone from my looking politely interested as Cas and an annoyingly perfect-looking real estate agent led me and a strangely quiet E from room to room around the house to my starting to envision the house if I lived there. No, much worse. I was envisioning the house as it would be if Cas and I and E and at least a couple more kids lived there.

To begin with, Cas had tricked me. Instead of taking me—as I expected from his description—to a house somewhere in the suburbs, all sterile neighborhood covenants and neighbors wondering why Mrs. Wolfe was using dangerous chemicals in her backyard, he'd driven me less than six blocks from my current home.

Here I have to explain how Goldport works. You see, it's not so much a city as a bunch of neighborhoods jammed together. Oh, sure, we have a downtown and a token few skyscrapers, most of them office buildings. But they are token, and that's the point. If you go in one direction from there, you come across the area of little shops, diners, coffee shops, and—survivors of the sixties—a lot of head shops and such.

But extending in each direction from those areas are pockets of neighborhoods. One of them was the area I lived in, which used to be stately Victorians but had been subdivided to become student and young couple housing. Another way from there were neighborhoods like my parents', inhabited mostly by middle-aged and older artsy people employed in intellectual professions. The small shops in those areas catered to a better category of customers, or at least charged more.

And then there were the more exclusive areas, some of which had once been like mine—subdivided, inhabited by people starting out—but had since become more exclusive and expensive, recovering some of their Victorian middle-class appearance. This house was one of those, painted white and set within a garden, surrounded by an iron fence. It had been recently restored, as had most of the houses around it. It was a step up from Ashton's neighborhood, as a whole, but not such a great step. It was not like the massive patrician houses that took up the streets a few blocks away. There I would have been in as much trouble as in the suburbs. No, worse. Not only would the dowagers wonder why I was playing with chemicals and wood in the backyard, but they would wonder why I never wore a nice dress; went out dressed in ratty jeans; never gave teas or parties. As for E, there was no amount of curbing that would make E fit in such a neighborhood.

But this house . . . well, the neighbors were likely to be as nonconventional as I was. I started by noting that I could still walk all the places I liked to walk with E, including the diner and the little coffee shop around the corner. And it was within walking distance of the neighborhood elementary school—one of the nicest schools in the city. Which meant that I had a better chance of having him go to this school than the school in All-ex's area. And that E would eventually need to go to school was one of those necessities of life I might not like but was growing used to.

But I withstood the appeal of the front yard, the flower beds, the roses—now bare and pruned back, growing around the porch. I even withstood the front hall, with the little bench, where E, covertly, tied Ccelly to the stair banister as soon as Cas and the real estate agent turned their backs.

It was far harder to withstand the sunny family room with the built-in bookcases. Though I'm not as devoted to mystery as my parents, I did grow up in a home filled with books, and I do love reading. These were spacious polished oak bookcases in a room with windows all along its longest side. The bookcases glowed, and I could imagine my books on them. And Cas's books, which tended to be science fiction and fantasy, since he dealt with mystery all day, every day. And E's books, down at the bottom, all the young adult science books he liked to have read to him. I could imagine nice, comfortable sofas with plain blue cotton slipcovers— for easy washing—and E and Pythagoras nestled in one of the sofas, with a book. I could imagine some nice oak coffee tables, coated with polyurethane so they could withstand glasses of lemonade and milk. I could imagine summer afternoons, with the windows open and the breeze washing in, bringing the smell of the rosebushes.

After that point I was lost. I might as well forget telling myself that I would not, under any circumstances, consider moving and give up the apartment lease. I might as well stop telling myself that I didn't want the pretty house and playing happy family with Cas, either.

By the time we reached the spacious kitchen, I could see myself cooking on the built-in stove, and I could imagine the kids gathered around the beautiful table I'd inherited from my grandmother: E, and Junior, and the little girl. All waiting for their pancakes. I had no idea where they'd come from—and Cas would probably kill me before letting me call a kid Junior—but they were as clear and present as the image of the table in the bay-windowed breakfast nook. Junior had my eyes and Cas's chin, and the little girl looked like a replica of myself at her age. Which meant I'd better make sure if we did buy this house that I had a fire extinguisher for each room.

I couldn't stop thinking of the arson we were supposedly investigating then, but it left my mind again as we went upstairs to the bedroom area. One of the rooms was just perfect for E. I could imagine him growing up in it, with posters of cartoon characters being replaced by musician posters on his wall, and the books on the desk progressing from young adult books to whatever his interest turned out to be. I could imagine him at eighteen, sprawled on the bed and talking on the phone. It was so vivid I almost told him to move his feet off the bedspread.

Then I realized he was only three and was, in fact, by my side, his hand in mine. I looked down at him, and he looked up and nodded "E's room." Which meant, I don't know what, except that perhaps it was a shared dream.

The bedroom right next to the master's would be the

nursery, of course. Which is when I realized I was utterly lost and tried to concentrate on the conversation Cas was having with the nice real estate agent.

But I couldn't really, because they were talking about how the people who had initially renovated this had been making a business of it until recently, when the real estate market had stopped dead. Now they were left with this house—and, I understood, others as well—on their hands.

The back building was the best part of it. Not only did it have a garage, which was not a given in this part of Colorado, but it was adjacent to what had once been a carriage house, which was wide enough—and floored in practical concrete—for both my refinishing needs and for Cas and Nick's playing with cars. In fact, it already had a lifting platform or whatever it was called, so the guys could get under the cars with minimal effort. I imagined the carriage house divided by plastic, and my side kept dust free, lined with shelves of chemicals, and . . .

At the door, the real estate agent shook both our hands, earnestly, while E—covertly—untied Ccelly from the banister. "I'm sure the owners will be very amenable to discussing price," she said. "The place has been on the market for more than six months, after all. And I happen to know they want it off their hands."

That last comment made me think, again, that we were here because the house was threatened with arson, somehow. And I felt suddenly this shouldn't be allowed. It was my house. Surely they couldn't torch it.

But then I heard the price that was being asked for it, and I nearly swallowed my tongue. The Goldport Police Department pays its officers relatively well. Still, I

CHAPTER 14

The Principal Suspect

I was so confused by the developments that I didn't think clearly till a while after Cas had dropped me off with a kiss and a reassurance that although he might have to work late, he'd be coming back to spend the night. Which just underscored how crazy it was for him to have a separate place, I guess. But he was going to put an offer on the house and . . .

While E told Pythagoras all about the nice room they would have, I moved through my place in a haze, pretending to straighten up. A whole house. The idea was so odd. Oh, I'd lived in a house before—I mean, my house, not the one I'd grown up in. But my house, shared with All-ex, had been a small starter home in the suburbs. I'd always felt vaguely out of place in it, like it was too new, too . . . too neatly arranged to fit me.

This house, on the other hand, might have been made

for me. Oh, it was clean, and the floors were refinished and looked lovely, but the house, itself, had nooks and crannies. It had places to hide and places to grow. It was a house with character. A people house.

I had to resist the impulse to hit a few of my normal places to get used furniture at bargain prices and start buying pieces to refinish for the new place. I had to resist it for several reasons, not the least of which was the fact that I had just the money for the rent in my bank account, and unless one of my pieces on consignment at the various furniture stores in Denver sold, and soon, I'd be scrambling for grocery money next week.

So, before I started buying things for the house I wouldn't move into until three months from now at the earliest, I must buy or find some pieces I could make money from. Or finish that table in the back and sell it.

I shivered. The idea of working on the table, with the visible bloodstains, gave me the creeps. And what if someone had really been killed on it? Or against it? What would I do then? I couldn't sell the table and potentially destroy evidence.

But what if the table hadn't been part of a murder? But then why would someone disguise expensive, smooth oak as cheap pine? And why would someone have gone to my dad to ask questions?

Was the pop-eyed blond Jason Ashton? And why had Peter and Collin talked to Sebastian about me? And what would Cas think if he found out how far into this murder investigation I was, if it was a murder, without telling him anything about it?

I stood in my kitchen, looking at the counter I'd just finished wiping down, and sighed. I hated to do this, truly, but before I came clean to Cas, before I even considered letting him know what I'd been up to, I had to figure out if Jason was the guy who had gone to my dad—possibly with intent to scare him.

Which meant, I would have to take risks. Again.

Actually, what really bothered me was that I had to take E with me. But there was nothing for that. Ben was at work—a distressing habit of his—and my parents were . . . sadly, my parents. So I would have to take E with me.

Fortunately, he didn't resist much, just taking one of his books about lab rats with him and pouting because I wouldn't let him take Pythagoras.

I wasn't sure at all what I was going to do, particularly after Sebastian had warned me away from the place. I had some vague idea that I was going to sit across the street and watch the people who came and went into the house. But before I got there, I had decided the thing to do was to ring the doorbell and ask to see Jason Ashton.

It turned out to be completely unnecessary. When I got there, kids were playing in the front yard, in the cool but sunny afternoon. And at the door, leaning against the frame, was a man, clearly watching over them.

He was not Sebastian. He did not have that kind of sex-appeal wattage. But neither was he the pop-eyed blond that my father had talked about. His hair was brown, slightly receding. His eyes were also brown and, though he must have been in his late twenties or very early thirties, had a little pattern of wrinkles at the corners, which indicated he laughed a lot.

He wasn't laughing just then, I noted, as I approached with E by the hand, after having parked in front of the house. His eyes had a pensive, almost haunted look.

When I reached for the latch on the garden gate, he came toward me. "Hi there," he said. "May I help you?" though the tone was *Please go away and leave me alone*.

I squeezed E's hand a little tighter and hoped I wasn't making a terrible mistake. "I'd like to talk to Jason Ashton," I said.

"I'm Jason Ashton," he said, looking a little taken aback.

I extended my hand. "Hi, I'm Candyce Dare. May I talk to you? Just a little?"

"Uh," he said. "I don't mean to be rude, but I really am not in the market for a religious conversion, and I don't buy encyclopedias."

Interesting. So my name was total news for him. This would seem to imply that Sebastian and whatever his name was, the blond, were both acting on their own, or perhaps in concert with each other.

"That's fortunate," I said. "Because I don't want to talk to you about either religion or encyclopedias. Look . . . I understand this must be a stressful time for you, but . . . I've come across something that might give us some idea what happened to your wife, and I'd like to talk to you about it."

"Maria?" His face lit up with something like wild hope. "You've heard from Maria?"

"Oh, unfortunately, nothing like that," I said. "But . . . If I may . . . Can I ask what you know about when she disappeared and what happened?" I was having serious trouble thinking that a man who became so enthusiastic about the idea of finding her had done away with Maria Ashton. On the other hand, it was possible he was a really good actor. Or crazy.

"I don't want to talk to reporters, either," he said.

"I'm not a reporter. Nothing connected to it. I promise. My fiancé is the chief investigator on the case," I said. I got my wallet out and finished for a business card. "This is what I do for a living."

He looked at the card for Daring Finds, then back down at me. "I don't understand. Furniture refinishing?"

"The problem," I explained, "is that I don't want to tell you what I think I found, because it might worry you unnecessarily. You see, I think I have some . . . leads, but they might have nothing to do with the case. I really don't know much beside the fact that your wife disappeared more than a month ago. I could, I suppose, have asked my fiancé more about it, or even have gone around you and badgered everyone . . . I did talk to your neighbors once." I indicated Peter and Collin's house with a nod. "But I thought it would be better to come and talk to you and get the truth from your mouth."

He hesitated, playing with my card, then shrugged. "Okay, fine. I'm moving anyway." He paused. "Do your friends call you Dyce?"

"Yes, why?"

He smiled, just a little, a smile that didn't alter the fact that he looked immensely sad underneath it all. "Ah. Because when I was talking to Officer Wolfe, he answered the phone to someone named Dyce."

"Yeah," I said. "I must have called about something."

He nodded. "Well . . . it's just, I don't know how much Maria would want known, but I could tell the police thought she'd disappeared voluntarily, and that's entirely possible, but I was wondering . . . I mean . . ." He shrugged. "I don't know what she wants me to tell people. I know I told the police about it . . . but . . ." He seemed to notice E for the first time. And that his kids were clustering around us, looking at E.

The kids were a little girl about E's age and two boys a little older, and they looked like good kids. The little girl looked a lot like her dad; the two boys looked darker and more exotic.

"If your little boy wants to play with Isabella and the boys, we can talk by the door while we watch them."

Since E was already pulling his hand away from mine, I presumed he wanted to. In no time at all, the four of them were running all over the tiny lawn, looking like they'd known each other from birth.

Jason smiled a little at their playing. "It's good to see them having fun," he said. "This has been very hard for them, too. Now . . . what did you want to know?"

"What happened when your wife disappeared," I said. "And why it took you so long to report her missing."

He looked at me and narrowed his eyes, not threateningly but more like he was thinking. "Because I was hoping she'd come back," he said.

"So . . . you argued and she walked out?"

He shook his head. "We never argued," he said, then gave me a little tight, self-conscious smile. "I mean we never argued before she disappeared. We argued a bit, like normal couples do, usually about truly stupid things—you know . . . who left the lid off the sugar bowl and who forgot to feed the cat and water the plants."

"Yeah. But you didn't argue before she disappeared?"

He shook his head.

"Well, pardon me, then, but wouldn't that be all the more reason to have actually gone to the police the minute she left?"

He sighed. "Well, no. See . . . See . . ." He visibly struggled for words. "Although we didn't argue and there was no logical reason for her to leave me and the children, there were . . . There was a reason for her to want to disappear for a while to . . . to deal with things and . . . and find her balance again, and I thought that's what she had done."

"Find her balance?"

His jaw worked for a while, while he remained silent. "You see," he said, "Maria was having these problems, and she went to the doctor. We thought she might be pregnant, because she would fall asleep for like fifteen minutes at a time, in the oddest places, and in the middle of doing stuff, and it was a lot like the first three months when she was pregnant with Isabella, so we thought . . . But it turned out she had narcolepsy."

He saw my total confusion. "It's a sleep disorder. It's not mental, you know, or psychological, but it is in the brain. The brain doesn't produce a certain protein that regulates sleep cycles. That means she wouldn't sleep at night, and then she would fall asleep at unpredictable times during the day. We both work very hard. I mean, we both go to school, and she had the kids, and I work at the lumberyard part-time. Well, I did till last week. So it wasn't like . . . I mean . . . it has no cure, but there are medications for it, so maybe we could control it. So she started taking the meds and all, but it takes time to adjust to them, and meanwhile she . . . needed help. Watching the kids, and making sure she was okay around the house and stuff, so we had to have one of our friends always with her, and . . . I think she felt useless. Or as if she was a burden on me, which was totally not true. She kept saying that the kids and I would be better off without her."

"So you weren't afraid she had committed suicide."

"Well, no," he said. "Because people who commit suicide don't take all their clothes, the kitchen table, and a chair."

"Oh, she . . . took stuff?" I was thinking of the table. He wouldn't tell me about the table if he'd been the one to kill her, right? Or if the table was somehow involved? But the man at the semi-permanent garage sale had told me that he'd bought the table from Jason Ashton.

"Yeah. Our friend Sebastian normally stayed with her. He's our oldest friend here in town, and he's the most reliable of our friend group. So he stayed with her while I was at work. But he works as a handyman, and he can't afford to turn work down, not in this market. So he had to go and fix someone's leaking washer for an hour, and he says Maria told him she would be okay, so he left. When he came back, the kids were in bed and asleep—this was in the evening—but Maria was gone. She did not take her car, which is weird, but she'd taken a bag with all her clothes, and the kitchen table, and a chair."

"Isn't it weird?" I said. "I mean, that the only furniture she'd take was the kitchen table?"

He twirled my business card between his fingers. "Not really. The table came from her aunt's house, and she was very attached to it. If she was going to take something from the house, it would be that."

"But if she was only going to be gone for a few days . . ."

"I figured she'd rented a place somewhere and taken the table so that she could feel at home. You know, something she knew and was comfortable with? And I figured it was until she could figure out her medication and the dosages and come to terms with her illness. She had trouble because she was convinced . . . Well, some of the medicines you take for narcolepsy are antidepressants, and she was afraid people would think she was mentally ill."

"Ah. And when . . . when did you decide to go to the police?"

"I wanted to give her all the room she needed," he said. "We got married right out of high school, you know, have been married for almost ten years, and I trusted her. I thought she would do the best possible, and I trusted she loved me and would eventually come back to me."

"Trusted?" I said. "But not anymore?"

He shrugged. "I don't know. I have trouble believing that she doesn't love the kids, at least, even if she's mad at me or feels she can't come back to me. But that's not it. What I'm afraid of," he said, "is that something happened to her."

"Why?"

"It's like this," he said. "I got an offer from a university in California. I just finished my doctorate in classical studies, and you know—or perhaps you don't, but I know—how difficult it is to get a position in academia right now. But this place in California, no, not UC Berkeley, but a small, private college you probably never heard of, offered me an assistantship, and it has a good possibility of advancement, plus I'd make enough that I wouldn't need to moonlight at Home Depot. It's the kind of thing that's too good to pass up. So, even though I'd been giving Maria room to decide she wanted to come back, I realized I needed to get in touch with her and tell her about this. Because, you know, if she finally decided to come home, even if there was someone here to tell her where the kids and I had gone, it could be a problem.

I mean, she'd wonder if I really cared for her because I hadn't even bothered to tell her in advance."

"Yeah," I said, feeling sorry for what appeared to be a nice man in a terrible situation.

"The only lead I had to contact her was her doctor. I hated to tell the doctor I hadn't the slightest notion where she'd gone, but it was also my only way to get to her. So I called Doctor Ludo."

"And?"

"And he hadn't heard from her since the week before she disappeared. In fact, she'd missed one appointment, and they were concerned because her medicine would be running out soon."

"So then you told the police?"

He nodded. "Yes." He hesitated. "And now, if I may, why do you ask? What . . . what has made you investigate?"

"I bought the table," I said.

"What?"

"I bought your kitchen table. At a garage sale."

"But . . ." He frowned. "Did Maria sell it?"

I shook my head. "Not that I know." I told him about my interview with the man running the garage sale.

Jason looked puzzled. "But I didn't sell it," he said. "I thought . . . Do you have a description of the man who sold it?"

I shook my head.

"But surely you buy used furniture all the time," he said. "What was so special about this one that you had to investigate it?"

So I told him. About the gummed-up top, but not about the blood. I didn't want to tell him about the blood.

I'd decided there was enough in this, right now, to go to the police. Or to Cas, who was the more familiar, closer, and less scary form of the police. To him I could tell things like what Collin and Peter claimed to have seen— that is, Sebastian helping Maria out of the bathroom. I certainly was not going to tell this anxious, sad man about it.

"I want to see the table," he said.

I hesitated. "It's in my work space, and I don't want anyone to go in without me there; besides, perhaps the time has come to talk to Cas . . . to the police about it."

To my surprise, he nodded. "Yes. Of course. I wish you'd told me earlier." He shook his head. "I mean, I wish I'd known earlier. Maria would never, ever, ever have done that kind of half-assed finish on the table, so I wonder what went wrong. I mean, someone could have robbed her. She could be somewhere in the high country without the means to get back. Or . . ."

I know both our minds went there at once. *Or she could be dead.*

He looked at me, his eyes widening in horror. "I just want her to be well," he said. "And . . . and I'd like her to come back. Yeah, I know she didn't believe she was as much use to us after . . . well, she thought that we'd be happier without her, and she kept saying she'd get an apartment and get out of my hair, which is why I didn't think anything about . . ." He put his hand on his forehead. "I just want my wife back."

He might, of course, be the world's greatest actor, but I couldn't help believing him.

CHAPTER 15

The Loose Ends

I got into the car with a flushed, happy E. "I left Ccelly with them," he announced.

"Huh? Oh," I said, which was about my level of coherency.

"Isabella liked Ccelly, and she doesn't have a Mommy just now. I have a Mommy, so I told her she could keep Ccelly for company."

"That's very sweet of you, honey," I said. Which was true. It was also a little odd, as I'd never before heard of a child giving away his imaginary friend. But then, my son was nothing if not original.

"Yeah," he said. "I left her a sack of oats, too. You don't mind?" He looked worriedly at me.

"Of course not." For all I cared, he could give away all the invisible, imaginary oats he wanted.

A Fatal Stain

I drove for a few moments in silence, and then E said, softly, "You'd never just disappear, Mommy, would you?"

This, too, was one of the sweetest things E had ever said. Look, I have no illusions about my fitness as a mother. Even if I wanted to have them, I couldn't. It seems like every other week All-ex throws one of my failings in my face. I am, it appears, insufficiently sensitive to E's delicate development stages. I don't give him organic, full-fiber food. I don't dress him in shoes that support his growing arches or in clothes that won't dent his self-esteem when he meets better-dressed peers. Add to that that I've failed to teach him to hold up his place in society with the right manners and that at three he has yet to learn a second language—which means, if I am to believe Michelle Mahr, that he'll never make it into one of the better-rated preschools. This, in turn, will keep him from getting into the most exclusive kindergartens, and it will all end, by degrees, with E digging ditches for a living in some back-country town.

Or, at least, that's what All-ex tells me. Though I'll note his attempt to have E learn to play piano went badly wrong. I never got the full story out of Michelle, who can't seem to explain herself when she's also having hysterics. However, I believe it was something about how E had set fire to the teacher's hair. But surely that couldn't be true, unless it was accidental, or I'm sure I'd have heard something more about it. Of course, it was entirely possible E had simply set fire to the piano. He had a very forthright way of showing when he didn't care for something.

I knew when Mother's Day came around, if E ever got me a mug that said *To the world's greatest mom*, it was proof he hadn't learned to read yet. Otherwise, it would be because it was the only thing he could buy on his way to see me.

But to hear him ask me not to vanish gave me a sort of inner happy feeling. Okay, it was sort of a minimal type of praise. After all, how many times do we go around wishing people would vanish, especially people we didn't particularly like? But it was praise, nonetheless, and I hoped to hold on to it, to remember when E was a stormy teen who hated me, hated me, hated me.

So I said, "I will do my best not to."

"Thanks," he said. Then, as though he'd scoured his mind long and hard for a compliment that wouldn't be a lie, he said, "No one makes pancakes like you."

I realized I was about to drive by the house with the semi-permanent garage sale, and it occurred to me it wouldn't hurt—before I talked to Cas—if I asked the man for a description of the person who'd sold the table. I mean, I had thought that Jason was plausible and truthful, but frankly, it wouldn't be the first time I was fooled. I mean, I had married All-ex after all, even if I'd corrected the mistake as soon as it was humanly possible. So it's not like I could claim an infallible knowledge of men. Or women, or even small animals. Or, possibly, my parents, who sometimes acted like aliens.

"I'm going to go talk to this man, okay?" I asked E as I parked my car and reached for the door.

He gave me an evaluating look. "At the icky garage sale again?"

"Yeah," I said.

E looked worried. "You're not going to buy me any of that stuff, right?"

I laughed. My son, the fashion arbiter, refused to let me buy stuff from a déclassé garage sale. "No. I just want to ask the man a few questions."

It wasn't until I was out of the car, though, that it occurred to me if I just trooped up to the man and asked him about who had given him a check, he was likely to become defensive. Just a little. So defensive, in fact, that it was entirely possible he'd give me wrong information just to take revenge.

Between the sidewalk and the pathetic spread of things on the lawn, it occurred to me that the best strategy—since I didn't have a lie detector available— would be to get the man relaxed. And the best way to do that would be for me to buy something.

I cast a desperate eye over the flotsam and jetsam of other people's lives that had come to rest on this lawn. I'd seen better pickings in Dumpsters. At least those that didn't contain dead bodies. Well, those, too, but you sort of had to work around the dead bodies.

Then I noticed a virulently green-gold box. At least, at first I thought it was a box, till I got closer and realized it was a wooden trunk. The sort of thing where, presumably, brides had kept their trousseaux. Or the type Grandma kept her quilts in.

Only anyone keeping quilts in something that was painted bright, virulent greenish-gold, as this one was, would find that everything inside had turned overnight into polyester in a paisley pattern. To make things worse, it had huge golden knobs on it. I opened the top, looked inside, and realized that this was a modern, very cheap piece.

It wasn't that it was badly made, as such. I mean, it was real wood and not veneer, though I couldn't quite establish what the wood might be, besides "pale and smooth." The paint was a very thin layer, probably applied by sprayer, and it was a weird shade between green and gold, so you could kind of see gold flecks in it.

The style was familiar, only because I'd recently seen it—ridiculously overpriced, of course—at one of those cutesy Asian import stores that sell paper umbrellas and baskets, also ridiculously overpriced. I remembered having looked at the pieces in horror and wondered who actually bought them, even if they were comparatively cheap and made of real wood.

But now I had to buy something, and other than headless dolls, which even the doll hospital could not fix—even if they'd been old and antique, which they weren't—or what my son would undoubtedly class as icky clothes, and too small and babylike at that, I had nothing.

Except this.

The man who ran the garage sale approached. I knew this, because I could smell him at a distance. He loomed over me, his shadow, momentarily, obscuring the golden shimmers in the awful green paint. "Lovely piece," he said. "Very classy. It's amazing, really, that someone got rid of a piece that good. People moving out of state," he said, and spit, his spit landing just beside the trunk. "They don't have any choice but to sell, of course, but that piece there, I bet, cost them a pretty penny. It's very new, too, none of that old junk you see around."

I could tell it was very new, and I refrained from telling him it was new junk. Instead, I stood up, afraid next time he spit he would hit me by accident. I fished my wallet from my jeans pocket and looked in it to realize I only had ten dollars. "How much do you want for it?" I asked.

"Oh, a piece like that is easily worth a hundred dollars."

That I could believe, since it had been marked exactly that at Ye Tacky Import Shop. However, I wasn't going to tell him so. Instead, I said, "Um . . . all I have is ten dollars." I was already calculating, in my mind, whether I could ask him to hold it while I drove to Ben's office and asked Ben for a loan. A twenty or so. There was no way I was going to pay the man the same price this thing had cost new.

The problem, of course, was that Ben would probably commit me immediately after. One look at this trashy piece and he'd know I'd lost my mind for good. But I had to buy it, at least if I was going to be able to ask the man any questions about the supposed Jason Ashton. And besides, really, what room did the man who had been imitating a human burrito on my sofa have to talk about my sanity?

But the man, after a moment of drawing breath in, looked over my shoulder into my wallet and said, with ill grace, "Well, if that's all you have."

It was all I had. Quite literally. That is, it was all I had other than the money in the bank, which would go to pay the rent in a day or two.

These days, of course, the refrigerator tended to be stocked. It was very hard to get Cas to stop buying milk, eggs, and bacon. Heck, he'd been known to stop by Bread Alone and get the freshly baked loaves and sandwich fixings, too. Which to my mind was just his way of showing off his wealth. And with Ben staying over, the fridge and freezer would probably end up even more full. It was Ben's way of repaying me whenever he'd had to crash on my sofa for any reason. Though I might add that in the list of crazy reasons that had ever caused him to crash on my sofa, avoiding a conversation with Nick might be the silliest.

Which was something else I'd have to deal with soon but which had nothing to do with the fact that I didn't have to like it when I was dependent on the guys for food. When I'd got divorced and found myself alone with E and confronted with All-ex's erratic memory when it came to child support—and my not wanting to challenge it, or point out I needed it to be able to feed E, because All-ex might use that to prove I wasn't fit to have joint custody of the child—all I could do was vow I'd never again be dependent on anyone. I'd worked hard to build my skill at refinishing and my business contacts. I didn't want to owe Cas anything.

On the other hand, it occurred to me that marriage, after all, meant owing each other something. Sharing. And I'd agreed to marry Cas, which meant I had no business being aloof. I was either going to be his wife or not. And if I was going to be his wife, it meant letting him get food and, yeah, pay for the roof over my head. In return, I would have, after all, to have the kids, and probably— if I could find the time after all the refinishing—clean the house and do his laundry and all. I didn't think that Cas would be crazy enough to let me cook. Or at least not often.

As this was going through my mind, I handed my last cash over. The man looked toward the car and said, "This is pretty heavy. Is your boy going to help you carry it?"

Perhaps E projected bigger through glass. "No, he's three. Can you give me a hand?"

He gave me a hand, which meant enduring his smell

all the way to the car. We slid the trunk, top down, into the back of the station wagon, which, for once, was free of other cargo. Cas often said I used it as other people would use a warehouse, to store various finds from my shopping or scavenging trips, and only moved the objects to the shed when I had run out of space.

It was partly true. The real truth, though, is that I never moved them to the shed until I had the elbow room and the time to deal with them. Both of which were in such short supply right now that I'd not even bought any pieces to finish.

And now I had to finish planning the wedding. And, apparently, I had to come up with a bridesmaid. This was somewhat of a problem. I'd never had many friends, and of the few I'd managed, Ben was the only one I'd kept after my divorce. All the others—who were really more friendly acquaintances than friends, by then—had taken All-ex's part in this. Possibly because All-ex was less likely to embarrass them.

This is not to say I lived a life in isolation, of course. I knew tons of people and had tons of contacts. This was the problem, though—the few friends I'd had growing up in school and such, the girls with whom I had shared confidences, the ones whose parties I'd attended, had either moved out of town or lived and worked in such different circles from me that I'd hardly even said hi to them for years.

The truth was that since I'd got divorced I'd been so busy making a living and so afraid that everyone I'd known before would disapprove of the way I made a living that they'd make snide remarks or act like I'd lost my mind. So I'd simply cut off most social contacts.

Which left me with a very odd dilemma. Who could be my maid of honor? I had no cousins. Other than Mom—who was an only child—I had no female relatives. So who could I conscript for the embarrassing role in my wedding? I mean, I didn't think that vets gave sex-change operations, so even Pythagoras couldn't be my maid of honor. Cas had a best man and a male attendant. No, two, since he was also having Nick's brother as a male attendant. This was downright selfish of him. The least he could have done was have a female cousin or a sister. Didn't he know I'd eventually need a maid of honor?

Thinking along these lines, I closed the back of the car. The man was threatening to lumber away, and I was, by gum, going to get my ten dollars' worth of information.

"Wait," I said. "Did you get this trunk from Jason Ashton, too?"

He stopped and frowned at me. "Who?"

"The man who sold you the table I bought before."

His look, as memory cut through the fog of whatever he was on, seemed to say I was clearly obsessed with this Jason Ashton guy. But he shook his head.

"Oh," I said. "I was hoping—" I let what I was hoping drop. "I wonder if he's the Jason Ashton I know? Is he a tall, dark-haired guy?"

"Nah," the man said. "Short, blond guy with big popped-out eyes." He made an expression curiously reminiscent of my father's. "Talks like this, too," and he made a high, nasally sound that bordered terrifyingly on a whine.

"Did he . . . Did you see his driver's license?"

He shook his head. "Nah. What for? I mean, I was paying him, not he me."

"And you paid him by check?"

"Yeah."

That was about as far as I could go. I wanted to ask him if the check had ever been cashed, but I suspected he already thought I was stalking this guy. So I said, "Oh, well. I wondered if he had other stuff to sell."

"I don't think he did," the man said. "He was driving a rattrap of a car, and all he had were some baby clothes and that table."

I nodded. Again, I couldn't ask for a description of the rattrap of a car. But Cas could, and possibly would, once I put all the facts in his lap. At least I hoped he would, instead of thinking I'd finally slipped the last cog of sanity and contact with reality.

I said, "Well, thank you," and jumped in the car, happy to be away from the man's smell. I wondered if no one ever sold their stock of decorative soap, but I suspected if they did, the man running the sale would be so unfamiliar with the substance as to think of it as cheese, or perhaps cooking lard.

"Mom?" E said. In the rearview mirror, I could see he had his head turned back and was looking at the brand-new trunk. "That's so . . . green."

"Yeah, I know," I said. I was still vaguely afraid that Cas would have me put away for insanity, but right at that time, I wanted, more than anything, to get home and talk to Cas about the whole thing.

CHAPTER 16

The Matter of Bridesmaïds

When I got home, the light was blinking on the answering machine, and when I clicked it, I found it was Cas saying, "Dyce, I'm sorry. We're staying over. They've identified the body, and Nick and I are making some phone calls. We'll probably have something here, Chinese or whatever. There's some cans of soup, and you could make grilled cheese sandwiches." I loved how he sounded tentative. "I'm sure E would love that."

E probably would have, but I'd had no time to more than get the can out of the pantry when Ben came in with Chinese. "Nick called," he said. "To say he wasn't coming home for dinner, so I figured . . ."

I didn't even want to ask where "home" was, considering. Instead I said, "Uh . . . I thought you weren't talking to each other."

He managed to give me a completely blank look. "What? Of course we're talking to each other."

"Right," I said. In my mind, the line went *Stomp once for yes, twice for no.*

But he was opening rice containers, and E was jumping around like a maniac, saying, "Combination, combination, combination."

Given all possible foods in the world, including chocolate-covered chocolate bars layered with chocolate, E would choose combination fried rice every time. Not only that, but when he starts eating it, he can't seem to stop. In fact, there must be some form of special mechanism in his stomach that transports all the food to another dimension because he will eat an adult portion—far more than any sane toddler should be able to fit in a normal stomach.

Ben, of course, knew our tastes as well as he knew his own. He'd got hot-and-sour soup for the two of us and chicken curry for me. For himself, he'd got Peking duck, which he only liked at this particular restaurant. He got the plates and started distributing the food, while I got milk for E and soda water for myself.

Pythagoras came nosing around, rubbing on legs, and I got him tuna, which was probably a bad idea, as everything we were eating was suddenly suffused with eau de cheap tuna.

Because I couldn't tell Ben about the murder—or possible murder—of Maria Ashton, I told him, instead, about the house I'd gone to see. "Oh, yeah," he said. "Nick told me."

From the way he set his mouth, there was something

painful about the whole subject, and I wasn't even about to guess what. "What do you mean Nick told you?"

"Well, the first time, Cas dragged him along to look at it."

"Ah," I said. "And what? Was someone murdered in it once or something? Did he sense a ghost lurking in the shadows? What is the problem with the house?"

He looked up and frowned. "Don't be stupid."

There was no talking to him when he was in that mood. I could have argued that I wasn't stupid at all and that there was no reason I could see for him to look like that. Also, that it was almost impossible to read his mind when he was in this mood. Almost. I could sometimes figure it out, but it took a game of twenty questions, and I simply didn't have the energy right now. It occurred to me that if I managed to be this bewildered, after knowing Ben for most of his life, then poor Nick must be baffled. "Stomp your foot once for yes, twice for no," I said, cheerfully, eating my curry noodles.

He glared, and I was afraid he'd take the noodles and storm out the door, so I just made a mental note to look up the house in the news before we were irrevocably committed to buy it.

Instead, I concentrated on getting E to finish eating. As usual, when he ate this much, he was half asleep by the time we finished the meal, which was just as well, as I could then give him a bath and put him to bed.

Ben insisted on reading him a book, which must have been an excuse not to talk to me about the house—as if I were stupid enough to try that—because his idea of reading books to E included much too much ad-libbing. He was quite capable of reading a line like "The young lady was always happy" and add his own codicil of "because she was taking Prozac by the truckload." What he'd once done to a reading of *The 101 Dalmatians* could not—or should not—be reproduced in front of young and impressionable audiences. And the fact that E actually preferred the version of "The Three Little Pigs" in which Practical Pig decides his brothers are too stupid to live and roasts them and invites the wolf to the barbecue was something that would probably come back to haunt me in the form of therapy bills in ten years or so.

But this time what he read E was a nonfiction book called *Groovy Greeks*, which he must have brought with him, because I'd never seen it. And although the book didn't say anything about Nick—not even in the ad libs— it seemed to be about Greek civilization and its history written for about a fifth-grade level. Which meant that E got to ask questions until his eyes were so heavy that he fell asleep, with Pythagoras vigilantly perched on top of his chest. How E could breathe with that weight was beyond me, but he clearly could.

And once they were both asleep, Ben truly could not avoid coming out, turning the light off, and risking talking to me.

I came out of the room with him and sat on the sofa. "Sit," I said. "I found some stuff about the murder, and I want to talk."

"Murder?" he said.

"Almost for sure. The woman, Maria Ashton."

"Oh," he said.

Yeah, I definitely was going to look up the history of that house before I bought it. But aloud I said, "Yeah, look, I went and talked to her husband."

"You what?"

So I had to tell him the whole story of what Dad wanted. He absolutely refused to believe that Peter and Collin could have betrayed his secrets or mine. Ever. "No, they wouldn't talk," he said. "No. Sorry. Faulty assumption."

"Well, whatever," I said, and told him about the blond guy with the pop-eyed look. Then I told him about the guy in the semi-permanent garage sale.

"I see," he said. "So . . . someone figured out you had that table and went to talk to your parents and stuff. May I ask how you paid for the table? Cash?"

"You mean, the table in the shed? Nah. I was out of cash, so I gave him a check. He said that was all right."

"I see."

Which was very good, because I didn't. In fact, it was all clear as mud. Then I told him about Jason Ashton and how I couldn't really reconcile the man with the idea that he'd killed his wife.

"I know what you mean," Ben said. "I have met him once or twice, and he seems like such a nice guy. I mean, not good looking or anything, but like concentrated essence of nice. I don't think even if he caught his wife in flagrante delicto he would think of killing her. More likely he'd ask her if she wanted the place while he moved elsewhere."

"Or offer to get a bigger house so the other guy could live with them," I said, and hastened to clarify. "It's not that I think he's whipped, just one of those very rare men who don't put themselves ahead of others, you know, and who are willing to do anything for the ones they love, even if it means sacrificing their wishes or ambitions."

I must have said something funny again, because Ben was staring up at me, with an intent look.

"What? Do I have curry between my teeth or something?"

"Uh, no. It's just . . . Never mind."

I realized he probably thought I was being sexist. "I don't mean it's just rare in men," I said. "It's rare in women, too. In this case, I meant *men* as in *humans*, because . . . well, people in general, particularly in this day and age, I guess," I said, rushing ahead, trying to cover whatever I had said that had made Ben stare at me that way. It wasn't a hostile look, but it was a profoundly discomfiting one. "Well, we're all self-supporting adults by the time we marry, and it's annoying as heck to give way. I mean, look how uncomfortable I am with Cas buying a house for both of us. Given a choice, I'd rather we each put half down, but . . ."

The stare was back. "Yeah," Ben said, breaking in. "But you are right. I, too, have trouble believing that Ashton would kill his wife in cold blood, much less then refinish a table in that stupid way and sell it. At any rate, that never made much sense, you know, Dyce. If someone killed Maria and got blood on the table, why would he sell it? Isn't it possible whoever bought it would just go ahead and refinish it and then find the blood? If it were me, I'd just spray paint it with black or white or something, all over, several coats, and tell people I liked it better that way. Or dismantle it and put it way back in the attic or basement. I mean, all these Victorians have those areas. Crawl space maybe. Whichever tenant ventured to those places down the line—and it wasn't likely to be soon—would find it. I mean, people don't in

Victorians. There's always this feeling that something really nasty might be lurking in the crawl space, isn't there, and if and when someone did, they wouldn't even know when the table was from and would be unlikely to trace it."

"I know," I said. "Frankly, that puzzles me, too, unless someone took the table because he or she panicked, and also to give the idea that Maria had taken something with her." I told him about her taking her clothes. All her clothes, including the maternity ones, and added, "And though Ashton didn't tell me that baby clothes were also taken, the guy at the garage sale says Ashton sold him those, too."

Ben frowned. "He might not know the baby clothes were missing. I mean, they don't have babies right now, right, so why would he notice there were no baby clothes in the house?"

"Point, but that again argues for his being innocent."

"Yeah," he said. Then he got this weird sideways smile he gets, when he finds something terribly amusing. "Not that the two of us have ever been wrong before, of course."

The vast panoply of the many times we'd been wrong, without even touching the times we'd been wrong because one or the other of us had fallen in love with a bastard, didn't need repeating.

"But I still think," he said, "you're wrong about Collin and Peter. They wouldn't have talked. Seriously, they wouldn't. They've been my friends for years, and some of the stuff they don't talk about is stuff even you don't know."

I gave him a long side glance.

"Stuff you don't want to know, truly. Stuff you don't even want to think about."

"Yeah," I told him, but in the sort of tone that let him know I wouldn't buy it, even offered at a discount. Not that I really wanted to know everything possible about Ben. I suspected even Ben didn't want to know some of the stuff about Ben. But just on principle, because if I didn't know something about him, then no one else should know it, either.

But I didn't want us to be mad at each other—look, I don't own a TV. It was talk to Ben or go to bed and read a book, and right then I didn't have any books I really wanted to read, having left my parents' home before they could shove an improving tome at me. Or the latest book they'd fallen in love with, at least.

I still thought his friends had told Sebastian—and perhaps some unspecified crazy—where I lived. But that, too, didn't bear arguing. So instead I told him about my mom's efforts to have me accept Fluffy as a maid of honor. This amused him enough that he was laughing hysterically. "You don't mean it," he said. "You can't possibly mean it."

"Yep. The cat that hates me. But she'll have a wisp of material in some nice color around her neck."

He opened his mouth, closed it, then opened it again. "What about wasshername who used to be your friend in school?" he said. "You know, the skinny little girl with the big—" He motioned over his chest to indicate what she had that was big.

"They were not that big." Ben had issues with breasts. As in, he thought all of them were much too big. I think he'd been traumatized in childhood by watching Benny Hill's skit with the giant pursuing breasts.

"Right, but you two were thick as thieves. If I remember until the end of high school. What became of her? You two no longer talk?"

"Ben, I hardly talk to anyone," I said sullenly. "Except you. And you only because you didn't give me much of a choice."

He looked concerned. "Uh . . . should I ask . . ."

I shrugged. "No. It's E. He doesn't seem to bother you. And he probably wouldn't bother a bunch of my old friends, either, but see, by the time I came back to Goldport, after college, many of them had moved out, and I was busy setting up house with All-ex. And then, you know, even in the early days, I had this feeling my friends would know something was wrong. The friends I still had, that is. And then, suddenly, I was divorced and there was E, which prevented my making more friends. Heck, most of the time, between looking after him and refinishing enough stuff to sell to keep pancakes on the table, I barely have time to sleep." I made a face at him, because he looked much too serious. "I'd penciled in *Make new circle of friends* for after E goes to elementary school, two or three years from now."

"Uh," he said. "And for when had you penciled in *Find new boyfriend and get married*?"

"I hadn't," I said. "Cas just wouldn't take no for an answer."

"Right," Ben said. "Seems to run in the family, that. So you're stuck getting married and you don't have a maid of honor or, I suspect, any bridesmaids, right?"

"Right," I said. "And if I push it, and Mom can't make

me take Fluffy, she'll find some beginning or self-published author and convince her it's good publicity to be my maid of honor. And then my dad will convince her there will be a murder."

Ben got up and went to the kitchen. He came back shortly with two beers. I had no memory of his buying beers, but Cas rarely bought them, so perhaps Ben had left them there the last time he'd come over. I hated that my fridge had become the United Nations, with various interacting fiefdoms assigned to various interests. Not that either of the guys had ever complained about my drinking their stuff or eating anything they'd brought over. But all the same, the fridge didn't feel exactly mine anymore. The only thing I felt safe eating or drinking was stuff I'd bought and remembered buying, which at the moment restricted me to the cat's food and half a stick of butter. I felt very much like a parasite.

But not such a stupid parasite that I'd turn down a good beer. The bottles were clearly from a microbrewery and had a cutesy label with a bunch of dogs and *Barking Mad Ale*. Turned out to be a pale ale, malty and unobjectionable.

Ben took a sip of his, and said, "It would almost be worth the trouble and aggravation," he said, "just to see your mother try to push some anonymous, struggling writer on you. And to see how panicked she became when your father was . . . himself."

"You have a mean streak, Benedict Colm. What have struggling writers ever done to you?"

"What have struggling writers ever done *for* me?"

"Oh, I don't know. Remember that dark-haired guy who did a signing at the store when we—"

He grinned. "Has anyone ever told you a good memory is unpardonable?"

"Jane Austen," I said, dredging it up from high school memories. "The least that Cas could have done, honestly, was have a sister. Or Nick could have been a girl."

This made him laugh so hard he had to swallow the beer hastily, so it wouldn't come out of his nose at speed. "I'll tell him you said that," he said. "He'll be hurt." He paused for a moment. "But you . . . I mean . . . Have you considered asking my mom or one of my sisters?"

"Oh, heck, Ben. I don't think I've been to your parents' place in over a year. Last time I was there, E did something to the dog while I was talking to your mom. I have no idea what it was, but the dog wouldn't come out from under the table, afterward."

"The dog is a scaredy-cat. Okay, that sounds funny, but it's true. And there's nothing E could do to the house or the family that my siblings and I didn't try at least once. Seriously, ask my mom. You can have her as matron of honor. Get one of my sisters as maid of honor. They clean up okay. One of them should be free. They'll probably do it for the cake. Incurable sweet tooths. Mom will be honored. She always liked you. Besides, it will get her mind off weddings."

"Oh?"

"Nothing material. The woman just has weddings—or something—on the brain."

"Ah," I said, feeling, once more, that everything was clear as mud. Mud glimpsed through ten-inch-thick metal plates. At midnight. With a blindfold on.

"Meant to tell you I talked to this woman at work, and she got her dress from this place in Denver that she says sells discount wedding dresses. Like, you know, last year's? But they're designer, and she says they have a great selection. Surely you'll find something there. Wanna go next week?"

I almost said yes; then I remembered the dress by Cthulhu and the funereal dress, and I thought that because Ben thought a place had a great selection—or for that matter, just because Ben thought I needed a dress—it wasn't necessarily so. I could go to a discount store and pick up a skirt suit. Cream or peach or something. It would do. "I don't know. I don't think I need a dedicated wedding dress. For that matter, I'm not sure I needed a dedicated wedding. Perhaps I'll just—"

He put what remained of his beer down on the cheapest coffee table in the world—it was so bad I'd never tried refinishing it, much less selling it—causing it to buckle, and said, "Candyce Chocolat Dare, you are not buying your dress at a discount store. If you want a skirt suit—"

At which point the phone rang again, and I answered it.

"Sorry, hon. I will be home to sleep, but it will be another two hours at least. So if you need to go to bed, don't wait up for me. We're still working on this ID."

I should have asked him if the dead person was Maria Ashton. Though, of course, you'd think he'd tell me, since I'd mentioned her before and all. But he didn't tell me, and I was too much of a coward to ask.

CHAPTER 17

Never Did Run Smooth

I drank another two beers with Ben that night. Now, I realize that for most people three beers isn't exactly something to get worried about, but for a woman who had spent the last two years unable to afford grains except in the form of flour for pancakes, three beers were an awful lot.

At any rate, I was never that good with alcohol. The last time I'd drunk any significant amount, I'd ended up climbing the statue of the miner downtown and sitting at the top imitating a chicken, until one of my friends— this had been during vacation from college—had thought to call Ben on the cell phone, and Ben had talked me into coming down. Or, at least, he had told me he had instructed my so-called friends to take pictures of me and send them around.

I couldn't remember the whole episode very clearly, but I was halfway sure that at least one of the little wretches had gone ahead and taken the picture and probably at this very moment there was a picture of me in some photo service—or a video—called *Woman in Short Skirt Imitates Chicken atop Statue of Miner*. I'd always been too afraid to look.

At least I was fairly sure the beers hadn't caused me to climb any statues—mostly because the closest thing to a statue in the house was E's Darth Vader doll, and if I'd tried to climb that, it would be squished flat and E would be howling for my blood. Since I couldn't hear any sirenlike yowls from my ever-beloved progeny, it stood to reason that the doll was fine, and also that I hadn't tried to climb any statues.

I also had to deduce, with my extraordinary investigative powers, that I had at some time gone to bed, and that I'd still been enough in possession of my faculties to have undressed, dressed in my pajama pants and T-shirt, and put my dirty clothes in the hamper. At least I was wearing my normal sleep attire, I was in bed, and my day clothes were nowhere around.

Cas was asleep, facedown on the bed, with his head in his arms, snoring gently. I put my arm over his shoulders, as much to reassure myself that he was really there as to look over his head at the clock.

It was pushing seven in the morning, and I probably should get up. Besides, I felt a great hankering for coffee just then, even though I did not have a hangover. I sat up, and Cas opened his eyes. I told him what I was doing, and why, and he looked over at the clock. "Ah," he said.

"I should get up, too. Have a long day ahead of me. And I talked to the agent, and she's bringing the papers over for us to sign, for the offer, this afternoon at three."

"Oh. To the police station?"

"Yeah." He got up, looking quite nice in his boxer shorts and nothing else. Me? I refused to look in a mirror till I'd had some coffee. I was fairly sure my hair was all over the place and that my face had somehow become all puffy and wrinkly during the night, so that I looked more like Sir Winston Churchill than like myself. In fact, the only reason I had agreed to marry Cas—at least that I was willing to admit to—was that he was capable of looking me in the face when I first wakened and telling me I looked beautiful.

Since he was an officer of the law, and therefore not inclined to lie, this must mean that he was mostly blind. And when you find a man whose blindness leads him to believe you look wonderful in the morning, before you even wash your face, you secure that man's affections with all the alacrity of a Victorian bride proposed to by a prince.

"Uh . . . who got murdered in the house?" I asked. I swear the words were out of my mouth before I'd thought about it. Weirdly, he didn't even look surprised.

"Don't know," he said. "As far as we can tell it's a male, aged about thirty-five, but we haven't been able to identify him in any of our databases, so we're sending the dental impressions out this morning, though you know, given the fire, those were pretty damaged, and fillings might have run out, and—"

"There was a fire?" I asked. "In the house?" I was wondering in which room it had been, trying to imagine the interior blackened by fire. I wondered if we removed the tile and all the beautiful oak woodwork, whether we would find burnt timber beneath. "It was in the family room, wasn't it?" I asked. "That's why they have all the nice oak bookcases up."

He stared at me for a moment. "Dyce? What in hell are you talking about?"

I waved my hands. "The family room. With all the bookcases. They probably put up the bookcases to hide charred stuff. There are probably other bodies behind there. And the stupid thing is, I was willing to buy the house because of the oak bookcases, because I thought they made the room feel warm. Warm. It must have been warm enough to—"

He laughed. "Dyce, no. We're talking about different houses."

"We're buying another house?"

"No. I was talking about the condo fire we're investigating. The corpse is male, and we haven't been able to ID him. We're going to send out the dental impressions, perhaps as far as Denver, and then we're going to start asking the neighbors—who aren't very close, but might still have seen something—if anyone has been around that house in the last few days and what he looked like. If we get a description, we might be able to identify the vic." He looked at me.

I was too busy registering relief that the body in the house couldn't possibly be Maria. Not unless she'd had a sex operation in the meantime, and anyway, I doubted that those showed up if all you had was a skeleton. "Oh. I thought you meant the house we're buying. What was the murder there?"

He frowned. "I don't think there was one. Why?"

"Ben."

"What? Ben thought there had been a murder?"

"Ben told me there had been a murder," I said, then thought over our exchange carefully. "No. Never mind. It wasn't that, but he gave me the impression there had been a murder. He said Nick went and saw it with you." This was almost accusing.

"Well, I had to make sure it was worth it before I took you over there under false pretenses, and Nick was with me. But I'm fairly sure I didn't tell Nick there had been any crime in the house, and I doubt Nick told Ben any such thing."

"Ben acted like there was something wrong with the house," I said, stubbornly.

"Ah. Dyce . . . In case you didn't notice, the house next door to it is also for sale."

"So there's something wrong with the house next door?" I asked. I was fathoms deep in the deepest mud, doing the backstroke while wearing a blindfold. Any minute now, I'd hit my head on the remains of Atlantis.

"Er . . . not that I know. Look, let's not make a simple thing complicated, okay? Just come by the office at three, we sign the offer, and everything is fine, okay?" He smiled at me. "That way we can start finding pieces for it, and we'll have it all ready to live in by the time we get married."

It sounded lovely. And if he thought I was going to sign that offer before I went to the library and looked up the history of the house, he had another thing coming. But there was absolutely no point antagonizing him until

I had reason to, so I said, "Okay," and got out of bed, and opened the bedroom door.

The mummy had brought his friend, scruffy zombie. The mummy was still lying on the sofa, completely wrapped in a white blanket, which he must have had in the trunk of his car the night before. But now there was another body on the floor. I was fairly sure this one wasn't a mummy because he wasn't all wrapped up in white, with his arms by the side of his rigidly held body. Instead, he was sprawled on the floor, his arms above his head—the better to bring them to a forward position when he headed off screaming, *Brains!*

Instead of the white blanket, he was wearing . . . no. He was inside a sleeping bag. An orange, camouflage sleeping bag, designed, I guessed for those rare times when you needed to fit in inside a violently orange forest, possibly made of Play-Doh. And I would swear he was a zombie, because his dark, curly hair was a mess; his face looked three shades paler than normal, highlighting the slightly olive—no, greenish—tint of the skin; his mouth was slack; and—very important—he had dark circles around his eyes. If he had neck bolts, he'd be Frankenstein, but without neck bolts, we'd have to assume zombie.

I was about to make some comment about ever-multiplying cheap horror-movie critters when Cas leaned into me from behind and put his finger on my lips, as if to command silence. "In the kitchen," he whispered in my ear.

So I went to the kitchen, but Cas wouldn't even let me bang some cups around to wake the sleepers. Clearly, he thought the curse of the mummy would kill us all. Instead he said, in a whisper, "Don't."

"But they have a home," I said. "Two homes."

He nodded. "I know. But they need to talk."

"Oh, yeah? The only way you'll get those two to talk is to make them stomp their feet for yes or no."

"Okay, but for that to be effective, we'd have to put metal shoes on them." He winked at me. "And yeah, I know it's tempting just now, but we'd regret it in the morning. Seriously. They do need to talk, and I'm hoping they do."

I nodded and started to get coffee going as quietly as I could.

"For one it would be truly annoying if my two grooms-men weren't talking to each other at the wedding. For another, because it's not like they've broken up. They're just being weird. And I get plenty of weird from—" He stopped. I assumed, for charity's sake, that he meant that he got plenty of weird at work. I mean, what could be more normal than my household, with the two horror critters in the living room, the son who had an invisible llama, and not a single female friend?

"Anyway, my life is weird enough," Cas said. "I can't take another source of weird. And Nick's nonconfidence confidences are driving me insane. It's like, *Guess what's wrong in my life right now, for the prize of a burger and some really crunchy fries.*"

"He gives you fries for guessing what's wrong?"

"He takes me to lunch and then determinedly doesn't pour his heart out to me."

"Hey, Ben brought a six-pack of microbrews over. For the same purpose, I think."

"Wonderful. If they're not going to talk to us, the least we can do is get them to buy me alcohol, too."

"So you told Nick—"

"Nope. I just invited him in for a coffee, and he came in, and Ben was asleep on the sofa. So Nick went to his car and got his sleeping bag."

"Nick often hide in orange forests?"

"What? Oh. I think it's designed for hunters. So they don't get shot by accident."

Which made perfect sense, of course. First, you made it of camouflage, so that they could blend into the forest, and any deer who were so observant as to look around for people would fail to see them, and second, you made it virulently, offensively orange so that if any hunter was wandering around looking for deer sprawled in sleeping bags on the forest floor, he wouldn't accidentally shoot a fellow hunter. "Nick hunts?"

"Not that I know."

Right. We were now well into primeval silt. Listen, when this mud had been deposited, fathoms deep at the heart of a dark ocean, dinosaurs had still walked the Earth. I'd find them, too, the moment I removed my welded-on blindfold.

The coffee started percolating, and Cas started scrambling eggs. There is this noisy element to eggs; they are not silent food. You have to crack the shells and use some kitchen utensil to scramble the contents. And, at any rate, the bacon that Cas had put in a very large pan was going to crackle and fizz. And the smell alone could wake the dead. Or, in this case, the undead.

I knew it had succeeded when a long, low moan came from the living room. It sounded so macabre and odd that I almost jumped out of my skin, and would have, if it hadn't been followed by, "You? What are you doing here?" in Ben's indignant tones.

This was followed by Nick sounding about three octaves lower than he normally did. "Sleeping. At least, I was till you moaned like a ghost or something. What happened?"

"You're here!"

"Yeah."

"But this is not your place."

"No. Or yours. Why isn't it yours?"

"What? I wouldn't rent here if—"

"No. Why aren't you in your place?"

"Because I'm here."

"Benedict Colm!"

"Okay, fine. Because you have a key to my place."

"Oh." That sounded . . . not quite offended, but wounded. And neither of them seemed to have given the slightest thought to the fact we could hear him. "You're trying to avoid me?"

"No."

"Uh."

"Okay, Nick, if I were trying to avoid you, I wouldn't you know . . . call you and stuff."

"Right . . ." I couldn't hear it, not really, but by now I knew Nick well enough to know he was rubbing his hand on his chin, producing a noise somewhat like running your nails over sandpaper. "Right. But you're trying to avoid us spending the night in the same place?"

"You know what you're like in the morning," Ben said. "You always want to talk."

"Yeah," Nick conceded. "Like now."

"Yeah, but we're not home," Ben said.

"Noted. Ben, can we talk. I mean, really?"

"Not even. Cas and Dyce are listening to everything we say."

I felt my cheeks heat.

Nick chuckled. "So they are. So . . . lunch. My office. We'll go to the deli."

"People will listen."

"Right. Take a coat. We'll grab sandwiches, and we'll go park somewhere and talk."

"Right," Ben said.

Cas lifted his hand, with the obvious intent of giving me a silent high five. I wasn't sure this was the best idea in the world. And I was proven right, as the mummy—now converted into the human burrito—came shuffling into the kitchen, his bare feet protruding below the blanket.

"That," he said, glaring at me, "was bad of you."

"What was bad of me?" I said. "I swear it didn't involve statues."

"What?"

"I didn't climb any statues."

"I see, so it was you?" He looked at Cas, more in sorrow than in anger.

"Me? Never climbed a statue in my life. Closest I ever came was trying to get onto the roof of my college dorm."

"You told him," Ben hissed.

From the sounds, the reason he felt free to vent this was because the zombie had gone to use the bathroom.

"No. I just invited him for coffee."

Ben crossed his arms on his chest. "Great. Just great. Now we'll have to talk. And if we talk, he'll decide I'm crazy, and then . . ."

Cas's eyebrows went up. "Maybe he likes crazy. Let me tell you about his ex sometime."

But it was a mystery that was destined not to be solved, because Nick came into the room before Cas had time to reveal his deep, dark secrets, or even his somewhat shallow, vaguely shady secrets.

With E joining us shortly after, we ended up in a complete confusion, as all three guys tried to eat, shower, and dress in less time than it normally took Cas alone to get ready for work. The confusion was so great that I swear Ben's tie was slightly askew as he left. This meant that his colleagues would view it as a sign of the apocalypse and make critical financial decisions for their clients based on this fact. This in turn meant the market would collapse, and by late afternoon, there would be brokers dropping like flies from their office windows, all because Ben had insisted on playing mummy on my sofa.

For lack of some common sense, the market was lost.

They managed to get out, though, even if at times the whole process resembled a Chinese fire drill.

I was left washing breakfast dishes as E took a bath. And then the phone rang.

CHAPTER 18

Suspicions Everywhere

I picked up the phone with my hand slippery from dish soap, dropped it, and picked it up again. Which just goes to show you that phones are things that conspire against me.

When I finally got it to my ear, a man wasn't exactly yelling but saying rather insistently on the other side, "Hello? Hello?"

"Hi. Yes?"

"I don't know if this is the right number. I looked in the phone book. Dyce Dare? Of Daring Finds?"

I'd recognized his voice. "Jason Ashton?"

"Yeah," he said. "Sorry. I lost your card."

No, he hadn't. He'd folded it up until it had become so crumpled that it was unreadable, a process he'd started while I was still there. But, of course, I wasn't going to say that. "Yeah. It is Dyce. How can I help you?"

"That table that you . . . You said you had the table Maria took."

I felt a sudden disappointment. If, in the middle of all this, the man I'd thought heartbroken over his wife's disappearance was obsessing over the lost table, I washed my hands of humanity.

It's not that I particularly wanted to keep the table. Actually, if the table had evidence of a crime, I not only didn't want to keep it, but I wouldn't keep it. The police got a mite touchy over stuff like that.

It's more that it seemed like a petty and stupid concern for him to have when his wife was missing.

My voice could probably have created glaciers as I said, "Yes?"

"Well, how do you know it is the table my wife took?" he said.

"The man from the garage—" I stopped.

"Yes, but he also says that it was me who sold it to him, which I can tell you it wasn't. So . . ."

"No, the description doesn't fit you," I said.

"So can I come over and see it this evening? If it is Maria's table, then the police can start tracing where she might be, right? Given the lack of her going to see her doctor, I'm afraid something happened to her, like . . . someone kidnapped her or something."

I thought of the bloodstains on the table. "Uh. I'll be home after about . . . four, I think," I said, and thought maybe I should uncover a bit more of the blood while I still had the table in my possession. Of course, the problem with that is that I would have to find someone to watch E, which right then wasn't likely.

"I won't be home till five, anyway, between school and work. I've given notice, but I'm still working."

"So, five thirty?" I said.

"Yes," he said, after a pause. "That would work. Have you . . . talked to anyone about it?"

"Not really. I meant to tell my fiancé, who is an investigator with the department, but he's investigating murder and arson, and there were other complications." I'd be cursed if I was going to sit here and explain to him that my best friend's very complex love life had kept me from discussing something far more important with Cas. "So I didn't have time to tell him."

"Oh. Just as well," Jason said. "That way, if it's important, I can tell him, and that will be far more serious, and they can start investigating in earnest."

I agreed and hung up, to find E looking up at me with a betrayed expression. "You didn't ask him how Ccelly was doing?"

"Oh," I said. E was washed and trailing a towel. Since the towel had been given to him by Ben, who seemed to acquire a serious case of the either deeply weird or terminally cute when it came to dressing anyone else—I suspected because he kept such a tight rein on his own tendency to any sartorial splendor—it had a little hood with cat eyes and nose. He had the hood on and looked even more like he was impersonating an angel child than ever. Not that it was convincing. I knew what evil—or at least sheer mischief—hid in the heart of E. "Tell you what, the dad is coming here this evening, and you can ask him then."

E didn't seem particularly convinced, but he is my son

and always operates on the principle that a half—or even a quarter—loaf is better than none.

He allowed me to shower without setting fire to the house while I was in the bathroom. In fact, the angel child impression continued. When I came out, he was on the sofa, reading to Pythagoras. I left the bedroom door partly open, so I could keep an ear out for what was going on, and was putting clothes on when I realized my son was having serious difficulties with one word. Which puzzled me a little, as he knew by heart every word in the little picture books that Ben and I read to him, to the point where his lips would move along with our reading as he recited the words.

I focused on his voice and realized he was saying, "Inkssst, inkset, inssssseeeeet."

Right. Probably a new book on bugs that he hadn't had time to memorize yet, and he didn't precisely remember the word that Ben—must have been Ben because I don't read books about insects to my son; I draw the line at rats—had pronounced. I combed my hair, tied it firmly back with a scrunchy, and hurried out to the living room to find the book that E had on his knees was not a picture book. And I hoped to heaven that no one had been reading that book to him, since it looked like a dictionary, or perhaps a particularly fat volume in an old encyclopedia.

"What are you reading, baby doll?"

"A bisgraphy. Mom, what's inseshts?"

"Bugs."

"No."

"Yes. You know, little critters, like spiders and stuff. Remember that tarantula you wanted at the pet shop, and

Ben was going to buy it for you, but I said that it would get eaten by Pythagoras?"

"No. That's a bug. Maybe. But not an *I-N-S-E-C-T*. Spiders are arcsenids." He spoke so intently and—my realizing belatedly I'd spoken without thinking—so close to right I didn't bother explaining that he'd mispronounced *arachnids*. Also, he could spell *insect*, so that wasn't the word he was gagging on.

He got out of the sofa, carrying the book, open in his hands, and pointed me at the line. I choked. "Uh . . . incest . . . uh . . . how . . . er . . . uh."

"What's an incest, Mommy?"

"Oh . . . uh . . . something I'll tell you about when you're thirty, if you don't figure it out before then." I took the book from his hand before he could hold on tighter and looked at the cover. A biography of Julius Caesar. A flip to the overleaf revealed the inscription "S. Nikopoulous." Right. Stravos Nikopoulous. Nick. Nick, who was a policeman and for the love of heaven repaired vintage cars on the weekend. Why was he reading a biography of Julius Caesar, where more than half of it was annotations—as a quick flip through the pages revealed?

I'm not, at least I hope not, one of those people who assume one is stupid because one doesn't have a graduate degree. At least I hoped I wasn't, because the closest I'd come to any kind of degree was two years here and a year there and then a failed marriage. And my dad had a high-school education, though Mom had managed a bachelor's in English literature. But, in the name of all that was holy, what could Nick's profession or hobby have to do with . . . a biography of Caesar?

And, more importantly, what was my three-year-old

doing reading it to the cat? It could scar the cat for life. Cats had run away from home for less than that. "Why . . . Where . . . Why were you reading this? It's Nick's."

"It was on the coffee table," E said, looking guilty. "And I like Rome."

"Uh . . . and you can read."

He nodded. "I didn't mean to," he said, defensively, and blushed. "I just . . . I found out last month I could read. I don't know how." He twisted his hands together. "Honest, I really didn't mean to."

"I don't think it's a hanging offense," I told him. It might in fact curb some of his more enthusiastic attempts at self-entertainment. I grabbed the book under one arm, grabbed my purse with my other hand, sort of shoved the handle up my arm, then grabbed E with the suddenly free hand. My next body I want three hands. At least if I'm supposed to manage anything more challenging than a hamster.

I managed to open the door with the book-hand and my foot, then close it with my elbow, all the while keeping Pythagoras in the house with careful deployment of my other foot. The idiot cat is convinced he'd love to go roam the neighborhood and be a wild cat. I'll point out that the one time he got out, he tried to claw his way back in through the door. Of course, it probably wasn't his fault, as he was scared by a squirrel that jumped up on the front stoop next to him. You can't expect a wild cat to face squirrels like that, because squirrels are, as everyone knows, the source of all evil. However, since he had the capacity for memory of cream cheese, he still kept trying to get out. And I didn't want him trying to claw through the front door while I was gone. He might actually get all the way through on sheer desperation. I mean, two squirrels might gang up on him.

Once the door was closed, I tested the handle and marched my prisoners—boy and book—to the car. The book, thrown on the backseat, would go to the police station when I went to sign the offer—if I went to sign the offer. First on the route, though, there was a trip to the library, where maybe E could find some more books on Rome, and then a trip to my parents' bookstore, because after all, now that he read, my parents would want to get him mysteries.

Okay, this last was totally and completely self-serving and probably unworthy of me. I mean, the child hadn't actually, as such, done anything to me. Well, not on purpose. The ravages of birth and all that were not his fault. The ravages of melting crayons on the radiator were, but there wasn't much I could do about it. Besides, I'd done worse. No, when it came right down to it, I was very much trying to throw the baby from the sleigh in order to slow down the wolves. If my parents—okay, they were odd wolves, with glasses and dentures—were busy covering E in books, I would get fewer armloads handed to me with the demand that I read them now, and maybe even—with luck—fewer handed to me with the guarantee that this book would change my life.

I had to say that though I'd loved one or two mysteries in my life, and though a few—particularly some chick's (I was lousy with writer names) musketeer mysteries—had become regular rereads, I had yet to meet a mystery that would change my life. I mean, what would this book do? Come in, do the dishes, bathe E, give him civility lessons? Perhaps fill my bank account in the process? I'd be more than eager for a book like that, but so far, no luck. I suspected we'd need much better technology. Or something.

The library was nearly deserted on this Tuesday morning. It was not story-time morning, but all the same, I dragged E to the children's area of the library and explained to the young lady on duty that E liked books on Rome while writing furiously on a pad left conveniently on the desk that she was not—absolutely not—to let him check out anything rated above sixth grade. She looked at me as if I was completely insane, and I last glimpsed her heading into the picture-book area with E. I wished her luck in that endeavor. At least E wouldn't try to escape, because he was absolutely and utterly in love with books and had never actually left the library when I'd left him alone.

Mind you, I suspected that, now that he could read, I might very well find him in another and completely different section. That was a risk I was willing to take, as I went through the corridor and door into the local-history area of the library.

This part of the building was always fairly empty and was usually staffed by one of the descendants of local blue bloods. In this case, the descendant was a woman about my age but infinitely better dressed. Again, a blonde. I think there is an archetypal blonde that was put on this Earth to annoy me, and I keep finding reflections of her everywhere. Oh, it's not that every blonde annoys me, mind you, just the ones with perfect nails, perfect eyebrows, and mirror-smooth pale hair.

But in this case, she thwarted all my intentions of

hating her at first sight by being very nice, very attentive, and doing everything she could to help me.

She searched everything archived in the computer, as well as all the microfiches, but we couldn't find anything on the house. Still, I didn't feel reassured.

I emerged from the local library to find E (miracle!) still in the children's library, having amassed quite the selection of books, including *Rotten Romans*, the companion to *Groovy Greeks*, and a couple of books on Roman legions, including what they wore and how they ate. Also, an infinitely more appropriate book on Julius Caesar, which I was *practically* sure didn't include *Lock up your sons and your daughters; home we bring the bald seducer.*

The kind lady at the desk tried to tell me those books were highly inappropriate for a three-year-old. I told her it was okay; the inappropriate book was in the back of the car and would be going right back to its owner. She gave me an strange look, and I decided not to explain.

Back in the car, with E's books secured, I drove to my parents' store, where Dad, manning the counter, gave me an odd look, then said, "Must you bring that creature in with you?"

"That creature," I announced dramatically, "is your only grandson, and he can read."

"He is?" My dad looked at me. "Are you sure of that? He doesn't look a thing like Ben."

Which was indeed fortunate for all concerned, but particularly Ben and I, because we'd never gotten that drunk, at least not while together. "Yeah, I know," I told Dad with a bright smile.

"And another thing, Sherlockia," he said. "If anything happens to the books, it's entirely your fault."

"Yeah, yeah, I know," I said. I'd never be allowed to live down the time that E had spilled his juice bottle on the new paperback section. "I'll keep E in a tight rein."

"E?"

I gestured. "E. My son."

My father looked at him again, as though he were yet again a new and wondrous object. Something never seen and scarcely imagined. "I wasn't talking about him," he said. "I was talking about the rude young man with the petulant accents who told me that if you don't stop sticking your nose where it doesn't belong, he'll come here and burn all the books. He told me that I was supposed to keep you from meddling. Clearly"—Dad drew himself up to his full height—"he completely misunderstands the situation."

"I'd say," I said under my breath, thinking that Sebastian must have been very busy indeed.

"Because," my father went on, as though I hadn't spoken, "I have never yet managed to control you or tell you to stop anything. I mean, if you did what I'd like you to, you'd be a PI with a decent business. None of this crazy going around with however many men and getting shot at. No, you'd have a proper office and be versed in all the best forensic techniques. But no, you had to do your own thing, and marry . . . Who did you marry?"

"It hardly matters," I said, and patted Dad on the arm. I never knew how much of a contact with reality he had at the moment, and at least half the time he seemed certain that I had married Ben at some point. The rest of the time he seemed to think I was some sort of a fancy escort.

And yet the rest of the time, he thought I was about six and in elementary school. "I'm divorced now, and truly, I'm not running around with any men."

"Are you sure? Because he said you should stay away from someone named Jason, or it would be the worse for you."

"Right." I was starting to thing Sebastian, the sex god, was far more interested in Jason than it seemed. Or at least determined to keep me away from Jason. It made absolutely no sense, since Jason was not exactly my type and besides I had Cas. Also, Sebastian had definitely not struck me as swinging that way, so his interest in Jason could not be of that type.

I frowned, as I followed E to the juvenile mystery section, where he discovered detectives in togas. I hoped that now, with enough books on hand to keep him happy for several hours, it was safe to go to the police station.

But as we were leaving the store, Dad gave me a look of warning and said in a voice that could have come from an entire Greek chorus, "I warn you, if something happens to the books, I won't be responsible for my actions."

I hoped nothing would happen to the books, but as I got in my car, I thought the store was stocked so full of books it was a tinderbox waiting to go up. And there was at least one arsonist running around Goldport.

CHAPTER 19

Groovy Greeks and Rotten Realtors

Before we drove off, I called the consignment store in Denver, and found that three of my pieces had sold, and they'd made a—new for them since they'd always sent a paper check despite my repeated requests— automated deposit of my portion of the proceeds. They wanted more pieces. I stared at the trunk in the back of the car and decided that although there might be nothing I could do with it, at least I could look for more, small pieces I could refinish and take up to Denver. Of course, refinishing would have to wait for the weekend, and I'd have to convince Ben to babysit. So hopefully he got over whatever the drama was in his life, so that I could get back to taking advantage of his good nature when I needed work time.

But my two first favorite used furniture stores had nothing, and the salvage store yielded nothing but a set of three copper lion-mouth pulls. I bought them, at fifty cents apiece. They're the sort of thing that will lend class to any piece. But I wished I'd found a piece they'd go in, as well.

With some of my newly acquired money, I bought E and myself organic burgers at Cy's and then compensated for the offensive healthiness of the food by drowning it in milkshakes, thick with fat and sugar. And marshmallows, because we got the Rocky Road milkshakes. The gods must have been with me, too, because I managed not to spill any of those saliencies on my chest, which always seemed to maneuver to be in the way of falling liquid, and E got nothing on his little coveralls or his red jacket. Instead, he collected most of the leftover on his face, where I could wipe it away with moist wipes.

I refused to imagine what child care had been like before premoist wipes. Perhaps archaeologists were wrong, and there had always been moist wipes. Sometime in the future, they'll find a cylindrical container in a cave, with the telltale pull-through top.

So we both looked like respectable people as we headed into three other stores—where I looked in vain for serviceable furniture—and finally to the police station, with Nick's book under my arm and E by my other hand.

The receptionist gave us a smile and didn't say anything as we sailed past. Which meant that Cas would be in his office at the back. He was. And, bonus, Nick was with him. And looked considerably more animated than he had this morning. Or the day before. Or any time in recent memory. Which I hoped, for purely selfish reasons, meant the drama between him and Ben was at an end.

At least if they settled down a bit, I could—and would—impose on Ben to babysit while I saw what I could make of that green trunk.

So I smiled at him, a little nicer than I might otherwise have done, and dropped the book on the desk, on top of the papers he'd been looking at. "You forgot this at my house," I said. "Why in heaven's name did you need to bring a history tome with you, when you came to sleep on the sofa? A little light reading?"

He looked at the book like it contained all the ashes of his ancestors or something. "What? I didn't take that."

"Right. Well, someone did, because E was reading page six. He wanted an explanation of Caesar's bad habit starting with *I*."

"Icksets," E said, and nodded.

Cas groaned. "Please, tell me he didn't say what I thought he did."

"Oh, he did say it," I said, cheerfully. "But I've got him more appropriate books."

Nick blinked down at E and the book E was holding up. "*Rotten Romans*," he said in a fading voice. "How . . . interesting."

"With recipes for dormouse," I said, encouragingly.

Nick looked up at me. "What, no *Irksome Irishmen*?"

"No," I said. "The Irksome Irishman gave E a book in that series, though. *Groovy Greeks*."

A weird, surprised smile twisted Nick's lips. "How interesting," he said. He grabbed his book.

"Why do you have that book, anyway?"

"What? I like history," he said, managing to sound just as defensive as E when E told me he hadn't meant to learn to read. He mumbled something about snobs, grabbed his papers, and left the room.

"So," I said, looking at Cas. "The talk worked or not?"

Cas shrugged. "I'm as at sea as you are."

"Maybe we *should* nail horseshoes to their feet. In the interest of their understanding each other better when they stomp."

Cas looked immensely cheered at the idea, but before he could say anything, his receptionist came in and announced the real estate agent.

At which point, the talk became completely nonunderstandable. Honestly, I seem to have contract stupidity. I can read anything else, including big, fat tomes like the ones that Nick, apparently, felt like carrying around for the purpose of proving he could. But the minute you put a contract in front of me, I became illiterate. Or an official form of any sort.

One of these days, I was going to figure out I'd sold my soul to the devil accidentally because I'd filled my matriculation forms wrong when I'd first signed up for college.

This time, at least, I wasn't in it alone. Which meant if I sold my soul, Cas would, too. This wasn't precisely comforting, but at least we'd have one of the nicest, coziest arrangements in Hades.

And when the woman was done with the contract and had our signatures on it, she said, "And now, where is Mr. Nikopoulous's office?"

Cas pointed her in the general location of Nick's office, and when she left, I looked at Cas. "So why does she want Nick?"

"Nick is putting an offer on the house next to ours."

"What?"

"Well, you know, it is not quite as big, and he figures he'll have to pull up the carpet and refinish the floor before he moves in, but then again, he has a place to live meanwhile. Also, the way he sees it, he doesn't need as big a place as ours."

I calculated mentally exactly where this fit on the game of chess he and Ben seemed to be playing. Correction, the game of blindfolded chess, played in a pitch-dark room at midnight. From the Irksome Irishman remark, I assumed that not all had been decided. Which meant they were probably still sparring over who got to move in with whom.

This meant by buying a house, Nick was trying to call it a checkmate. Interesting. And entirely insane. So Cas and I would have the coziest arrangement in Hades, except that Nick would probably be sharing the general area with us, right after Ben brained him with his bio of Caesar. Seemed just about right.

"Anything new on the arson thing?" I asked Cas.

He frowned at me. "Eh. Somewhat. It looks like the burning of the place was accidental."

"You mean, someone was playing with matches?" I thought of the equipment in the back of Sebastian's car. "Or blowtorches?"

"No," he said. "I mean someone was cooking meth and things got out of hand."

I stared for a moment. "You mean . . ."

"I mean, we're now evaluating samples from all the other houses," he said, "to figure out whether the same thing happened. It would make a certain sense, since the houses are always houses that have been empty a long time and that are away from other occupied properties. By the way, I told All-ex we would be keeping E because we wanted to go shopping for wedding clothes this week, at irregular intervals. We're going to be shopping for clothes, right? Because you know E will tell him if we aren't."

"Yeah, we can," I said. "But not at Dresses by Cthulhu."

"New shop?" he asked, sounding confused.

"Yeah. They call themselves The Pink Rose, but don't let them deceive you. In the back—"

"They keep a multitentacled seamstress?" he asked. "Plying multiple needles at an amazing speed?"

"Probably," I said, not willing to admit I was being silly. There apparently was a lot of that going around. "So you think this is a meth ring? Which means it would have nothing to do with All-ex?" This was a bit of a relief. I mean, I didn't particularly want to have to tell E his daddy was a criminal. I could see it now. *No, honey, Daddy just enjoys living behind barbed wire and wearing orange. He thinks One-Armed Art is better company than Michelle. No, no, he really enjoys talking to us across safety glass. It's very fashionable.* I could see that if I worked the thing right, E wouldn't need to know the truth until he was twenty, maybe thirty. But sooner or later, he would have to discover the truth, and he'd probably get upset. Almost certainly.

Besides, if he tumbled onto it earlier, there was a good chance he'd deploy his alleged lock-picking abilities and then he, too, would end up in jail. I'd have to figure out how to take them pancakes with nail files in them. And those would have to be much thicker pancakes than normal.

Cas shrugged. "Probably not. Right now, I have no idea if it's even a ring. We haven't seen any increased meth circulation in town, so whoever is doing this is a dumb fool."

"A now-dead dumb fool?"

He frowned. "One of them, almost for sure, but we're waiting for results from the lab, because right now all we have is a corpse. We don't even know if he was dead or alive when the blast went off."

"Ah," I said. And then, "I have to go."

"Why? You could wait. There isn't much more I can do here today, until those reports arrive. I could take you and E out to eat and—"

I shook my head. "No, you don't understand, I'm meeting someone."

Suddenly he sharpened up and became all policeman. "Who?"

I could of course have told him it was just some friend—but why would he believe that, when I'd lost most of my friends in the recent vicissitudes? I could tell him I was going to see someone about furniture, but he wasn't likely to believe that, either. And besides, I didn't want to lie to him.

So I sighed and plopped down on the battered metal chair across from his desk. Cas's office is a work in progress, as I guess is most of the police station. The desks and chairs have seen better days but he'd put really nice pictures on the walls and a rug on the floor. It looked homey, strangely, despite the dented chairs and chipped desk.

I sat down. E was on the floor reading *Rotten Romans*.

"It's Jason Ashton," I said.

This time, Cas dropped into a chair and raised his eyebrows. "Explain," he said.

I explained. In detail. Including the bloodstains on the table. By the time I finished, Cas had his face in his hands, his elbows on the desk. "Dyce, what am I going to do with you?"

I didn't say *Marry me* because I was afraid he'd decide that was way too far-fetched. So, instead, I said, "Uh . . . I don't know."

"Me neither," he said. "And I suspect neither does anyone else. When were you planning on telling me all this?"

"When Jason identified the table, of course," I said.

"Of course," Cas said. "The fact that he might be lying and coming over to eliminate you has never occurred to you, right?"

"Um . . . not really. I think he's nice, Cas."

Cas stared at me for a moment, then sighed. "And he might very well be, but you see, in the police, we can't just go based on how someone looks. Supposedly, he sold that table, and then he said his wife had taken it with her. I don't need to tell you that in nine out of ten spousal murders—"

"The criminal is the other spouse?" I said. "No. But he couldn't make himself a bug-eyed blond, which is what the guy at the garage sale said he was."

Cas shrugged. "Could be an accomplice. I'm paid to think of suspicious circumstances and things that can go seriously wrong. So you should have told me."

"Maybe," I conceded. The problem was that at some level I agreed with him. When he talked to me about stuff like this, I always emerged feeling like I'd been totally reckless and also a bit foolish.

"Yeah, more than maybe," he said. "I tell you what—I'll come with you. We'll bring E and his Romans. And I'll meet Ashton with you. If he has any bad intentions, the fact that I'm there should be enough to thwart them. If he doesn't have any bad intentions . . . It all depends on whether that table was the one Maria took or not, doesn't it?"

I nodded. I didn't like it. I couldn't even say for sure why I didn't like it, but I didn't. It had to do with the fact that I'd told Ashton I'd be there alone and that I'd never told Cas anything. Now he was going to think I'd been lying and perhaps setting a trap. At best, that would make him defensive. At worst, it might make him lie about the table.

But there was nothing to do about it, as Cas convinced E to get up and he followed me in his car to my place.

CHAPTER 20

Someone to Watch Over Me

As it was, I half-expected Ben and Nick to converge on us as we approached the driveway, because that would really set the cap on this mess. Then Ashton would think that I'd called everyone I knew to my aid or something.

But we pulled up on the driveway and beside Ashton's brown, dinged beater Toyota. He had been behind the wheel and came out of the car. The way he managed not to look like he was surprised, much less upset at Cas being there also, was pretty convincing.

Cas, on the other hand, acted with an odd mix of protectiveness and possessiveness, going around me to stand in front, holding out a hand to Ashton. "Hello, Mr. Ashton. We've met before."

"Oh, yes," Ashton said, and blinked up at him, in a confused way. He looked even smaller, more rumpled, and more inoffensive next to Cas. "Dyce . . . er . . .

Ms. Dare said that perhaps she bought at a garage sale the table that my wife took with her, and I thought I'd look at it before we bothered you with it, because, you know, she might be quite mistaken."

"Yes, of course," Cas said, and then added, "Did she tell you about the bloodstains?"

Jason Ashton stopped. He'd been reaching a hand to shake mine, but he just froze in midgesture. "What?" he asked, and shot me a terrified look. "What bloodstains? What do you mean bloodstains? Where were the bloodstains?"

He looked like a man on the verge of a heart attack. If he were acting, he shouldn't only be on the stage; he should be in movies. He would probably be the best actor ever, in fact.

Cas shook his head. "Maybe they're not blood. Dyce wasn't sure. There are some stains. Perhaps you know something about them?"

"There were no stains," Ashton said, frowning. He took a deep breath. "I wish I knew where Maria is and what happened to her. This is insane. I can't believe she would disappear this long. And if the table is stained, it wasn't when she took it." He paused. "Perhaps that is why she got rid of it?"

"Perhaps," Cas said, appealingly.

He managed to sort of guide Ashton up to the house. As we got in, he said, "Dyce's workshop is at the back, and it's easier to walk through the house than to go around."

"Yeah," Ashton said, but he was in a daze. As we walked through the house, he went first, with me right behind him, and Cas, holding E, at the back. But in the kitchen, Jason Ashton turned back. He was visibly nervous. I thought he was afraid of looking at the table, of confirming that it actually belonged to his wife, of knowing something he didn't want to think about or believe. "Where were these stains?" he asked. "On the top? On the legs? I mean, we used to have this dog . . ." He frowned. "But you couldn't remotely confuse that with blood, could you? Or maybe you could? Does it look burned, because dog—"

"No," I said. "It looks like some dark substance was spilled all over it and penetrated the wood. It's hard to tell though, because of the—"

"He'll see," Cas said, clearing his throat, and I guessed that it didn't suit his plans to have Ashton know that the table had a weird top finish. "It'll be obvious."

"Okay," I said, and stepped into the back hallway ahead of Jason Ashton, to open the door to the backyard. Then I held it open, while he stepped through it.

The backyard wasn't big. It was not nearly as large as either my parents' backyard or the backyard of the house—I still had trouble believing this—we were planning to buy. There were maybe twenty steps between the house and my shed.

To this day, I can't tell you why it felt wrong. It just did. As far as I could tell, there were no footprints on the ground, and the door wasn't ajar or anything, only the place felt wrong, all of it; the entire area around the shed felt as though something was seriously out of kilter.

And then I realized there was a hiss coming from the shed—a hiss just on the edge of hearing. And I thought of all the things I had in there that could make that sound. There were chemicals and jars of stuff and . . .

Out of the corner of my eye, I saw a flash of light blossom and shine through the window high up on the wall.

I didn't think. I didn't have time to think. I had a feeling I should jump back, but Ashton was almost at the shed, so I jumped forward, grabbed his wrist, and jumped back, pulling him.

We collided with Cas, who was carrying E, and all of us went crashing and careening against the back door, which opened. Cas and E got shoved through the door, and Ashton and I barely had time to cover our heads.

There had been a boom sometime along the line, only I was too busy trying to get back to pay attention.

Now there were other booms and a muffled succession of pops.

Something big and heavy hit me on the head, hard. And darkness fell.

I woke up in a fog of smoke. Thick smoke all over, and fire engines echoing all around. It was raining. No. It was water, but not rain. A paramedic—had to be a paramedic because he was wearing a surgical mask—was leaning over me, and from somewhere in the fog, Cas said, "Is she . . ."

"She's fine. Just got knocked out when some debris fell on her head," the paramedic said.

I demanded a recount. My head felt like it was on fire, and my lungs felt like they were about to burst. If the paramedic thought this was being all right, I had news for him. But I had more immediate concerns, to wit, "E? Is E all right? What happened to Ashton?" I asked in the general direction Cas's voice had sounded.

"E's fine and Ashton's getting taken care of," he said, and now his face came through the smoke, looking at me. His hair was all up on end, and he had a smudge on his cheek. His eyes were red and tearing, obviously from the smoke. He was the best sight I'd ever seen.

"E's okay?"

"He's in the front room with Ben."

"With Ben?" I said, confused. "How long was I out?"

"About fifteen minutes. Ben was in his car, heard about the explosion on the radio, and drove here. He says he knew where it was immediately. He managed to get E to the living room by telling him, with great authority, that you'd be fine. Apparently the rest of us aren't as trustworthy," he said with a grin.

"He's been ordering E around at least as long as I have," I said. "And with the same mixed results, but sometimes it works."

Cas squeezed my hand, and since the paramedic had left, I tried standing up. I felt dizzy and vaguely drunk, and my head hurt; plus, my hair felt weird.

"Your hair caught fire," Cas said, as I put my hand up to it. "On the right side. We managed to put it out before it got to the scalp. Ashton is worse off; he has burns all over his arms. He put one over his head and one over yours, which is probably why you didn't get hit worse. Also, his jeans caught fire."

"Uh," I said, which was about my level of eloquence, as I was led into the house and all the way to the living room. Someone had closed the door between the dining room and the living room. Since this was a pocket door that had been jammed, and I'd never tried to close it before, someone had expended a great deal of effort in this. Cas now opened it with visible effort and pushed me through it and into the living room.

The air was surprisingly clear, the windows open, both with fans in them—the ones I used in summer—blowing air in.

The air in front of the house was just a little hazy, not black with smoke like in the back. "We're lucky how the wind is blowing," Cas said.

"There are still . . . I had chemicals back there that . . ." I tried to explain inhaling the stuff back there wasn't good for anyone, but then it occurred to me the quantities I had weren't that great. Though they would feed the fire and guarantee that no piece of the shed stayed unburned, I doubted they were more than about one-tenth of the total material burning. Most of it would be old wood and old shingles.

"Yeah, but most of it was right at the beginning. And the firefighters are bringing it under control," Cas said. He closed the pocket door behind us.

"Mommy!" E said and ran to hug my knees, leaving Ben on the sofa, holding *Groovy Greeks* open.

I patted my son's head distractedly and realized there was a third person in the room before Cas and I entered it. He was tall; had overlong blond hair that always looked a little unruly, reminding one of a leonine mane; and had a way of looking almost terminally relaxed, even in his suit pants and with a dress shirt on. His name was Rafiel Trall, and, with Cas, he was one of two senior investigators in the Serious Crimes Unit of the Goldport police. He was also one of Cas's friends dating back to their days in college. Or at least they were friendly acquaintances. Cas said that Rafiel didn't really encourage close friendships, seeming to prefer to keep his distance. He also seemed to be a bit of a ladies' man, never settling for one woman and changing his clothes several times during the day, in a way his colleagues thought denoted clandestine encounters.

Whether this was true, I didn't know. I'd always liked the man when our paths converged. He was polite, professional, and generally a nice person, even volunteering to watch E when Cas and I wanted a minute to talk about something important in his office. Cas had said that he thought Rafiel had a girlfriend just now, but there hadn't been time to give me the full gossip.

He now smiled at me and nodded, and I realized he was here in an official capacity and that it was his job to talk to me.

"Uh," I said. It seemed to be my most common word just now. In fact, I probably could give it the sort of intonation that would make it into an entire dictionary, but I'd probably sound like I was imitating a chimp. And because that is how my mind works, I had to make an effort to stop myself from scratching in a simian fashion and saying, "Uh uh uh."

Instead, I went over to the sofa and sat down. Rafiel came over and looked as though he'd sit on the coffee table, but a "No," from Cas, and Ben hastily getting up and standing by the window, made him change his mind and sit beside me, a little way away, instead.

He took a small tape recorder from his pocket and said, "Do you mind?"

I shook my head and instantly regretted it. Maybe my head wasn't as hard as everyone kept telling me.

"Okay. So do you know what happened?" he asked. "And do you feel well enough to talk about it?"

"Oh. Yeah," I said. "The shed exploded, and I guess I got hit with a piece of it."

Rafiel looked like he was considering what to ask next, then said, "Did you expect this to happen?"

Here I have to confess something. Having—absolutely through no fault of my own, and certainly not to gratify my parents—been involved in two murder investigations before, I knew this tone of voice. And it annoyed me.

Perhaps it was because I was, after all, engaged to a policeman and got to see policemen, as it were, in their natural environment. I don't know. I suspect it was more than that, though, because even the very first time that Cas had used this tone on me had made me less than happy. Now it made me feel snippy and ill-used.

Partly it was because it was this extremely calm, almost insanely even tone of voice, the kind you might use to speak to a child or someone who is very ill. It was not the tone of voice two adults ever used. Second, I knew it was the tone of voice they used on those they suspected of having done something wrong. They thought this would lull the suspect into telling all—possibly so relieved at not being beaten and dragged away in chains that they cracked like a ripe nut.

Several people in the past had accused me of being a nut, and now I cracked. "Oh, yes," I said, in a tone of exaggerated friendliness that would, under other circumstances—and now that I thought about it, maybe even under these ones—have led people to take me directly into the madhouse. "I have been piling up explosives for years. It was only a matter of time till they blew. I facilitated this by keeping a small—"

"Dyce," Cas said, in a warning tone, while Ben snorted, the kind of snort that said I had finally lost my mind, and, frankly, this time he wasn't looking for it, because when he'd found it last time it had been covered in Cheez Whiz and cat hair.

Rafiel smiled, reached over, turned the recorder off, looked over at Cas, and said, "You know, you're technically not even supposed to be here."

"Why not?" Cas asked. "Regulations and all. Second officer present, and I'm very conscientious."

Rafiel sighed and mumbled something under his breath that I swear was "One of these days I'm going to eat him." Since he'd never impressed me as being one of Ben's fraternity, I refused to ask what he meant. At any rate, he continued. "Look, why don't you go out back to stay with Ashton, and send Nick in."

"Well, first because Nick and that idiot"—a head gesture toward Ben—"are having some sort of tiff I don't even understand, and since the idiot . . . Oh, pardon me," he said, at a sound from Ben. "Since *Mister* Idiot is not likely to leave, you'd find yourself in the middle of a soap opera—"

"Which would be markedly different from where I find myself now, sure."

"And second," Cas said, as if Rafiel hadn't spoken, "because you are handling Dyce entirely wrong and will only get nonsense from her. Unless you think she would let me and her son—let alone Ashton—march out there when the shed was about to explode. Or that, having done so, she would delay precious seconds to grab Ashton instead of just jumping back in the house and keeping E and me safe."

Rafiel looked like he was counting to a hundred in his head, possibly in Sanskrit. After a long period of silence and intense concentration on something inward, he said,

"Right. Okay, then." He reached over, erased the portion recorded, and then said, "Let's start again."

Once more, he asked if I knew what had happened and could I talk to him. Then he asked if I knew the shed would explode. This time he used a normal human voice, so I had no excuse to give him the runaround. Instead, I told him the truth. That the shed contained flammable materials, that these flammable materials might go off at any moment, of course, but would need a spark. And that I was very careful not to leave anything around that might create that spark, even unplugging the fan so it wouldn't freakishly burst into an electric fire.

"I see," he said. "And yet you jumped forward, you grabbed Ashton, and you jumped back. All before it blew."

"I heard something, I think," I said. "It sounded like a hiss, though that's . . . I mean, it was so slight I wasn't sure. And then I saw a red flash through the window, and, of course, since I've always been afraid of fire in there, I reacted."

"All right," he said at last, after he asked me a few more details. "That sounds plausible." He paused. "Now, tell me why Ashton is here."

So I told him about the semi-permanent garage sale, the table, everything leading to the talk with Jason this morning and, finally, to us coming here.

He was just turning the recorder off, when Nick opened the pocket door with some effort, and stuck his head in. "I have Ashton in the kitchen now, and the smoke has died down, so we can talk there. The explosives guys are looking through the shed."

If our police department had explosives guys, it had

gone up in the world. Most of the trouble in town consisted of those darn students playing pranks or leaving graffiti. And not much of that, since the college had never made the party-college directory. In fact, Cas had once told me that for three years in a row it had made the "Best College for Daytime Naps" category, but I think he was joking.

At any rate, Rafiel got up from the sofa and followed Nick out. I noticed there was some sort of look between Nick and Ben before Nick turned away, but I couldn't even guess what, and I started wondering if it was illegal to nail horseshoes to their feet, so they could stomp out their messages. I mean, they couldn't say it was cruelty to animals, right? Although humans are technically animals, they usually don't get dropped at the SPCA.

"No," Cas said as soon as the pocket door closed. "I don't think we can, Dyce. You know how it is, even though it wouldn't be cruelty to animals, someone is bound to complain that it's assault and possibly maiming."

"What?" Ben and I said, in unison. I refused to believe that Cas could read my mind.

"No, I can't read your mind," he said, creepily enough. "But I know I was thinking that sooner or later we're going to have to nail horseshoes to the feet of both of the goofballs, so that, since they won't talk, they can communicate by stomping once for yes and twice for no."

Ben made a sound much like an outraged horse, but Cas went on. "But they're likely to complain we assaulted them. And then, you know, I'm almost their size, but there are two of them, and you're not almost their size, and the force tends to get a little funny if I go around shooting people with tranquilizer darts." He looked up at Ben, all innocence. "Even if it's for their own good."

"We can talk," he said, under his breath, in the tone of someone who is highly insulted. "We do talk to each other. We are resolving our differences." And then, in the face of our silence, "Almost."

Which is when we realized that E was missing, and we found him in his room, with Pythagoras, looking out his back window at the men dealing with the remains of the shed—one tilted window and a bunch of indistinct remains. All of them were wearing the sort of hazmat suits that made them look like space aliens. And E was explaining to Pythagoras that it was okay and they were just policemen who dressed funny.

"We have an explosives unit?" I asked Cas.

He shrugged. "Not exactly, but because of the risks of terrorism and all, we got some funding, and we've contracted with a firm that specializes in industrial accidents here in town, and who will look at the scene first—before the Denver guys who normally help out get here—so that if there should be rain or snow, or whatever, we have an investigation of the scene before all that. They're part-time policemen, as far as legalities are concerned, and had additional training in techniques that conform with ours. They're going to take samples, that sort of thing."

"So . . . we don't know what caused the fire?" I asked Cas.

"Probably not meth cooking," he said.

"Oh, thank you."

"I wasn't accusing you," he said. "But considering the other house, it had to be mentioned. However, I doubt anyone would choose to do that in your shed, within watching distance of neighbors, upstairs and all."

He paused for a moment. "Tell me you have renters' insurance," he said. "Including for catastrophic accidents."

"She does," Ben said. He was standing behind E, watching the work on the shed. "I made her get it, considering the stuff she works with."

He didn't say that he'd paid for it most of the months, as I'd refused to, telling him it was completely unnecessary, and I wouldn't pay for it when I could use money for other things. It seemed like I owed him an apology and also would need to pay him back as soon as I could afford it. When that would be was something else again—as it occurred to me I'd just lost all my tools, all my chemicals, and all the small pieces in the shed. And the table. In fact, all that was left of Daring Finds were one or two pieces on consignment in stores and the horrible green trunk in the car. I felt suddenly very tired.

"Good," Cas said, and put his arm over my shoulder, signaling that he understood my feelings—or at least knew that one hard truth at least had just hit me. "You'll be okay, Dyce. I'll lend you money to start you off, if you need. But I must tell you that you can't stay here."

"What?"

"You can't stay here. I'd suggest you come to my place at least until we figure if the explosion was due to . . . well . . . enemy action, or just an accident. Besides, I don't think anyone is going to be staying here, not even your upstairs neighbors." His hand massaged up and down my arm, as he spoke. "The roof caught fire, a good portion of it burned, and I don't think it will be safe or structurally sound enough for anyone to live here for a few days at least, more likely weeks. They'll have to cover the roof with tarps, and, you know, it will get cold."

"But . . . I can't stay with you," I said, before I fully thought it out. I knew I couldn't, but I had to think frantically to realize why I couldn't. You see, it wasn't right. Oh, sure, most of the time Cas stayed in my house overnight. He also bought food, but that was all right since he ate here so often. Ben did the same, although Ben wasn't supposed to, and normally didn't, come and spend the night.

But if I went and lived with Cas now, he would lend me money to restart the business—or not—and I'd just be living in his house and kept by him. Even as a wife, I would feel uncomfortable if I didn't have something of my own to rely on. But, more important, I wasn't his wife. And that would feel like I was just sponging off him.

Of course, I couldn't tell him that because it wasn't rational. Not that I had ever refrained from telling him stuff that wasn't rational in the past. Oh, no. I'd told him just about everything that crossed my mind, and so much of that, so often, wasn't particularly rational. But this was the sort of irrationality he was likely to resent and hold against me. So I had to find another excuse, fast.

Fortunately, the main thing I learned from my fruitless schooling was how to make up plausible—or so wildly implausible people believed them because they thought no one would make such a thing up—excuses. I was a professional when it came to the art of piling BS high and deep. So I said, "If I stay with you, and take E with me, it will technically violate my agreement with All-ex about E. He could claim that E is at risk and bring up all the stuff about how boyfriends of the mother are more likely to hurt a child, and you know . . ."

"Oh, come on," Cas said. "We're engaged. We're almost married. He can't possibly be that stupid."

"Oh, yes he can," I said, firm in the conviction that my ex-husband could in fact be as stupid as anyone and often twice as stupid. "He's good at it."

"Much as I hate to disagree with you, Cas," Ben said, "Dyce is absolutely right in this. Her ex-husband is absolutely capable of being as stupid as anyone."

Cas looked like he'd argue the point, but instead he said, "But you can't possibly stay here. I could book you a hotel."

He was doubtlessly thinking that then he could stay at the hotel with me. I honestly hated to burst his bubble, but sometimes one has to do these things. If I stayed at a hotel, I'd have to pay for it—I'd just have to—and that would eat through the less than a thousand dollars I had in the bank. Money I was going to need to buy chemicals and tools. Besides, there was no way I could restart the business immediately from a hotel. I mean, I know there are some hotels that let you have pets, but I had yet to see a hotel advertisement that said *Refinishing encouraged in our spacious rooms*. And I had to restart the business right away, or some of those consignment shops in Denver would allot my space to another vendor who could make them more per square foot. I'd fought hard to get and expand the floor space they gave me. I explained this last part to Cas and then said the inevitable. "It will have to be my parents," I said. "Mom will let me use the garage."

This was bad news all around, because although it

was true that Mom would let me use the garage, and although it was true that my father probably wouldn't notice if Cas moved in with me there—except perhaps to reproach me for being unfaithful to Ben, if he was having the sort of day when he thought Ben and I were an item—Mom was likely to notice and to give us that look of not-quite disapproval. And besides, two weeks with my parents telling him the plots of the best books coming out, urging him to buy some book or other because it would improve his police work, or reproaching him for not doing things literally *by the book*, and Cas would commit homicide. And no matter how justifiable it would be—I had considered it several times myself—the police were likely to take a dim view of his killing my parents. They could be quite stodgy that way.

And then, as though the bad news needed piling on, Nick came in looking grave. He put a hand possessively on Ben's shoulder, but when he spoke, it was to Cas, and it was all official. "Bad news," he said. "Or good, depending on how you look at it. The piece of the table that hit Dyce on the head? Ashton identified it with a high degree of certainty as being the one his wife took with her."

CHAPTER 21

You Can Go Back

It seemed like old times, climbing my parents' rickety staircase from the backyard to the kitchen door on the second floor.

The house had once belonged to my grandmother and had, therefore, like most Victorians in this area, a kitchen on the ground floor as well as an entrance room, a parlor, a powder room, and a glassed-in back porch. Now all of those were given over to the bookstore, with bookcases against every available wall as well as framing the windows and the fireplaces and marching in ordered rows through the middle of the rooms. These days, the kitchen on the bottom floor was used to prepare cakes and refreshments for big signings and parties.

When I was in high school, Ben and I used to hide out in the kitchen and eat leftover cake and whatever appetizers had been put out for the parties, while the adults circulated, talked books, and tried to look important. Immediately after the end of high school, Ben had seemed to find one particular beginning writer who had come for a signing very fascinating, but since the writer had departed back to his home somewhere in the East, I would presume nothing came of that.

I suppose when my dad lived in the house alone and filled it with books, he'd used the kitchen downstairs, at least when he remembered he needed to heat a can of soup or something. Having seen my father's attempts at housekeeping since then, I had to assume my mother had cleaned it with a blowtorch before she allowed it to be used for anything public.

But when my mother moved in and the store became a store, they needed a kitchen on the second floor. And then they needed access directly to the second floor, so that every person they invited over didn't have to come in through the bookstore. (Also because, after a while, they'd had to block that door with a bookcase. I remembered being five or six and finding disoriented customers who, with the best intentions in the world, had gotten so lost wandering through the store's labyrinthine confines that they were now browsing mysteries in Mom's kitchen or living room.)

So Mom had got on Dad to build a staircase to the second floor. Let alone that I had no idea how she had managed to focus him on reality—or hammer and nails—long enough for this to happen, I was in awe at the moment of insanity in which she thought this was a good idea.

At the best of times, entrusting Dad with anything more lethal or potentially dangerous to his own life and limbs than a pen was a chancy business. But, presumably, she'd handed him a saw, nails, a hammer, and very large, very heavy boards.

Or maybe he'd got the boards himself, since they bore the hallmarks of having been grabbed more or less at random by someone heedless of quality, strength, or weight. Or, for that matter, size and shape. They had also been minimally sawed—if sawed at all.

Instead, Dad had taken these varying-size-and-shape boards and built a one-story-high staircase with a landing halfway up that resembled nothing so much as a cat's cradle in wood.

And yet it worked and had worked for the entire time of my childhood, when, sometimes, dozens of family friends gathered on that landing to watch the Fourth of July fireworks set off at a nearby park.

At this point, I felt fairly safe climbing it, even though it swayed and creaked like a sailing ship under a gale. I kept thinking that, by all that was holy and rational, this thing should not be able to stand, but when had anything around this house been rational, anyway?

So I climbed up, with a cat carrier in one hand and E by the other hand, and felt like I'd felt a dozen times before—coming home from college—only this time with cat and son. Or when I'd first left All-ex and lodged with Mom and Dad for a brief while.

My mother opened the door as soon as I got to the top. I swear she has the landing bugged and possibly covered by a spy camera. Mom looks nothing like me. She has white hair, is skinny, and has a china-doll prettiness. She didn't even stare, despite the fact that the hair on one side of my head was about one inch long, with frazzled ends. If she thought anything at all, she probably thought I was trying out a new hairstyle.

Instead, she threw the door wide and said, "Come on in. I assume you want to discuss the bridesmaid thing again? I've been talking to Fluffy about it, and we've decided not to press you on the subject. I mean, if you're not comfortable having Fluffy as your maid of honor, we're not going to push it. Are we, baby?"

Baby, who was by her dish—yes, porcelain, with *Mommy's Fluffy Princess* painted on the side—arched up and hissed for all she was worth. I gave her a look that said I didn't care if this was the second life she'd hated me, I could still light an embroidery hoop on fire and make her jump through it.

She yowled. I dropped the carrier and E's hand.

In the next moment, E and my mother—together—were prying Fluffy from the leg of my jeans.

"I don't understand," Mom said, picking the cat up and petting her, while examining her for . . . I don't know, trauma at having attacked me? "She never acts like this for anyone else, does she-ums? No, she doesn't. Baby is the bestest kitten in the world, she is."

Fluffy purred in an entirely artificial way while giving me the evilest glare any cat had ever given a human in the entire history of interspecies relations.

"Never mind me," I told my mother, who was not, in fact, minding me at all. "I'm sure my leg will be perfectly fine. It's not like cat claws can lead to lethal infections or anything, and if they have to amputate, I'll just have a peg leg put in with a stiletto heel at the end; that way I'll always be perfectly dressed."

Mom nodded. Which just goes to show you. I have no

idea what it goes to show you, but it definitely does. She had Fluffy upside down and was petting the cat's belly while reassuring her that everything would be all right. Why everything shouldn't have been all right—for the cat—while the wretch was licking my blood off her claws, I don't know.

"I'll just go up to my room, shall I?"

Mom nodded while telling Fluffy-ums that she was a "good, good fluffy kitteh." Heaven preserve us from a *bad fluffy kitteh*, in that case.

"Fluffy is a good guard cat," E said, pensively, as we walked up the staircase toward my room in the attic of the house. I suppose when one grows up with me as a mother, one learns to make the best of things. But I had to burst his bubble. "Not really," I said. "She is just really good at guarding against me."

"Well," he said, cheerily, "maybe that's something."

"Ah, just wait until she pees on your bed. Or mine." The third floor had two bedrooms facing each other. One was my parents' bedroom, and the other had been my childhood bedroom. But, eventually, around adolescence, I'd realized there were things that no girl should hear. Like, for instance, the endless discussions about the ending of novels that had just come out. Which totally ruined my fun in reading them and, besides, kept me up half the night and caused me to fall asleep in math the next day.

And so, with my grandmother's rather formidable backing, I'd moved upstairs to the attic, a room that ran the entire length of the house, though not the entire height. The roof sloped so that on the edges, it was about two feet from the floor. This had been okay when I was shorter, and was still okay, I supposed, if I minded my head, but I'd come close to braining myself several times by walking full force into the sloping sides.

But it had a desk against the tiny window that gave out onto the roof—and now two beds, one for me and one for E, at opposite ends of the room.

Coming into this room was another trip into the past because when Ben was tired of his noisy and ebullient family—who I always found fascinating but he seemed to find less so—he'd come here to do homework with me, and we'd inevitably end up on the floor, talking about everything but homework, over the mess of books.

I remembered the dinky tape player that I'd taken from downstairs without anyone ever noticing and the spirited arguments where we took the world apart and put it back together again, and I had a moment of wistful fear that E wouldn't get that when he entered school. But he probably would. He probably would also get in a never-ending world of trouble that would cause me to be called to the school multiple times a week, but nothing could be done about that.

And then I closed the door to my room and released Pythagoras from his carrier. E was carrying a bag with Pythagoras's litter box, litter, and dishes, which I set up in a corner of the room. The last time we'd had to stay over, Mom had tried to get him to share a litter box with Fluffy. Which, of course, meant that Pythagoras had ended up peeing on a pile of books in the living room and had almost got thrown out the second-floor window by Dad, who called him a vandal.

This time, we wouldn't let that happen. I'd left the bag of clothes for myself and E in the car.

The room had never, at the best of times, had really

good light, but I used to have a floor lamp and a desk lamp, which I'd taken with me to college and which, in the fullness of time, had been left somewhere when I'd got married and moved to a real house.

E went to his bed and rooted underneath for the stuff he'd left there the last time he'd stayed over—which was not the last time I'd stayed over, as Mom and Dad had kept him over a weekend when Cas and I had been so foolish as to go to Denver for New Year's.

Mom assured me the fire department people were really quite nice and that one of them remembered the last time they were called to the house, when I'd tried to make homemade fireworks, so they weren't surprised at all to see E do the same.

But fortunately, as Mom had explained, they'd found a series of Agatha Christie coloring books and given E a large box of crayons, and that had taken care of the rest of the stay.

Now E took out *Murder on the Orient Express* and his red crayon and went back to working on the interrupted coloring. I stared for a moment, wondering where Mom and Dad had found these books. I had a suspicion they were printed by some tiny press and served a demographic consisting of my parents and twenty other people like them, worldwide.

I considered my options as I rolled up my pants leg and examined the deep claw marks on my skin. Much as I hated to, I thought I would take E out for burgers at Cy's. Or perhaps to the George for breakfast. Breakfast was E's favorite meal of the day, and he'd gladly eat it all three meals.

I'm not going to say that my mother is a bad cook

because it wouldn't be exactly right. Mom is a fair to decent cook and an excellent baker. She is, however, mostly an absentminded cook. Meals tend to happen whenever they happen, and you might very well get cookies instead of dinner.

Also, they, too, were in the habit of living off the leftovers from signing parties. Mind you, it was, in many ways, an economic necessity. Sometimes you threw a signing party and only half a dozen people showed up, though you'd bought food for fifty. That meant you had little cheese balls and vegetables and chips and dip that you'd paid for and that were not covered by books sold at the party. The food had to go somewhere, and where it went was the fridge, where Mom and Dad lived off of it for a while.

Normally, I'd at least check and see if the fridge was stocked, but two things deterred me. One was that Fluffy would be patrolling the kitchen, and although one peg leg might be acceptable, I felt fairly sure that if I had two stiletto-like peg legs, people would notice and perhaps remark on them. Besides, I had a feeling that Cas wouldn't like it.

The other thing was that I had E. And feeding E on cheese balls and chips—though perfectly acceptable and likely to give him his daily dose of preservatives and colorings, which, as everyone knows, are absolutely needed for one to live a long life and have healthy color— was likely to be frowned upon by All-ex and Michelle whenever they heard about it. Michelle shopped only at Organic Foods. I knew this because she always brought one of their bags when she had to come near me. I was fairly sure that she used it as a protective device, kind of like a cross to a vampire. I was pretty sure of this because there was absolutely no reason for her to have a bag with her when she came to see me, much less every time she came to see me. Organic Foods was a few blocks from her house, in the opposite direction of the route she had to take when she came to my place.

Also, Michelle often packed organic muffins—with the consistency of ill-mixed cement and the general taste of sawdust—and fruit when E came back home. Exactly as if she was packing for him to go into the desert and live with savages. Which meant it behooved me, in return, to make sure that E got a bit of nonorganic-type food. Organic in the Michelle sense, of course. Although Pythagoras might be quite capable of eating coins, screws, and, on one memorable occasion, a roll of piano wire, I didn't think E would be interested in nonorganic substances.

But when it came to that, a shake at Cy's would be considered an indulgence. Living off of chips and cheese balls probably not.

So I'd take E out for dinner. Then I'd come back up and bring our clothes up. And somewhere along the line, before going to bed, I'd ask Mom if I could use her garage for refinishing. If I hit her at just the right time, she probably would not have the faintest notion what I was asking her and would say yes without thinking.

This meant that tomorrow I could start refinishing the horrible green trunk. And looking for other small pieces to finish. And determinedly not thinking of Jason Ashton, or Maria Ashton, or the bloodstained table that had gone up in flames in my shed. But not gone enough that it hadn't been identified.

CHAPTER 22

Return of the Mummy

I woke up while E was still asleep—and with great hopes he would remain so or at least behave while I did the rounds of the various places where I usually found furniture, I headed downstairs. To stop in the hall between the two rooms.

On one side was my parents' room, the his-and-hers bedside tables crammed with books and, in Mom's case, notebooks, in which she made notes for book recommendations for her very own mystery book blog, *The Missing Clue*, part of their online bookstore website. The website was one of the biggest sources of revenue for the store and truly a brilliant idea on Mom's part. It was also the reason why these days she spent more time at the kitchen table, working on her laptop, than at the store.

Mind you, when she sold books online, she then had to go downstairs and wrest them from Dad. Dad had this thing about selling books, his idea being to surround himself with books and then bask in knowing he was insulated from reality by all those lovely words. You could always tell it had been a good sales day when Mom was all happy and Dad looked like he was going to break down and cry.

Their bed was neatly made, and I could hear Mom talking to Fluffy downstairs. But the other room, the room that had been my own, once upon a time, before I claimed the attic, was occupied by . . . the mummy.

The mummy, of course, was Ben completely wrapped up in his blanket, perfectly immobile and facing up. He said the fact that he could roll himself up and sleep all night like that was the sign of a clean conscience and a peaceful nature. Personally, I thought it was a sign of being crazier than should be allowed by law, and possibly the sign of a control freak.

What it shouldn't be, however, was in my parents' house. If he wanted to play *Return of the Mummy*, he should at least rent a hotel room. Of course, ideally, he should be with the zombie somewhere, making beautiful music, or whatever it was they did, and no, I didn't want to know. I just didn't want any more of the soap opera.

So I stepped into his room and said, "Benedict Colm! What are you doing here?"

He woke and sat up, straight from the waist, in perfect horror-movie style. But I never figured out what he would have answered, because at that moment, my mom yelled from downstairs, "Children? Breakfast is ready."

Ben's lips said, *Children?* soundlessly, and I said, "This is what you get for coming here to sleep. What do you think you're doing?"

He got up, wrapped in his blanket, doing his imitation

of a human burrito with feet. "I was sleeping. I thought that was perfectly obvious."

"Oh, please, Ben. Good Lord, so the man wants to buy a house and have you move in with him. It's not like he asked you to sell your soul. Can't you behave like a normal human being for a change?"

Ben stared at me for a moment and blinked. "Buy a house?" he asked, as though I'd suggested that Nick wanted to get Ben to his secret lair and feed him to the piranhas in the tank of doom.

"Oh, look at the time," I said, realizing that Nick hadn't got around to confessing that particular misdeed. "And Mom is waiting breakfast."

I ran down the stairs before he could say anything else, taking advantage of the fact that he wasn't yet fully awake.

Downstairs, the breakfast spread proved that there had indeed been an unsuccessful signing. At least, I think that even in my parents' house, a breakfast spread of celery sticks, carrots, broccoli, and cauliflower surrounding jalapeño spread could only happen for that reason. But it's not like my mother had forgotten I didn't like spicy foods, particularly for breakfast. No way. She'd also set out a large bowl of cheese puffs, a bag of salt and vinegar potatoes, and—probably left over from Halloween's Spooky Mystery Day, two months ago—a massive bowl of candy corn.

She was sitting at the table, with Fluffy on her lap, working madly at her laptop. When I came in, she got that just slightly disappointed look that she got when she expected Ben and she got me. I suspected she'd had that look in the hospital when she first saw me, too.

I noticed that she'd started coffee and edged around

her—and Fluffy—to get a cup and was seated safely at the table eating candy corn—for the energy—when Ben came downstairs, having showered, dressed in his stay-at-home uniform of chinos and button-down shirt with no tie.

"Aren't you supposed to go to work today?" I asked him, to ward off questions about that house-buying thing.

He shrugged and petted Fluffy on the way to get a cup of coffee. "Nah. I had some time off coming, and I think I need to deal with . . . stuff."

"You know, I could get horseshoes today. It wouldn't be hard to nail them on, either."

"Oh, are you going to buy a horse, Ben?" Mom asked, perking up. "But I wouldn't let Dyce shoe it. She might be okay with her little furniture stuff, but she doesn't know a thing about horses. She'd probably get herself kicked in the head."

"She's sure to get herself kicked, at least metaphorically," he said, glaring at me over the rim of his coffee cup as he sipped his coffee. "Guaranteed."

Mom typed something in her blog and beamed at one of us, then the other. "Well, since you have the day off, and Dyce is here—"

"Please don't suggest I go shopping for dresses with him. I have to go and get stuff to get the business on its feet again. By the way," I said, stuffing my mouth full of candy corn and speaking around it. "May I use the part of the garage that's empty for my refinishing stuff?"

"You know," Ben cut in, "the only thing that exceeds Dyce's empathy for people in emotional turmoil is her dainty eating manners, isn't it?"

My mom looked completely confused, and I struggled to swallow the candy corn. And the phone rang. Ben grabbed it—no, he pounced on it as if he were expecting a call that told him whether he'd live or die. And his face fell. "Yeah," he said. "She's here." And handed me the phone.

It was Cas. "Hello, sunshine," he said. "How does the world look this morning?"

"With a high incidence of candy corn and jalapeño cheese for breakfast," I said. "A way too high incidence of Ben, who is still being weird, apparently, and a mild to moderate tendency to shopping for refinishing stuff."

Cas didn't say anything, but I knew he was smiling. It's hard to explain, okay? But after a while you get to know your significant other like that.

Then he cleared his throat. "Well, I thought you might want to know that your shed blew up because of a bomb—which makes some difference for the insurance policy, but not much, since Ben bought you the best plan. Your landlord is dealing with them, but I don't know if they'll let you come back. You might have to move out. Good thing our offer was accepted, huh?"

I felt my heart lurch and a vague sickness settle in the pit of my stomach. Okay, so I'd signed the offer for the house, but did these people really, truly have to accept it? And that fast? It seemed like unusually fast turnaround. It seemed like the future was rushing at me.

"I figure," Cas said, "you can move into it in solitary splendor until the wedding. Or, at least, theoretically you'll be there in solitary splendor, and then I'll move in. So I asked for a closing date next week. Is that okay?"

I think I squeaked, but he interpreted it as meaning yes, because he said, "Okay, then I— "

I knew he was about to hang up, and I said, "Uh, Cas?"

"Yes?"

"What is the news, you know? On the Ashtons?"

"Oh. We . . . er . . . the table is . . . er . . . the table she took. And we did find human blood on one of the fragments . . ."

I noticed Ben was staring at me. "So. What are you doing about it?"

And I swear, like a bad mystery movie, Cas said, "We're continuing our investigations," and hung up on me. I stuffed my mouth with candy corn, washed it down with coffee, and found Ben still staring at me. "Most infuriating man in the universe," I said.

He gave me the ghost of a smile and sat down across from me. "Oh, you haven't spent much time with his cousin, have you?"

I couldn't help grinning, and Ben reached for a celery stick. "So," he said. "We're shopping for refinishing stuff, are we?"

"Yes," I said, hoping I read him correctly. "Mom, do you mind keeping an eye on E? You're not going anywhere, are you?"

Mom looked worried for a minute, then said, "He's not done with the coloring books, is he?"

"No, he has only done *Murder on the Orient Express*, though he might need another red crayon."

She smiled. "Oh, that is easy."

Ben and I hustled down the stairs and out to the circular driveway, where both our cars were parked. "My car," I said. "You don't want stuff to refinish in your car."

"Not to worry," he said. "I brought tarps to protect surfaces."

I was greatly impressed with this bit of foresight but also a little suspicious. "To protect them from old furniture and chemicals, right?" I said. "Not to protect them from Nick's blood after you kill and dismember him, right?"

Ben stared at me for a moment, his eyes growing wide. "Why," he asked, "would you even think of that? Ew. I love Nick."

"You've been avoiding him for a week."

Ben sighed. "That's completely different. It's just . . . I'm afraid he'll think that I'm . . . I'm afraid of being too dependent on him, you know? I've always stayed fairly independent."

And suddenly I understood the whole insanity, because I had gone through the exact same thing just considering staying with Cas for a week or so. I sighed. "Yeah, I get that."

We got in the car, with him behind the wheel, which was the real reason that he didn't want to take my car. The man has this thing about me driving. He seems to think I'm the world's most dangerous driver, which only means he's never been in a car that my dad was driving. Particularly not while Dad was enthusiastically telling the passenger about a book he had just read, gesturing broadly, *and* forgetting to have even a finger on the wheel. At one time he'd picked me up from the airport on a return trip from a vacation, and not only had we ended up in Denver—not Goldport—but once there, he'd jumped a median on Colfax Avenue and gone across the traffic stream and into the parking lot of a McDonald's. He'd finally stopped only because the car had come to rest against a young sapling. And then he'd asked me where the tree had come from. That we made it back home, let alone in one piece, happened because I took the keys from his hands and insisted on driving back.

But to Ben I was the most dangerous driver in creation.

"But, Ben . . . if you want to live with him . . . I mean . . ."

"Yeah," he said. "Yeah."

"Is this because you can't marry him? I mean . . ."

He shrugged. "It's just more work. We can make a bunch of legal contracts to protect me . . . and him, as much as if we were married. It just takes a bit more work, but it's no big deal." He chewed the corner of his lip as we drove out of my parents' driveway. "I suppose we're going to the flea markets?"

"Yeah," I said. Taking Ben to the dive flea markets I frequented was a treat. Probably only because I have a low sense of humor, but watching Ben in his impeccable clothes edge away from dusty surfaces and look around like he feared contagion amused me no end.

Ben drove carefully along the narrow street with cars parked on both sides; it was a mystery to me how customers ever managed to park to come into the bookstore. "The thing is," he said, "I'm not absolutely sure I wouldn't be even more freaked out if it was possible for us to marry. Damn, Dyce, how can you have done it . . . and be about to do it, twice? Aren't you scared?"

"Terrified," I told him, and laughed. "But, you know . . . if you don't risk this sort of thing, then you are, by definition, going to be always alone."

"I suppose," he said. Suddenly he chuckled. "Sometimes alone seems like a really good option—you know, free to go where the wild wind goes and all that—and then I see Nick again, or we go and sit up on some stupid hill, with the convertible top down, and eat sub sandwiches together, and I feel like if I let this go without at least trying, I'll kick myself for the rest of my life. But I don't want to rush it, either, you know . . . I mean, it's just that I think the habit of staying together, every night, might be clouding my decision. So, I thought, if I spent a few nights away from him, maybe I'd see things differently."

"And did you?" I asked, curious.

"Yeah, I saw things considerably more lonely," he said. "It's totally stupid, but I think I've . . . Well, I think I have to give it a chance. He's overbearing. He seems to think housework happens to other people. He calls me weird names in Greek. He gets upset when I borrow his books without permission . . . but I think I'm going to at least give it a try."

"Ben," I said, somewhat alarmed. "From experience, your doing all the housework and his not liking you borrowing his books can be problems over time."

A weird smile broke out on Ben's lips. "Oh, well . . . It's entirely possible that he was in the middle of that book. It's even entirely possible I knew that and subconsciously tried to get the book, so he'd . . . you know . . . come find me. As for the housework, he knows he has a problem with that. His mom and Cas's mom do everything around the house, and his ex did everything around the house. He says he's not sure he can get broken into it, but he's perfectly willing to restore a few more cars on weekends or something and pay for a cleaning lady. And I'm okay with that. I mean, I have a cleaning service now; it's just when I'm at his place . . ."

"So you're going to move to the house next to the one Cas and I are buying?"

"Yeah, if he still wants me to. And if he's buying it. Is he buying it, Dyce?"

"Are you going to go crazy if I say yes?"

"No, I just want to know. You know, I liked the way he put his hand on my arm, yesterday, like he was afraid the fire in the shed would come out and hurt me."

Okay . . . having been down that path a couple of times, I knew silly love when I saw it. "Yeah," I said, because there was no point arguing. "And yeah, he put an offer on the house. I don't know if it was accepted. Our house . . . well, our *future* house has this garage, where they can restore cars."

"The other one has a four-car garage, so they can store cars there. And Nick was telling me that you'd be right next door and we could babysit E when he needed it. I'm not sure the man understands what a selling point is. *Hey, we can babysit E. He can set fire to our stuff.*"

I nodded, because I knew it actually was a selling point, though Ben would rather be cut into ribbons before admitting it.

We stopped in front of the flea market and went in. This time I got lucky, as there was a tall and elegant china cabinet, in pretty bad shape, cheap enough. I got it for under thirty dollars because one of the sides was scorched, clearly having been in a fire.

"Isn't that going to be hard to cover?" Ben asked, as we loaded it into the back of the car.

"Not really. I can either apply a veneer to it—and the other side is mahogany veneer, so that's okay—or I can put a sealant and then build layers of stain to imitate the wood. Which is how you fake a wood, with stain."

"Unlike that table?" he asked.

"Yeah," I said, and because it was on my mind, I told him what Cas had said.

"Um," he said. "Do you have some chemicals to buy?"

"Yes, why?"

"Because I figured we could go to the home-improvement place around the corner from the Ashtons, and then we could . . . go to Collin and Peter and ask them a few questions."

"No!" I said. "They told Sebastian Dimas."

"I don't think they did," he said. "But we can ask them that, too, if you wish. And if you're hell-bent on revenge," he said, with a smile, "I will point out there's a philharmonic rehearsal on Tuesday night, and it usually goes on till eleven or so, plus they usually go out afterward, and I suspect Peter didn't get to bed till two or three in the morning, so visiting them by nine is evil."

"And Collin?"

"What?"

"Does Collin also play at the symphony?"

Ben shook his head. "No, he's a lecturer of classics at CUG."

He didn't look old enough to be that, but I'd gathered from their conversation that he was in fact old enough. I just had trouble reconciling the sunny blond and classics.

In perfect harmony, we went by Do It Now Hardware and Lumber, where I bought some basic stains, plus mineral spirits, turpentine, and a no-fume remover that would work on everything including polyurethane, mostly because I had no idea if the green trunk had been finished with stain, paint, or Martian rocks. I also got half a dozen generic brushes, because it was easier to use and discard them than to try cleaning the really expensive brushes, particularly while I was working out of my mom's garage. On impulse, I got a small can of gold paint from the discount rack. And I grabbed assorted rags and a scraper and half a dozen other little things.

With them safely packaged and on tarps on the floor between the front and the back seats, I allowed Ben to drive me to the Ashtons' and park across from their house. Then we crossed the street and rang Collin and Peter's doorbell.

It took a while, and when the door was opened, it was by Peter, in a pitch-black silk robe. All tall and lanky and pale, with curly black hair, in that robe, he looked like he'd made a deal with Faust once upon a time. Not helped by the fact that he looked from one to the other of us with his eyebrows arched high. "Ben and . . . ah . . . Dyce. How nice of you to drop by," he said. But his expression said, *Do you two juvenile delinquents know what time it is?* "Collin is at the college. He had some conference or something, but . . . if you come in . . . I'm fairly sure I know how to operate the coffeemaker." His expression said, *But not at this time in the morning, when I'm more asleep than not. Do you two juvenile delinquents REALLY not know what time it is?*

To be absolutely honest, even though I thought that he had told on me to Sebastian and probably started the whole thing that had culminated in someone putting a bomb—a bomb!—in my shed and forcing me out of house and home, I felt embarrassed enough to just turn around and go away. But Ben, who is normally the socially sensitive one of the two of us, seemed completely tone deaf. "Yeah, that will be fine, Peter. And I'll make the coffee."

And then, he more or less herded Peter into his own kitchen. The fact that he knew where things were in the kitchen didn't surprise me. I had a feeling that when Ben had been with his ex, who was also with the symphony, they'd often ended up coming here to dinner or to hang out. Also, I knew that in that particular breakup, Ben had got the friends, or at least all the friends he cared to keep. I suspected he still often came over to hang out or talk, mostly because Peter and Collin normally threw his birthday party. That was probably going to change. Unless I was completely wrong, Nick would insist on doing it this year. Then I suddenly remembered the veiled questions about Nick and wondered how they felt about Nick and if that was why or part of the reason why Ben was so hesitant about the whole thing.

But mostly, as I saw Ben make coffee, and then get into the freezer and grab a pack of frozen waffles, which he thawed in the oven, all without Peter complaining—though it was entirely possible Peter was asleep—I wondered if Peter had told Sebastian I was investigating and why.

I asked the question as soon as it was socially possible. What this meant is that first Ben served waffles, with syrup. That Peter didn't act surprised Ben had just helped himself and served me a waffle meant that he was either more asleep than I thought or that Ben spent a lot more time here than I thought, which begged the question of why he hadn't imitated a mummy on their sofa.

But perhaps Peter had looked at Ben funny, because Ben said, "Sorry. I didn't mean to just help myself, but we stayed at Dyce's parents' last night, and you have no idea what her mom thinks constitutes breakfast food. Celery sticks. Jalapeño cheese. Candy corn!"

Peter smiled. "Absolutely my pleasure. Why did you stay at her parents' house? Still running away?"

Ben frowned. "Yeah, but it's no use. I think I'm going to give it a try."

Peter nodded. "Expected it, really. It seems like that sort of thing." He didn't seem upset and might have been vaguely worried, or just half asleep. "I'd have said he wasn't . . . but you know . . . These things are never like you expect them. Collin is not at all my type, either. But . . . this stuff ends up surprising you. So is that why you came over? For my blessing?"

Ben grinned. "No, not really . . . It's just that . . ."

And then he told Peter. About Sebastian visiting me. Twice. And about the explosion. And about all of it. All of it except the description of the guy who had sold the table to the garage sale. The guy who seemed to have either scared or confused my dad—the two not always being easily distinguishable when it came to Dad.

That was left to me. This after Peter had said, "I didn't tell him anything, of course, but I think he might have been babysitting the kids when you were here, and it only takes a second to snap a picture of a license plate. And if you have friends in the department, even a reception-ist, or a traffic cop, it is not that difficult to get the person's name and address."

That had not occurred to me. "But if Sebastian . . . I mean . . . If he came over to threaten me, surely he's involved."

"Not necessarily," he said. He seemed to be thinking. "I don't want to be telling tales out of school . . . I mean, these things are not my business, but . . . the Ashtons are very sweet and giving people. Until I saw . . . well . . . until I saw Sebastian in the bathroom with Maria, while Jason was gone, I never assumed there was anything untoward. Because they tend to adopt everyone who needs it. They have this huge Thanksgiving dinner, you know, with everyone who doesn't have any other place to go, and I understand from what Sebastian has said that he was living on the streets when they met him. He had a drug habit or something, and anyway, they took him and rehabilitated him."

While he was talking, I realized something. If she had been taking meds, and a narcoleptic . . . Jason had said something about her resenting having to be babysat. "He might have been helping her in the shower for health reasons," I blurted out.

And as they both stared at me, I sighed. "It's also not my secret to tell, but she was taking meds . . . She has a health condition that had just been diagnosed and that I understand could cause her to lose balance or worse."

For a moment Peter stared at me, then nodded, once. "Oh, that makes sense. Because, you know, though they were in there together . . . well, he didn't seem to be touching her, not *that* way, just . . . just sort of watching over her. It had that feel. And before you ask, we don't as a rule spy; it's just that the houses are so close together that sometimes you can't avoid a glimpse."

"I know," I said. "Ben used to play this game with the person who lived next door for a few months and who was . . . well . . . short and round. Ben used to try to guess whether it was a guy or a woman. When he caught an accidental glimpse."

"The weird thing is that I accidentally saw this person naked half a dozen times, and I still didn't know," he said. "My best guess was hobbit."

Peter smiled. "So you can see that if she had this

condition, whatever it is, it would make Sebastian even more protective. He says he'll be renting the house when Jason leaves, and he hopes Maria comes back . . ." He shrugged. "If I didn't know better, I'd say he treats them both as if they were his parents, though he's probably their age or older."

"Yes, but . . ." I said, and then decided to rush it. "You say they have a lot of . . . protégées?"

"A half dozen probably," he said. "Though I've noticed fewer recently, before Maria disappeared, and now I wonder if it was because she was trying to keep her condition a secret."

"Probably," I said. "She seemed to be embarrassed by it. Or afraid people would think she was mentally ill."

Peter drank his coffee. "I can see that."

"But among their protégées, did they have a blond, with pop eyes and . . ."

"Oh, of course. Winston de Leon."

"Beg your pardon?" I said.

"Winston de Leon. Yeah, he was by the other day, after you guys left. I think he lives somewhere nearby. Weird. I just realized he's been at the Ashtons a lot less since Maria disappeared, which is strange because . . ." He stopped, frowning. "Did you say something about a table? The first time you were here?"

I nodded.

"How odd. Because I'm sure that Winston was here and loading a table into the back of the car either the day that Maria disappeared or . . . around there. It's hard to tell, really, because of course we didn't know she had disappeared or that there was anything special about that day."

CHAPTER 23

De Leon Doesn't Sleep

We got out of there as soon as we could politely do so, and got in Ben's car. I'd trained Ben well. I didn't even need to tell him to call directory assistance. He did it himself. Of course, it occurred to me that it might not get us anything, since there was a good chance that de Leon had a mobile phone only.

But we were in luck, and Ben jotted down an address. Which happened to be a couple of streets away, in the sort of place where the Victorians were not only still subdivided into five or six apartments apiece, but also still very much owned by slumlords. Porches sagged and balconies looked like toothless mouths, favoring passersby with gaping smiles. Windows were covered in plastic, front yards grew mostly parts of plastic toys, the fences were chain link, and the dogs were snarling.

We found the address, mercifully dog free but

looking like it had needed a paint job since the Jurassic period, and went up and knocked at the door. No one answered. We knocked again. No one answered.

After a while, as we were about to give up, a guy came to the door. He was skinny and looked like he'd slept in his clothes, but he was neither blond nor bug eyed. He looked at us out of red-rimmed eyes, seemed to have trouble deciding whether we were one person or two, and said, "Dude!"

"We were looking for Winston de Leon," Ben said in his best *I'm here to serve a process* voice.

The young man in the doorway, who had either black hair or very dirty brown hair, made a heroic effort to focus his gaze, failed, and said, "Dude." And when that didn't seem to serve his purpose, he gathered himself up against the door frame to pull himself upright. "Dude," he said after some thought. "Dude is not here."

"Right. Could you please tell me where to find him?" Ben asked.

The man made yet one more manful attempt to focus on this *object* in front of him, from which words emerged. "Uh . . ." he said. "He doesn't have the stuff, you know? It's no use coming and trying to buy from him now, because he hasn't been able to make it. There was an . . . uh . . . accident."

"Thank you so much," Ben said, and grabbed my arm in a viselike grip and herded me down the steps and all the way into the car. I was in the car before he gave me time to talk. Not that what I had to say was that damaging, because mostly I was confused. "Stuff?" I said.

"I think, my dear," Ben said, "that Mr. de Leon has been doing a burgeoning business in . . . er . . .

over-the-counter pharmaceuticals." He started the car in controlled haste and drove away as though he expected someone to jump us, possibly with a chain saw.

But I was thinking. Drugs. An accident. Okay. I know that meth cooking is volatile, and I imagine there are hundreds of accidents a day. Okay, possibly a few less in Goldport, simply because it is a small town. On the other hand, such accidents are probably not rare. To link the "accident" to the guy who had died in the condo would be fanciful. It would be a matter of thinking that something must be linked to something else simply because the two were presented together. Having grown up in mystery fandom, I knew that readers often imagined romances between two completely unrelated characters simply because they were thrown together a lot.

"So," Ben said. "What is Cas doing about this? What is he looking into?"

"He told me he's pursuing inquiries," I said.

"That," Ben said, "is so . . . him! So we take this stuff to your mom's house, start whatever it is you do to furniture, and then I call Nick. I'll see if I can get more out of him than you can get out of Cas."

"What are the chances of that?"

"Oh, let me see . . . I've been spending time away for four days, and he bought a house without telling me. It's all in how I work those."

"You're utterly shameless," I said.

"Why, ma'am, thank you kindly."

CHAPTER 24

All in the Appearances

Which is how we ended up in Mom's garage, with one of Ben's tarps on the floor, the green trunk on top of it, and the no-fume stripper on it. After a while, Ben coughed. "Are you sure that thing is no fumes?"

"It says so," I said, defensively, putting my sleeve in front of my mouth. "No fumes for indoor stripping."

"Perhaps they meant the other kind of stripping," he said, and put his own sleeve in front of his nose and mouth.

"Perhaps we should step outside to give this time to work without choking ourselves?" I said.

We did, and Ben called Nick, but he wasn't in his office and his cell phone was turned off. "Which means he is in a meeting," Ben said.

"Or he's avoiding you," I said. Ben looked worried.

I went back inside and found, to my surprise, that the finish had already bubbled up. It came up fairly easily, too, with my new scraper. I scraped it onto an old news-paper, which I rolled and discarded outside the garage to minimize the fumes. What I was left with, without the horrible handles and the horrible green finish, was basically a square box done in some pale wood that might be poplar but was more likely some derivative of bamboo.

"Would you be terribly offended if I told you it still doesn't look like much?"

"No," I said, but I had an idea. There was an almost imperceptible gold indentation around the top of the lip. The wood was good, or at least unflawed and clean. There was no reason at all that I shouldn't be able to make this into whatever I wanted to. And the lion-mouth pulls I'd bought came to mind. If I stained the trunk a convincing mahogany or even walnut, highlighted that indentation with gold in a convincing enough way that it looked like a broken or just worn out inlay of gold wire, and then put the lion-mouth pulls in, no one would know this wasn't a nineteenth-century piece.

Oh, I wouldn't sell it as such. There is a fine line between faking and forgery. But it had been my experience that in choosing between a truly good piece that looked so-so and an utter fake—identified as such—that looked like the real thing and that fit with modern taste and decor—which the simple lines of this trunk did—people would always pay more for the fake. And I thought this piece might more than pay for itself.

I cleaned it carefully—because even a hint of refinishing paste left behind would ruin the final finish—then gave it a coat of mahogany stain. Now I'd let it dry, give it another coat, let it dry again, and, finally, I thought, give it several coats of hand-applied polyurethane oil finish. Because this had no pretensions to authenticity, there was absolutely no reason not to use it, and people nowadays liked that their furniture wasn't ruined when they failed to use a coaster.

I was humming softly to myself as I finished applying the stain and looked up to see Ben frowning down at me. "Okay," he said. "So now it's a dark-wood box. It still doesn't look like much."

"Hush now," I said. "Wait till it's done."

He looked doubtful, which just goes to show that the man didn't learn from experience. He had known me how long? And he still didn't know if I saw a way of making something look good, I could and would carry it off.

I was about to make a pointed remark in that direction when my mom came in. "Dyce, there is something in the house you'll need to look at."

All of a sudden, my happiness vanished. Look, you can't live with your parents that long—and certainly you can't live with my parents that long—without knowing the tone of voice that denotes truly bad stuff. And Mom had that tone. Also, her lips were all tight and stuff.

"Oh, no," I said. "Who did he kill?"

"Who?"

"E, of course. Who did he kill? Did he set something on fire?"

"Well, no," Mom said. "He did hit Fluffy on the nose with a coloring book."

"Oh, I'm sorry," I said, while inwardly I wondered what Fluffy had done to deserve it.

"Yes, it was uncalled for, but he said he had to make her let go of Pythagoras's tail."

"What?"

"She was being playful," my mom said and sniffed. "But E thought she was trying to eat Pythagoras."

"No," I said. Since I'd seen Fluffy try to do exactly that before, I didn't know why my mother thought she wasn't trying to do it just now.

"Yes. At most she was tasting him. I mean, there was almost no blood."

"Uh oh," Ben said from behind me, in his semi-official capacity as Greek chorus in these exchanges.

"But then E insisted on looking for the hydrogen peroxide, and I told him it was at the back of the hall closet."

"Uh-oh, uh-oh," Ben said.

Mentally I said, *Yes, thank you, Mr. Colm. This has been noted.* But aloud I said, "And then."

"And then," my mother said, tightening her lips, "he found the dresses and . . . objects."

This sounded utterly ominous. I said, "Knives? Guns? Poison vials?"

Mom looked shocked. "What? No. Just . . . You'd better come and see."

I went to see, followed closely by Ben, who frankly wouldn't be pried away, not even with knives, guns, or poison vials. We went up and into the kitchen and then to the hall closet.

The hall closet, strictly speaking, wasn't. It had, once upon a time, I think, been a dressing room between Mom's room and the stairs. But it had been used as a sort of catchall, probably before Dad inherited the house from his grandmother. When I was a child, it had been a fascinating place to find the unexpected, ranging from old cleaning implements, like a rug-beating paddle, to half-finished embroidery from my great-grandmother's era and, one glorious time, a wig that I had used to make a giant hair-spider to freak out my classmates.

It also had, close to the entrance, a couple of shelves where Mom kept the more prosaic cleaning implements and first-aid stuff.

The closet door was thrown open, and E was in there somewhere, talking to Pythagoras. "Yeah, I know," he told Pythagoras, in that disconcerting way he had of making it sound like Pythagoras could talk back to him. "I think it's cool, too. But that door at the back, I'm sure it leads to another world."

Now, thoroughly spooked, I called out, "E?"

My son emerged from a narrow passage between an ironing board and a vacuum cleaner. "Come and see, Mom." At least he didn't sound like what was back there was dire.

I went to see, with Ben right behind me, looming over me and breathing down my neck.

Past the stuff, there . . . there was a door. I vaguely remembered seeing it. Mom had always told me it probably had been a door to some exterior stairs. Since it seemed to be an exterior door and, moreover, since it was very firmly locked and I'd never been able to get it to open, I'd eventually come to accept it as another wall. I will confess I had spent a couple of happy summers collecting old keys and trying them in the lock, but none had ever worked.

Now E had turned on an battery-operated lantern and, clearly, had managed to open the lock. The door stood open and inside . . .

It was a closet. A proper closet, or perhaps it would be called a wardrobe. There were shelves at the top, with boxes. There were dresses hanging in the middle. And on the bottom there were . . . a pram, a trunk, and a few wooden boxes. At the back of that, there was another door, smaller, and this one almost for sure an external door. It was locked, though E had a wire in the hole.

"Don't open that," I said.

He looked up at me.

"It's probably just a wall behind there, but it might just be some boards, and I'm sure that leads out, and you'll just fall down the side of the house. Don't open it."

"But . . . There could be another world," he protested.

"Oh, there will be another world all right, if you fall and die," Ben said. "Come out of there. Stop fooling with that door. There's nothing behind that. And there's no more fantasy movies for you, young man."

The little wretch, of course, listened to Ben as he hadn't listened to me. He and the wretched cat, with a bloody tip of tail, went past me and toward Ben.

"I thought you might want to sell these. I mean, I assume there's a market. And I thought you'd want to use them to get money, you know, to furnish your new house, or something," Mom called from outside the area. "And maybe you can fix that pram. I'm sure it's an antique."

I was sure it was an antique, too. I was afraid to touch anything for fear it would dissolve into dust. And offering me all of this perfectly fit in with Mom's casual generosity. She didn't have a use for it, so she didn't see why I shouldn't have all of it.

But then, something caught my eye, at the extreme left side of the closet. It was a dress, and it had a veil with it, on the same hanger, and it looked like . . .

I touched it, afraid it would go up in a cloud of dust, but it wasn't even that dusty in there, because the door had apparently been sealed pretty tightly. I reached over and removed the hanger and looked at it.

The dress looked like cream silk, though it might have been somewhat yellowed with age. It was so simple that it looked almost severe. The only ornament was a belt embroidered with tiny pearls in the shape of roses and leaves. And it looked like my exact size.

"Try it on," Ben said.

"Uh . . . It will probably tear . . ."

"If it feels too fragile, you can stop. But if you can, try it on."

I went into the room that Ben had used the night before and put the dress on. It not only didn't tear, but it seemed to be at least as solid as any other dress I'd ever put on. It was almost a miracle. Of course, judging from the smell, great-grandmother had double ensured that the moths wouldn't eat it.

I put the veil on, awkwardly, since it was the sort of veil that covered both the back and the face. The dress had mutton sleeves, or at least I think it's what they are called. The sleeves fit tightly from wrist to elbow, and there was an infinity of little white pearl buttons keeping it cinched. I buttoned every third, just enough to keep it in place, then put the belt on and hooked it in the back, and walked out, pulling the skirt up a little, because I think it hadn't been designed for someone wearing completely flat tennis shoes.

"Perfect," Ben said.

Which unfortunately was exactly my idea. I now knew where I'd got my figure, since apparently Great-Grandma and I were not only of the same general size, but a perfect match, line for line. "We can make it a Victorian wedding," he said. "I know this place in Denver where we can rent period-appropriate tuxes and hats and all. What?" he said, at my look. "There was this party Peter gave a couple of years ago . . . Anyway, it will be great. I'll research the flowers, and we'll have the bouquets done to fit with the time. And maybe one of those other dresses can be copied for your bridesmaids."

"Supposing I ever get any," I said.

"Oh, come on. If there are pretty Victorian dresses involved, you'll have to keep my sister, Ellie, away with barbed wire. She's a member of several reenactor societies, from the Society for Creative Anachronism to various Victorian and heritage societies, and it's all for the dresses. Heck, she probably knows people who can make the bridesmaids' dresses."

We went back into the closet and took a tally. One of the boxes contained several hundred bone buttons, which Ben told me people who made reproduction dresses paid unreal amounts for. The other boxes contained bits of handmade lace, pearls for trimming, and various other bits and pieces of female frippery that could, probably—to be honest—if sold, furnish my house. The dresses included several morning and afternoon dresses and various other garments that must have made Great-Grandma the envy of society women in Goldport when she was young. Though truly, since at that time the society in Goldport consisted of a few pioneers and half a dozen Native American tribes—at least as far as my mental image of local history went—that wouldn't have been difficult.

However, when I told Mom that, she shook her head. "Oh, my," she said. "No. Your great-grandmother was British, and when she married your great-grandfather, he brought her to live here in some luxury. These were probably things she brought in her trousseau and that were either out of fashion in this area or that she found she had no occasion of using, society being much simpler here."

It was amazing how you could not know anything about your ancestors, even four generations back. No one had ever told me my great-grandmother was British, not even what her name was. My dad just called her Grandma. And, of course, my dad never remembered any details about people.

As Ben picked up a beautiful pink gown, much along the same lines as my dress, and said, "This will do perfectly for the bridesmaids," I thought I heard a distant scream, but I didn't give it much thought. I mean, look, the bookstore is downtown. So it's in one of the quieter streets of downtown, which means there is less traffic and general disturbance than in the outright commercial areas. But there are still people who scream for no reason.

Besides, this sounded like my dad, and it meant that he was probably trying to dissuade someone from buying a book, which happened at least twice a day and sometimes more. If he didn't have extra copies of a book, he became outright possessive about it and tried to dissuade potential clients.

So I changed back into my jeans and T-shirt, which seemed like quite a bit of a letdown after the fancy stuff, and we put the dresses away, and I closed the door, making sure it didn't latch. "I'll look on eBay," I told Mom, "and see what that stuff is worth. And yes, I probably can rebuild the pram. Seems to be mostly the leather that's damaged, and I can replace or fix that."

I was thinking warm thoughts of actually getting at

least most of the furniture for the house, so that Cas couldn't say he'd done everything for the new place.

We went into the kitchen, E explaining to me how he'd picked the lock and how easy it was. But the talk of wires, barrels, and tumblers sounded more like something from a bar than something relating to a closet, so I listened with half an ear.

Pythagoras sat on E's lap, while E ate candy corn. Mom had apparently locked Fluffy in her room. Not, mind you, to keep her from eating Pythagoras but because Mom was afraid that E might hurt Fluffy, or that I might hurt Fluffy's feelings. So we were in relative peace while Ben looked around in the various cabinets and made me and himself hot chocolate.

Then he called his sister, Ellie, and had some trouble dissuading her from coming right on over to look at the dresses. He promised we'd bring them by this evening.

And then, looking somewhat worried, he called Nick. I could see his expression clear as Nick answered. He walked away from me, his hand cupped around the phone, talking into it, from which I gathered relationship stuff was being said. Ben hates to have anyone hear him sound mushy. He stood by the kitchen window, looking out, and spoke almost in whispers. He smiled once or twice and nodded once.

Then, suddenly, his demeanor changed. He straightened his shoulders. He said, audibly, "Oh, no. Really?"

He turned around. "Dyce, they are looking for Winston de Leon, but he seems to have disappeared, and they think he might be looking for you."

"What?" I said, getting up.

"It's like this. They traced the sales to the garage sale and all, way back, and it seems that . . ." He took a deep breath, then hung up the phone and put it in his pocket. "They're leaving Rafiel and some other people looking for him and following leads, but they're coming here, because Cas thinks he might be coming here, and he doesn't want us alone."

"Why should he be coming here?" I asked.

"Nothing very definite," Ben said. "Or at least . . ." He shrugged. "He said something about looking for you. Has said so in the past. But mostly because Cas thinks you attract trouble like a magnet."

"It's not my fault," I protested.

"No," Ben said. "And we know it's not. But Dyce, it is true. You can't help attracting trouble. And trouble finds you even when you're hiding."

My mother, who had opened her laptop, looked up with a faint smile. "We sold another collectible edition of Dorothy L. Sayers," she said. "Really what people will give away or throw away or . . . forget, like those dresses your great-grandmother left behind, is just astonishing."

Mom was in a world of her own, and we weren't going to be able to call her attention to the present world or present concerns. It was just as well. I wasn't absolutely sure I wanted to worry her. Just six months ago, a madwoman had shot up the bookstore and hit one of the pipes in the bathroom. Between the water damage and the bullet hole through a couple of shelves, Father hadn't let me come into the store for a solid month. So it was best not to alarm Mom.

I left her blogging, and Ben and I went down to the landing, midstaircase, to wait for Cas and presumably Nick.

Who arrived, just minutes later.

CHAPTER 25

Following Inquiries

They came up the staircase side by side, causing it to shake beneath their feet. Of unspoken accord, Ben and I turned and walked up the stairs and to the kitchen. Yeah, we might be in love with these guys, but that didn't mean we wanted to be on the staircase when it fell.

Mom barely glanced up from her laptop as they came in. Pythagoras went and nuzzled Cas's ankle. He followed us to the parlor, as Ben and I led the two policemen there because I had no wish to talk around Mom.

E followed us with a fistful of candy corn that he tried to get into his mouth, with mixed results. Although he managed to have a mouthful of candy corn, he also left a trail on Mom's carpet. Which was just as well, in case we got lost and needed to go back.

The parlor, or living room, as Mom liked to call it—but which was more of a parlor, since it was nowhere near an external entrance—had been the scene of my attempt to play lion tamer, when I'd made the first Fluffy jump through a hoop of fire. Unfortunately, the hoop had been Mom's quilting frame. She'd been into quilting at the time, having been deeply into some quilting mystery series. And since the quilt had also caught fire . . .

Well, after the fire department had come and the disaster-recovery people and Fluffy, okay except for her fur being mostly missing, was found and taken to the vet, Mom had finally gotten to decorate the parlor her way, instead of living with the furniture, wallpaper, and carpet chosen by Dad's grandmother.

Now that I'd seen that lady's taste in dresses, I almost regretted it. Mom's taste was okay but bland. This might have been part of a suite in any discount hotel. The carpet was royal blue; the walls were cream. There were various family pictures on the wall, and the sofas were white and prim. Over the fireplace was a picture of Ben and I, in prom attire, blown up to about twice life-size. Nick, his hand on Ben's, pulled him toward it. I wasn't sure why, and at the moment I didn't much care, since Cas was kissing me for good.

"You look great," he said. "Except for your hair. You'll either have to cut it all short, or we'll have to find you a wig for the wedding. Otherwise our children will grow up believing Mom was some sort of very strange goth."

I looked up at him. I loved being enclosed in his arms like this. "I'd just make a spider out of the wig," I said. "So it must be short hair. I'll go see a hairdresser next week. For now I just want to get the business back on its feet and, I guess, get us some furniture for the new house."

I was so excited about the find in the closet that I poured

it all out to him before I remembered why they had come over. It finally hit me, as we sat on the sofa and he held my hand. "I was so worried about you," he said. "Yesterday."

This brought me back to de Leon and whatever danger I might be in. "Do you really think he'll come here?" I asked.

"Oh, yeah," Cas said. "Almost sure. See, it was him who told Sebastian about you, but he made it sound like you were harassing Ashton and trying to get a story to sell to some publication or other. He sold him the idea that because your parents owned a mystery bookstore, it was likely that you would sell the story to a true-crime publisher."

"But . . ." I said. "Why would he care that I was asking Ashton stuff?"

"Well, for one, because he didn't want Ashton to find out what had happened to his wife. We still don't know what that was, by the way, but the signs aren't good. That stain on the table—a piece was thrown clear and far enough that we could analyze it, undamaged by fire. Pure luck, of course, but it is human blood. We still haven't determined if it's the same type as Maria's blood, though it probably is. I mean . . . The chair"—he took a deep breath—"that she took with her was the same as the chair we found in the meth condo."

"Oh, no," I said.

"Oh, yes. Plus the garage sale guy . . . Remember your being utterly puzzled that he managed to make a living from selling that junk? And how many times you told me you just couldn't believe there were enough people willing to buy that stuff to make him a profit?"

"Yeah?" I said.

"Well, there aren't. Turns out he's running a side

business in drugs. He actually used to be the owner of a well-known electronics store here in town, but . . . he got a drug habit, and fell through the cracks, and eventually ended up working the supply side of business."

"And de Leon supplied him with meth?" I asked.

"Bingo. So when you came around asking about the other stuff de Leon had sold him—and, by the way, he did get a check in Ashton's name, because he wanted the garage sale guy to think that Ashton was the one selling him stuff. Long story. He had a check-cashing account at a service— got it with a fake ID. Anyway, when you asked the garage sale guy about the table, he got alarmed and put some pressure on de Leon, and apparently you paid for the table with a check, which, Dyce, was unwise, so the garage sale guy knew your name and address. Finding out who you were and all didn't take long, and de Leon first tried to send Sebastian after you. Part of it, of course, was that somehow you'd managed to make de Leon suspicious when you parked on that street and went to see Ben's friends."

"So he sent Sebastian after me."

"Yes. I don't think you know, but the Ashtons are what we call stray collectors, but they don't collect stray animals, which is annoying but arguably safer. No, they collect human beings with problems or down on their luck, and they bring them home and look after them." He shrugged. "It appears that Maria's parents did this, too, and never had a bad experience. So Sebastian used to be on drugs, and he has a record—"

"And he set the bomb?" I said.

"Oh, no. His record is mostly for completely innocuous stuff. Vagrancy and loitering and such. He was living on the streets for some time, after dropping out of college, but he says he's been clean for the last two years and it's probably true. He has no arrests in that time, and he has had several jobs, mostly of the contract and short-term type. He's also going back to college in spring and has got in touch with his family, but . . ."

"But you think he—"

"No. Once he explained the situation to us, he told us de Leon had given him a story about your selling Maria's disappearance to a true-crime publisher. He was only trying to protect his friends, and, frankly, he seems like a good guy. But here's the thing: he said that among the strays that they picked up, he was worried about de Leon, who still seemed to be on what Sebastian charmingly called the hard stuff. He said he also got the impression de Leon was using the Ashtons, instead of making a bona fide attempt at straightening out his life. Also . . ."

He hesitated and looked around. By the fireplace, Ben and Nick were talking earnestly with their heads together. I hoped this meant that Ben had conquered his fears and that they were going to make up. Not because I was a romantic—though I was—but because I really, really, really wanted to avoid any further intrusions of the mummy or the zombie into our lives. And besides, staying at my parents was trying enough. Staying at my parents with Ben might lead me to squeeze out of the window in the attic and onto the ground below, considering the whole thing a world well lost.

"This is the thing we have no way to verify," Cas said. "And if it weren't for the fact that the piece of the chair was in the burned-out condo, I'd have some doubts about taking it, but . . ."

"But?"

"But Sebastian says that Maria had told him something that led him to believe she was afraid of de Leon. He didn't give it much thought because Maria, having been diagnosed with narcolepsy, was on various antidepressants, as her doctor tried to find the right dosage to control the problem. As such, she was having mood swings, and she couldn't, quite, make sense of reality at times. So he thought she was just imagining things. But now, with evidence piling up that something terrible might have happened to her, he is afraid because the last time he saw her, he asked de Leon to stay with her for a couple of hours. He didn't like doing it, but he had to go out and do a job, or he would have lost that employer, who provided him with a steady stream of income. He owns a Laundromat that needed some pipe repair done. Yeah, we checked. So he left Maria with this guy for a couple of hours, because they were all afraid she would fall and hurt herself. Apparently, if the medicine is wrong, it can happen. Actually falling over or falling asleep standing up is often a symptom of narcolepsy, apparently. So he had to leave her with someone, even though Ashton had taken the kids to the doctor, since they were all sharing a cold.

"Well, when he came back, neither of them was in the house, and the table and chair and the other stuff was gone, and then, when he tracked de Leon down, he made a confused excuse, and Sebastian assumed that he'd gone off to make a deal, which Sebastian suspected him of doing all the time, anyway, and while he was out, Maria had taken advantage of being alone and left with her stuff, possibly in a U-Haul or something. Since they thought this was just a temporary aberration, and she'd come to her senses and realize she really was not a burden and her husband and kids loved her, they didn't tell anyone. And then, when a few weeks had passed . . . Well, neither they nor us could get a very precise idea of what had happened that day. I mean, people don't pay attention, you know?"

I knew. I was often surprised by how little people paid attention to odd events around him. "This still doesn't explain who blew up my shed," I said. "Or why you're here."

"Well, we traced de Leon. This is not his real name, by the way. We're not at all sure what his real name is, as he has something like ten aliases. He seems to be in his late twenties, and possibly, once having dropped out of college, to have drifted from place to place, living in odd and semi-legal ways. Anyway, what we could trace was a history of bombs, arson, and other . . . things involving explosives. And as far as the explosive guys can tell, that bomb in your shed, stuck under the table, had a timer that looks like other bombings he's been suspected in."

"How can he have that kind of record and be walking around?" I asked.

"Well, because it was never *definite* enough," Cas said. "There were maybe some indications he was guilty of this or that, but it was never clear enough for anyone to arrest him and bring him to justice. There were causes for suspicion but never for arrest, and he has the sort of associates who aren't particularly eager to help the police with their inquiries. If you know what I mean."

I knew what he meant. It seems like the easiest way to get away with crimes is to be either very rich or very poor and have a somewhat shady background. If you're rich, you'll of course be able to make whatever you do look perfectly legitimate, by dint of lawyers and various other tricks. If you're very poor and somewhat shady, they're likely not to be able to find anyone to testify against you, and besides, you can just pick up roots, move to another town, get a fake ID, and for all intents and purposes stop existing as the person the police were looking for.

"We've shown his picture to the few neighbors around the empty condos. With other pictures as decoys, of course, and they picked him out as having been in the neighborhood. We've identified the burnt remains, and it was one of his two roommates. The evidence is inescapable."

"Except?"

"Except he's disappeared. When I called you this morning, we were already trying to find him. And we have to find him, Dyce. I'm hoping that he means to come here and take revenge on you, since it's too late to silence the whole thing."

"You're *hoping?*" I said, feeling horribly betrayed.

"Well, yes," Cas said. "Because at this point we have to figure out what he did with Maria and where he hid the body. If he comes here, it will be difficult, but there's at least a good chance of catching him. If he takes a bus out of town, we might never find her body or know what happened, and think what that will do to her husband and kids."

"Oh," I said.

Which is when we heard Dad scream. And this time it sounded really bad. Like he'd just woken up from his semi-permanent daydream and found a monster in the store.

CHAPTER 26

Help!

The scream echoed from downstairs, and I was on my feet and running out the kitchen door and down the rickety stairs before even waiting to see if anyone was following. This is a big character flaw, see.

They did studies, apparently, on toddlers some years ago, and found that most toddlers, being sensible or at least conditioned for survival, run away from scary things. But then there is something like 1 percent of toddlers who will run toward scary things. I have no proof of this, and I doubt I could get a coherent report out of my mother or father—who would probably confuse me with some mystery character—but I'd always thought I was in that second group.

I was dimly aware of heavy footsteps behind me, and I assumed that Cas, and possibly Ben and Nick, were following me, but I was flying on automatic, all the way down the stairs and around the side path, to the front of the bookstore.

The door was closed, the way it normally was, but with a sign on it that said, *Come in, we're open.*

Everything looked as it normally did, from the two white wicker chairs on the porch—people actually used them in the summer but not so much when it was cold, as it was now—to the bookshelf of free books, which were the ones my parents rejected for trade. There were people who came by every week and gleaned reading material from that shelf.

I put my hand on the doorknob, shaking.

"Dyce, damn it." I expected it to be Cas, but to my surprise, it was Nick, and he was reaching over and pulling my hand away from the doorknob. Cas and Ben were right behind him, coming up the porch, in what they probably thought was a semblance of stealth. Ah! They still sounded like small elephants, or perhaps large ones.

"I have to see if it's locked," I said.

"No, you don't," Nick whispered furiously. "Get behind me."

Since he forcibly moved me around his body and behind him, I didn't have much choice but to obey, as he reached over, opening the door, and staying to the side, in case someone shot.

No shots erupted, but that's when I realized Nick, and Cas, too, had his gun out. "What?" I said. "What are you doing? You can't do that!" I was whispering, too, of course, because you always whisper around people who are whispering. Must be Basic Human Conditioning 101. "If you shoot a book, Dad will go nuts. He will go insane."

"Shh," Cas said, and, in turn, moved me around his body, and to stand in front of Ben, who put his hands on my shoulders, physically restraining me.

Nick and Cas went in, while Ben held me outside the door. I could hear them moving around inside, but listen, that store was a labyrinth. Forget minotaurs; my father could probably have hidden an entire village in there or perhaps a bunch of Tibetan monks. Considering how the bookshelves forked from each other, only bread crumbs or a bunch of string could ensure you came out all right again. Besides there were a hundred and one places where they could be ambushed and shot. Or worse. In my mind was an image of a bomb. I figured de Leon could time those bombs, or perhaps give them a signal to make them explode. I'd heard of terrorists using cell phones to set off bombs. What would stop this twit from using Dad as bait and then setting off a bomb and killing Cas and Nick? And as much as I would miss Cas, I also didn't want to deal with Ben if he had to get over Nick's death. No.

As my dad's voice yelled, "Help!" I pulled away from Ben's hold.

"Dyce," he said.

"No, you listen. Those two don't know the store. Remember how easy it is to get lost in there? I have to go in. I can find my dad. They can't. And if de Leon sets off a bomb . . ."

Ben became visibly paler, probably envisioning mince-Nick. "All right," he said. "I know the store almost as well as you do. We go in."

Which is how we ended up in there, walking around, following the sound of Dad's cries for help, which were echoed, immediately after, by furious whispering as, I suspected, de Leon told him to be quiet or else.

Okay, it was stupid, as we could easily have ended up shot if Nick or Cas had seen a glimpse of something or someone moving and shot first and asked questions later. But Nick and Cas were properly trained police officers, and I was sure they didn't want to deal with the administrative penalties—let alone the administrative paperwork!—for improperly shooting someone. So they'd want to make sure that they were shooting the right person.

Which is why, as I almost collided with Cas, he said, "Dyce, damn it," then, looking behind me, "And Ben. Just great. Nick," he called, in a stage whisper. "The footsteps were Dyce and Ben."

Nick appeared around the next bookcase and said, in the same sort of furious whisper, "Why?"

"Because you two don't know the bookstore," I said. "We do, Ben and I. We used to play here when we were little. I'll find my dad. Follow me."

They didn't look particularly happy about it, but really what could they do? So they followed me as I followed the periodic screams for help.

I half-expected this to lead to the kitchen, or the restroom, but no. It led, instead, to a little door, at the back, in what I thought was a closet beneath the old stairs that led up to the second floor. I had only the vaguest of memories of Mom and Dad storing the rarest books in that closet, the kind of books that sold for five hundred dollars and up. As everyone will probably understand, they'd never given me a key or given me much chance to explore in there.

Just as we got to the door, Dad screamed again—this

time sounding very loud, since we were only separated by a thin pine door.

"Dad?" I said, half in a stage whisper. Then I dove out of the way, as I thought de Leon might be in there with him, and he might have a gun and shoot through the door.

But no shot followed, and I thought I was being silly. This was my father, after all. Just because he was screaming for help didn't mean that he was in there against his will or with anyone else. It was quite possible, not to say probable, that my father was in there clutching a rare and collectible book to his chest and barricading the door against potential buyers.

"Dad," I said, getting up and getting as close to the door as possible. "What is wrong?"

"He wants to blow me up," he said. "Help. Get me out of here."

"Who wants to blow you up?" I asked, as my heart beat very fast, because this didn't seem like random locking himself in against the depredations of customers.

"I do," a voice said from behind us.

CHAPTER 27

The Smile on the Face of the Tiger

We turned around and there, at the corner of the bookcase that divided the new from the used part of the store, stood the man who was almost for sure Winston de Leon.

He matched the description, being skinny, not particularly prepossessing, with large bugged-out eyes and blond hair. "I do," he said again, and made a dramatic gesture, like a villain in a pantomime.

The men immediately, and with possibly foolish chivalry, formed a wall between me and this creature, while Cas turned back and whispered, "Go now. Go get help. Get out of here."

I had no clue what help he thought I could get, but he probably just wanted to get me out of the store. I wanted to get out of the store, too, but not leaving them behind, possibly to get blown to bits.

I managed to peer between Cas and Nick and see the guy wasn't carrying a gun. Instead, he had a cell phone in his hand. "If I press this button," he said, showing his finger just above a button, "it will automatically dial the bomb that's in that closet with the old man, and it will all go up in flames. This place"—he gestured around—"will burn like a tinderbox."

"But then you'll die, too," Cas said.

De Leon shrugged his skinny shoulders. "What do I care? You guys have destroyed everything I've built over time—all my contacts here in town, and everything I've worked so hard to do. I'd have to move again, with nothing, and you guys would probably be after me still, from town to town. All because that stupid bitch fell on the table and hit her head."

"Maria?" Cas asked, alert. "Maria Ashton?"

"Yeah, the Ashton bitch. Accusing me of all this stuff." He sniffed, violently, the kind of sniff that was part a need to clear the nasal passages and part disdain. He threw his head back, making a bit of blond hair flop backward and away from watery blue eyes, which looked like they would, with a little more effort, pop out of their sockets. "That I'd used her husband's name," he said, in a squeaky voice that he doubtless felt was a fair imitation of a woman's voice. "And that I could get him in trouble. And that I hadn't gone clean as I'd told them I would. As if anyone really expected me to go clean, just because they'd let me crash on their sofa and gave me food." He sniffed again. "There's hundreds of thousands of dollars to be made on the street, and they were always on me about stupid stuff like learning a trade. As bad as my parents." He sniffed again. "I don't want to be a menial laborer, like that idiot Sebastian. I want to be rich. I want to have my own place, and, like, a mansion, full of hot women, and a butler, and my own private jet and stuff."

He paused, and the finger hovered over the button. "But if I can't have that, then I'll go and take all of you with me."

"What do you expect to get from this?" Cas asked, and this time it was Nick who turned around and whispered, "Go, now, Dyce. We're going to need help."

"I expect you guys to arrange for me to get out of here without anyone bothering me and to get me a car to take me to the airport, and a plane ride somewhere. London. Yeah, I think London."

I wasn't sure if England had mutual extradition agreements with us, but I was almost sure they did, and I was almost sure that he'd be arrested as soon as he landed. "I'll give the phone to the stewardess over the ocean," he said.

And this, too, was misguided, because of course the moment he was out of the store, we'd be opening that door, and getting the bomb away from Dad.

"Help!" Dad yelled, and this time hit the door, as if he had thrown himself against it.

"Tell him to stop," de Leon yelled. "The bomb is on the floor, and he might step on it in the dark."

Which was a problem. The other problem was that I was almost sure the little weasel would push that button long before he was on the plane. And what if he sneezed or something.

Ben, between Cas and Nick, making a bulwark of defense in front of me, though he didn't even have a gun, turned around and whispered, "Dyce, go. Find help."

And this time, I went and found help.

CHAPTER 28

An Unlikely Savior

I tiptoed out to a corner of a bookcase, then got on my hands and knees and crawled behind the rows of bookcases to the door. On my hands and knees, because then it was far less likely that de Leon, looking at eye level, would see even a hint of movement.

Once I got to the door, I ran hell for leather down the porch and around the house. In my head, not very clear, was the idea that I would get E, and that E would go into the store and open the door with his magic lock-picking skills. I wasn't absolutely sure how we'd manage to do this with de Leon right there, but there had to be a way. Unlock the door, get Dad out, or even better, get the bomb out, and throw it to the bottom of the garden. And then, while Cas and Nick grabbed the little twerp, have quiet hysterics.

I didn't count on finding E just around the corner,

looking angelic, with his hands in his pockets. He perked up when he saw me. "Come," he said, pulling me toward the house.

"No," I said. "You have to come this way and open the door to rescue Granddad."

He shook his head. "No. I heard. But you have to come, the other way."

"How could you hear?" I said. "Were you in there?"

"No," he said. "The other way."

I had no idea what he was talking about, but one thing was for sure. Oh, of course you can get toddlers to do whatever you want to, if you use force. You can grab them and throw them over your shoulder and carry them anywhere. And you can physically restrain them and keep them from eating chocolate, or setting fire to the cat.

What you can't do is get a toddler to use a very specific and specialized skill that requires him to think, unless you get his buy-in. And I knew my son well enough to know that I wasn't going to convince him to pick a lock unless I got his buy-in.

"Okay," I said. "I'll go with you, but then you have to come with me and help me open the door to get Granddad out of there."

E shook his head. "That would be stupid," he said. "The bad guy would see me, and he wouldn't let me do it. He would blow up the place."

When I was first friends with Ben, his parents, who were—and are—Catholic and very religious, used to take me to mass with them. Since my parents weren't particularly religious—though Dad's grandmother had been well known for her work in the Unitarian Church here in town—his mother had taken it upon herself to teach me to pray. It had never taken. I once read some writer or other who said that people's ideas of God were based on themselves. I don't know. I think, myself, people's ideas of God are based on their parents. They extrapolate someone benevolent and disinterested who watches over them.

Well, if that was the case, it would explain why I never got my idea of God to jell. Because the closest I could come to understanding God would be as a man who wandered vaguely around the universe, looking for the book he'd left facedown somewhere and muttering stuff concerning the latest mystery he'd read. Also, possibly getting my name wrong.

However, as I followed E around the house, hoping there would really be something he could do to rescue my father, and unable to imagine what that would be, I found myself praying. Really praying. *God, if you get me out of this, and get Cas and Nick and Ben and Dad out of this, I promise never to be thoughtless again.*

We went up the stairs, into the kitchen. Neither my mother, nor Fluffy, nor Pythagoras were anywhere to be seen. I wondered if Fluffy had eaten Mom and Pythagoras. Perhaps E's plan was to take Fluffy to the bookstore, and get her to eat through the door, and get her to eat the bomb.

I promise I won't pick stupid arguments.

Up the stairs, to the middle floor of my parents' home, the third floor of the building, where the bedrooms were located. *I promise I'll learn to cook and clean, and I'll never again bug Ben about his behavior. And I promise I won't complain that my parents are so weird.*

The door to the closet was open, and Mom was . . .

inside the door at the back of the closet, only she was only visible from the waist up, and my first thought was that Mom was being swallowed, then she emerged fully, pulling Dad behind her.

I stared. I opened my mouth wide and stared at them as they emerged from the door that I'd assumed led outward, out the side of the house.

"There's a stairs," E said, smugly. "And the stairs go into the closet where Granddad was. So everything is okay now."

Like hell it was. Mom said, "You see, I realized your father's cries were coming from in there, and then E opened the door, and—"

I grabbed the lantern from the floor and went into the closet, moving past them.

"Sherlockia!" Dad said. "Where are you going? There's a bomb down there."

"Yeah," I said. "And there's my boyfriend and my best friend, and his boyfriend, too." And, to Dad's look of incomprehension, "And all those books, Dad. If the bomb explodes, the bookstore will go up in smoke."

Dad started toward me then, but I said, "No. Go back. Take E, Mom, and the two cats, and go to the garage. And stay there. Inside. With the doors closed. I'm going to try to fix things. Leave every door open all the way out to the stairs." I looked at them. "Go, now."

They went.

CHAPTER 29

Running toward Danger

Lantern in hand, hurrying down the incredibly narrow circular stairs, all the while wondering why and when it had been built, I realized I was running toward danger again. As I got down further, I could hear Cas's voice and de Leon's, but I couldn't make out their words.

It wasn't that the words weren't clear. They probably were, and I was fairly sure that this was why and how E and my mom had heard what was going on. But, you see, the blood was pounding in my ears. I also felt vaguely queasy, and there was this buzz that seemed to be in my brain.

I knew that at any minute, as I was running down, de Leon could get tired of waiting and push the button and send everything up. At least Mom and Dad and E and the cats would be safe. The garage was cement block, with a solid roof. There was very little chance of their getting hurt, even if the house went up in flames.

I ran all the way down the stairs to where another door stood open—my son had been busy indeed—and past that door, a little room lined with shelves, the shelves lined with books.

The bomb was obvious, right by the door, on the floor, as de Leon said it would be: an untidy package wrapped in duct tape and with wires and things coming out of it.

I grabbed it carefully with my free hand and clutched it to my chest; then I ran up the stairs, holding the lantern in my other hand and praying under my breath that I wouldn't trip.

Out of the back door, then out of the closet, I dropped the lantern, and now I held the bomb with both hands, expecting that at any second it would blow. At least, even if it blew now, it was unlikely it would kill the guys downstairs. Oh, it might cause a fire up here, but they'd still have the time to get away.

Weirdly, as scared of dying as I was, this didn't seem nearly as scary as taking the guys with me if I went. At least I suspected that death by explosion would be fairly painless, or at least instant, and then the guys . . . Well, they'd figure it out. And Cas would probably keep an eye out for E so that All-ex couldn't drive him completely insane. I hoped.

My mouth was dry, and though I knew I was running—running through the house, to the open door of the kitchen—I felt as though I was going very slowly and as if everything around me had gone very slow and very quiet, too.

It was like one of those dream sequences in movies, where the protagonist runs through a not quite real landscape. Perhaps the bomb had already gone off, and now I was a ghost, running this circuit forever, trying to make it to the back door.

The fresher, cooler outside air hit me in the face like a reviving slap, and I was suddenly aware that I was on the staircase, and looking down at the backyard, holding a bomb. A bomb that could go off at any minute.

My parents' backyard is huge. We hold the Mystery Lovers picnic there in the summer. The garage is at one end of it, but the other end is not only completely clear, but is also far away from the neighbors' house and their garage. There used to be an oak tree there, when I was little, one of those sprawling, massive trees, where one can hang swings and in whose branches one can build tree houses.

But I'd long since blown that to smithereens in an accident involving a bottle of gasoline and a grill.

There weren't even any windows on the garage on that side. And the garage was solid.

So I took a deep breath . . . and let the bomb fly.

De Leon had been right that it might go off by being bumped. Either that or, I thought, muzzily, de Leon had pushed the button at the exact same time that the bomb hit the ground, down there, sending up a shower of earth clods and pebbles that rattled all around me like hail.

My legs felt like jelly. I sat down and waited for the sirens.

CHAPTER 30

Alley Alley All Go Free

I don't know how long I sat there. There were indeed sirens, screaming their approach from all directions. Fire and police. I don't do things by half, no sirree; when it comes to tying up the emergency services of Goldport, I've always managed to tie up all of them at once. It's a gift; what can I say?

I sat on the stairs, and after a while, I let my head rest against the side rail. The backyard became a swarm of policemen and firemen, though there wasn't much for the firemen to do, except put out the straggling grass fire. And the policemen . . . I didn't know what they were doing.

Vague noises reached me, from the bookstore, footsteps, voices. Cars stopped in the driveway; cars drove off. I seemed to be in another world, far above it all and only slightly woozy.

Dad and Mom and E came out of the garage, carrying two cat carriers.

After a while, I became aware that E was sitting next to me. "Mom." He had a carrier with Pythagoras. "Cas said thank you and that everything is safe now."

"Yeah," I said. "I know."

"I made Grandma and Granddad put the cats in the carriers," he said. "So they wouldn't run away."

"Good E," I said.

"Granddad has gone to tell the books everything is all right."

"Good Granddad."

"Cas had to go to the station, with the suspect. He wanted me to tell you."

"Good Cas."

I'd come to the place where I had no energy and no strength to run anymore. I didn't think there was anything to do or anything I wanted to do, and at that moment in time, I would have been perfectly content to sit on that stair for the rest of my life, with the cold breeze in my face, while below me the police department and fire department swarmed in their inscrutable ways and Mom and Dad did whatever it was they did.

The world was a beautiful place, and I remained remarkably unexploded.

CHAPTER 31

Of Candy Corn and Men

It couldn't have lasted forever. Paradise never does.
Sooner or later, you get expelled and have to make your
way through the hardscrabble reality on your own.

In this case, the hardscrabble reality presented itself
as the phone ringing, somewhere, up there, in my mother's kitchen.

I dragged myself up the flight of stairs and into the
kitchen, where I picked up the phone, and heard Cas's
voice. "Hello, sweetheart," he said. "Are you okay?"

"Right as rain," I said.

I could feel him smile on the other side. "I'm sorry I
didn't come up to make sure you were okay. Nick went
up and looked at you and said you seemed to be okay,
but in shock. I thought . . . We heard the explosion back
there, when de Leon pressed the button, and that's how
we knew we weren't going to be blown up. I went back

and looked, before I brought de Leon to the station. That was a magnificent crater."

"There was one there before," I said. "From when I blew up the oak."

"Yeah, and I hope your parents don't get too attached to covering it up, because E and probably our kids will blow it up again. Probably."

I didn't say anything. The idea of E and E's siblings blowing up things was suddenly very warm and reassuring. "You took de Leon . . ."

"Yeah. He's talking. Actually the problem is going to be making him stop talking. He'd braved himself for suicide, and now that he survived it, he just can't stop telling us all about everything."

"Like?"

"It appears when Sebastian left him with Maria, he got in an argument with her, and he says he just barely pushed her and she fell over and bled buckets. So he put her in a trash bag, in the back of his car."

"The poor woman."

"It's not as bad as it sounds. She didn't fit in the trash bag, of course. He seemed to think she was in rigor mortis, but it appears her body was merely rigid. Narcolepsy does that. Only de Leon didn't bother to know anything about the illness, of course, nor did he realize people don't get in rigor mortis as soon as they die. So he thought she was dead, and he threw her in the car, and then he took the table, and really random stuff to make it seem like she'd left, and then he drove to that condo they were using and dropped the stuff and he drove off with her in the trash bag, because to him that was the most important thing to get rid of."

"Where did he dump her?"

"In Denver. Outside the hospital. He dropped her there, completely naked. By then, she was unconscious but, as he put it, *floppy*, so he decided rigor mortis had passed. She was still bleeding, but he thought she was dead. I imagine it was a slow bleed."

"I take it she wasn't dead?"

"No. She was in a coma for a bit, and she was very confused, and no one thought to correlate a woman dropped naked in front of a Denver hospital with what looked like a voluntary disappearance in Goldport. Yeah, my fault. I should have called the hospitals in all the nearby towns."

"So . . . she's alive?"

"Yeah. She woke up this morning. Since then she's been trying to tell the doctors who she was, but she couldn't remember her phone number or address. After-effects of concussion. She's called now and talked to Jason Ashton, who is very relieved, and it seems like the doctors think her prognosis is good, so . . ."

"All is well when it ends well?"

"Seems like it. De Leon then came back to the condo, bought some stain and varnish to disguise the table, and thought it was a great idea to dispose of the stuff at the garage sale. He and the garage-sale guy have both been talking and, well, as an additional bonus, your ex really had nothing to do with the arson. Which I'm sure you and he, too, will be relieved to know. Well, in his case, he'll be relieved to know that no one thinks he had anything to do with it, I presume." He took a deep breath. "I'll just finish up this report, and then I'll come get you, okay? We'll stay in a hotel for the night or something. I'm sorry, I can't stay at your parents'; they'd drive me nuts."

"Yeah, I know. They drive me nuts, too."

CHAPTER 32

Good-Bye, Ccelly

We were in the middle of moving everything into the house, which, even with my table and chairs, Cas's sofas and dining room table, and his bed and mine, and all of E's furniture, still looked like an empty place. I didn't mind. There would be furniture later. The little fake trunk had sold for an obscene amount. With the lion-mouth pulls in place, it looked vaguely medieval, and some decorator in Denver had fallen in love with it.

The profit would be enough to buy nice stuff to refinish for E's new room. And it could keep us in pancakes and Pythagoras in cat kibble, at least until the wedding.

Cas was theoretically staying with Nick until the wedding, having emptied his apartment and given the key to his landlord. Theoretically because, in point of fact, Nick was staying at Ben's until they could move into the house next door. Their move was delayed by the fact that Ben had hired Sebastian to pull up the carpets and refinish the quite beautiful oak floor underneath. Another week or so, and they would move in. I am glad to say that since the day I'd blown up my parents' backyard, I hadn't woken up to a mummy anywhere near me.

Dad and Mom had blocked those doors again, so that customers wouldn't be found upstairs, browsing through their bedside books. Pythagoras's tail tip had healed, and Fluffy, probably, remained offended by my refusal to let her be maid of honor.

Cas was bringing in his piano, with Nick's help, when I heard them talking with someone in the living room. I was in the family room, a scarf protecting my newly short hair from dust, putting books on the shelves.

I put the books down and went to see who had come in.

It was Jason Ashton, holding hands with a very pretty, olive-skinned woman about his age and looking happy and possessive all in one. I presumed this was Maria. Their kids were with them.

E came out of the family room with me, and the little girl—Isabella—ran to him. I didn't hear what they were talking about, because Cas grabbed my hand and pulled me toward the Ashtons.

"We just wanted to say thank you," Maria said. "Jason told me how much you helped and how, without you, they might never have found me."

"I'm sure it would have been all right," I said. "Sooner or later, you'd have told them your phone number and all."

She smiled and shrugged. "Yes, but probably not till after de Leon had hurt other people."

"Well," Cas said, "he's going to trial on something like fifty counts. I'm sure he'll be put away for a good, long time."

"Good," Jason said. "We're off to California, but Sebastian will stay in town, and we'd love to get news now and then, if you tell him stuff. We'll always be very grateful to you, and we hope the two of you will be very happy."

At that point, I became aware of a small hand tugging at my shirt. "Mommy!" E said, in the tone of a boy who had already called my name half a dozen times.

"Yes?"

"Is it okay if I send Ccelly with Isabella to California?" he asked. "Because Ccelly has gotten used to her, and she's afraid she'll be very lonely till she makes some friends."

The little girl's dark eyes looked imploringly at me. "Sure," I said. "Of course."

Moments later, we stood on the porch, waving good-bye to the Ashtons.

"Do you think they'll find good llama oats for Ccelly in California?" E asked, putting his hand in mine and sounding a little forlorn.

"I'm sure California has the best imaginary llama oats ever!" I said. "And you can write to Isabella and ask her to let you know how Ccelly is getting on."

He perked up. "And I can tell her everything I learned about the Romans."

"Yeah?" Cas said. "Like what?"

Honestly, he was going to have to learn better, if he was going to live with E.

"Like, they used to execute people by getting them bitten to death by inks, intsc, inx—"

"Insects," Cas and Ben and Nick and I finished, in unison.

Sow's Ears into Silk Purses

I'm not going to tell you how to take something in one form of wood and make it look like another. There are excellent books on faux painting that cover the subject at least in part. I will give you a cursory look into the processes involved, but this is something that's more art than craft and into which you'll have to wade at your own risk and learn from your own mistakes.

Most of the time it is used to make pine look like cherry or mahogany or another of the very expensive woods.

At the very bottom of this, of course, is just buying one of those cans labeled "stain" and applying the appropriate stain. It won't fool anyone, particularly if you apply it over pine and are striving for something with quite a different "figure" (the darker marks in the wood), such as mahogany, but if what you're looking for is, for example, making that cheap bookcase not stand out at first sight amid your antique ones, it will work well enough. A single caveat is to try it on a bit of the wood first, and make sure it matches the other pieces. I've found, for instance, that "cherry" stain often comes closer to the color of antique mahogany than the "mahogany" stain.

The next level is to procure a piece of the wood you want to imitate. Then prepare your piece. If it is—as in the built-in china cabinets in one room of my house— very rough, construction-grade pine, or if (not impossible with really old pieces) there's a coat of paint you simply can't remove completely, just sand it as smooth as possible, fill in any gaps and holes, and sand it again. Apply paint as close to the base color of the wood as possible; then sand again. Then, using something translucent (I use oil paint diluted in mineral spirits) and small brushes (or sponges, for some woods, like burled walnut), apply the figure over the paint. This is a trial-and-error process I can't help you with. Consult your model frequently. You might have to apply layers of shellac in between layers of figuring (to give a sense of depth).

Of course, this is not a piece you can leave merely waxed. You'll have to seal it and sand it. I've had the most success in this with the showy types of wood, like burled walnut, because the pattern is so distracting that people don't examine it too closely.

An easier and more satisfying "forgery" is to take poplar or pine pieces of relatively simple construction— you can often find them unfinished or cheaply enough. The piece Dyce finishes in this book is based on a trunk I bought at a garage sale. It was painted what can only be called radioactive green, and it had these large gilded medallions in the front. The whole thing was in screamingly bad taste, and my husband thought I was out of my mind to buy it.

But I'd looked inside the drawers, which no one had bothered to finish, and knew they were a pale poplar, with virtually no figure. Which meant they were a virgin canvas. And the trunk itself was just square, with a deep-set "cut" line running around the top in a rectangle.

When I tried to unscrew the medallions, I discovered they were plaster and very easy to chisel off. I used commercial paint remover to remove the horrible green paint, then sanded it lightly. Onto the clean canvas went a mix of black-walnut and mahogany stain, which came closer to a "walnut" color than straight out of the can. The inlaid line across the top I outlined with gold, then wiped it off, to give the impression of a line of gold inset and corroded by time.

When it was all dry, I gave it several coats of oil finish. With lion-mouth (with rings through them) door pulls through the holes that used to have the medallions, it makes a somber nineteenth-century-feel piece, which has done honorable duty as a piano roll holder next to our player piano for the last fifteen years. Those door pulls were bought from a furniture-restoring store, but they can now be found on the Internet, together with other suitably "old"-looking fittings.

My other great success as an impostor was buying a very cheap table with a "bubbled up" plastic-type top. Something most people don't know is that even in non-real-wood furniture, the legs are usually real wood because it's cheaper to do them that way. This table had column-like legs that twisted upward in a spiral. I stripped the legs of their plastic-looking veneer to reveal decent-enough pine, which I stained dark to suggest aged pine. The top I painted in successive coats as blue-green marble. It took forever, and I used not just a model but a friend who was a geologist as a consultant. But the result was convincing enough that the moving company wanted to charge me extra for the "heavy marble table."

If you're itching to replicate this type of success, or if you simply don't have access to good furniture (the table was done because I couldn't find anything up to my standards for the very large dining room we had at the time), buy a good book on faux painting, a set of student's oil paints, a set of brushes, and head out to your favorite thrift shop or flea market. Pick something small and easy to transform to begin with, and don't be discouraged by early failures.

Of course, no matter how good you become, you should never use your skills to fool others into buying a cheap piece as something more valuable. Fooling guests into thinking you have very expensive furniture, on the other hand, is a noncriminal and thoroughly fun hobby.

Just remember to tell the movers what is not real marble. Trust me; you don't want to pay marble rates.

A Note on Gifted Children

I didn't know I would have to explain this until my agent read the book and told me E sounded more like he was five or six than three and a half.

Since E is modeled on both my boys (who hate it like poison, of course), I was simply relaying things that they did at around three, three and a half. I didn't think it would seem impossible to other people until my agent mentioned it.

And now, it will seem like I'm bragging about my children. I am not. Let me explain gifted children, very briefly.

Giftedness, not as it's interpreted in the schools (where they tend to consider the top 25 percent of children gifted, and that top is often determined by which kids obey best or perform tasks most satisfactorily), is as much a blessing as a curse.

Again and again, I've run up against schools that have either no or inadequate gifted programs, because "gifted children already have an advantage," something that could only be believed by someone who never raised one of them.

Truly gifted children are a joy and a challenge in equal measure. Working with them consists partly of running to keep up and partly of being really frustrated when they don't pick up on simple things as easily as their "normal" counterparts.

You see, "gifted" is marked by "saltational development." What this means is that a gifted child might draw like Leonardo da Vinci but be totally unable to sound out the word *cat*. Or he might read a history of Rome written for adults but be unable to color within the lines. And then one or the other ability that has been lacking will suddenly leap ahead. It is also characterized by a multitude of interests, some of them odd or counterproductive at best (it's very hard to teach a kid to read when all he wants to talk about for six months is, say, the peculiar behavior of an anthill in the yard).

Gifted children are often classed as learning disabled or defective or both because giftedness is very hard to understand, even one-on-one and with more time than schools have. As a mother, I had to consult experts and learn to cope with my sons' idiosyncrasies.

Yes, giftedness, properly handled, can give people a leg up in life. Or it can turn into a curse that blights friendships and destroys careers. Education of the gifted child is where it should start being turned into an asset, not a handicap. It helps to remember it's not a quantitative thing—not that they're "smarter" or "better" than others—but a qualitative thing. Their minds work differently, and you'll have to learn how to help them cope with that and still become balanced and well-integrated adults.

If your child resembles E at all, I suggest you contact American Mensa, which in turn can give you local contacts to help with your gifted child. And good luck. Raising that child will be both the most exhilarating and scariest thing you've ever done.

Cast On, Kill Off

A KNITTING MYSTERY

Wedding bells are ringing in Fort Connor, Colorado, and the House of Lambspun knitters are abuzz with excitement. But when a murder interrupts the wedding planning, Kelly Flynn will have to solve the crime fast to ensure the killer doesn't wind up on the guest list . . .

Praise for the Knitting Mysteries

"A terrific series."
—*The Mystery Reader*

"A cleverly crafted whodunit."
—*The Best Reviews*

"A darn good series with vivid, breathing characters."
—*Mystery Scene*

DELICIOUS RECIPE AND KNITTING PATTERN INCLUDED!

maggiesefton.com
facebook.com/TheCrimeSceneBooks
penguin.com